Dead Shifter Walking

Kim Bair

Table of Contents

Chapter 1

I shifted uncomfortably, seated atop the makeshift desk Grams sat behind. Annoyed about this impromptu meeting, I peeked over my tense shoulder to see her steel gaze at the self-important Governor Hash. The hatred simmering below the surface was evident, but she wasn't allowing it to contort her facial features. Good for her.

I wasn't doing nearly as well; my jaw muscles twitched from unspoken words and my arms refused to uncross from my chest.

Pulling my attention back to the panel seated in front of us, I heaved an annoyed sigh. I wasn't much for the legal system, or legal anything, actually. I had my own set of rules, and I abided by those with fanaticism. I was tempted to kill each and every one of those stupid, idiotic vampires for coming out of the closet. And let's not forget about the lovely shifters who also decided it was a good idea to dump honesty on the general human public.

The truth of our existence had long been known, at least since the Salem Witch Trials, but I certainly didn't walk around with a t-shirt announcing, "Succubus." Most humans appreciated it that way, knowing there was something in the dark but not putting a face to it. Well, that had all ended now that their ridiculous human government thought they had some say in how we lived. The idiotic notion that the humans could control or dictate our activities was the reason I was sitting here guarding Grams, the head of our Supernatural Council, a council I had crafted and tended to for the last six years, making damn sure it was swift in action, just, and beyond reproach.

My system had worked wonderfully until the largest vampire House in the area, The Centennial House, decided they wanted a bigger piece of the ever-loving human pie.

Fucking vampire movies!

I was tempted to kill every novelist and screenwriter who glorified the undead. Contrary to popular belief, living forever is grossly overrated. After a few centuries, all the humanity leaked out of a vamp or shifter; only the powerful elite survived with their sanity. If out-of-control vamps didn't fall on a silver stake—yeah, that part is true—then someone like me came along and relieved them of their heads or hearts, depending on my mood. Contrary to vampire lore, sunlight didn't kill them, but their power, like that of most Supernaturals, was awakened at night.

As I rolled my shoulders, cracking my neck, I glanced at the Vamp Council on my left, decked out in soft black leather, chokers, and matching pale skin—the assholes. Across from them, to my right, were the shifters in all their big, bad, football-player glory, and directly in front of me were legalized human assholes, trying desperately to understand the supernatural beings who had always walked beside them. The Governor and his flunkies were attempting to pass judgment on who we were and what we did, all the while not really understanding a fucking thing.

"We simply cannot allow your kind to continue living the way you have, unchecked and unmanaged," Governor Hash stated, raising his beady eyes to the group assembled as he closed his paperwork, signaling that he was about to come to a verdict. "Therefore, we are going to relocate—"

I stopped him right there with a touch of my power. "Absolutely not," I said quietly, pushing away from the table to stand in front of him with my arms crossed over my leather-clad chest.

His eyes grew round. "You," he started uncertainly, "cannot tell me what to do—"

I chuckled. "Actually, I can and I will," I gritted, my power pooling in my core.

I took a step forward, bracing my legs apart and resting my hands on my hips. "This is what I will allow..."

He sputtered, attempting to regain control in the face of my brush-off. One look at me quieted him.

"I will allow one of your staff, approved by me, to monitor the clan meetings. Secondly, I will allow—" I stressed that word; setting up the proper power levels was important. Specifically, that he had none. Plus, I wasn't above killing them all. "—an enforcer to patrol your police files and deliver the head of anyone responsible for breaking the major laws of your society that are in agreement with our own laws.

"I will allow you to provide me with multiple candidates for an enforcer, with the final selection resting with me." I relaxed my stance, keeping his gaze. I knew the other clans would agree. The Supernatural Council was, after all, the head of all the clans, and what I said was law. Besides, there wasn't anyone or anything else willing and able to eliminate an entire city council to get this shit taken care of. But I was an Executioner. That was my job, and I loved it.

"And you speak for all these freaks?" he asked, his voice shifting up an octave, his fear coating the room.

I gave him a relaxed smile. Unfortunately, my genetic makeup did not include fear-inspiring canines, which I was certain had been a mistake.

"Anyone disagree?" I asked sweetly, not losing eye contact. Not a sound.

"Who gave you the right to defy the authority the citizens of St Ann have entrusted me with?" Governor Hash stood, raising his voice, turning red from anger. He wasn't much to look at: tall, skinny, with gray hair and thin, pale lips.

I checked my control; it was good. Fuck, it was perfect. None of my emotions leaked.

I stalked slowly towards him, rolling my hips in my soft leather pants and matching jacket. I had left my dual swords at home and was feeling a little underdressed, with just a few dozen knives hidden carefully under my silk cami and jacket.

Reaching his ornate, highly polished desk, I braced my hands wide, lowering my face to his own.

"I gave the right to myself," I whispered, "and no political dick bag is going to tear down any of the structures I have created. End. Of. Story."

I turned my back on him, walking towards Grams. She raised a dark blond eyebrow, questioning my methods, I was certain.

I tilted my head with a shrug. It was fun scaring him. I liked it. Did that make me more of a monster? Yes, I certainly hoped so.

"None of you will leave this building alive," the Governor threatened. The rustling of papers halted as the other clans began packing up.

I turned around, watching him pull on his tie.

"You mean those big, bad snipers on the roof?" I asked innocently.

I think the Governor might have actually growled.

"Don't worry," I said, settling my hand against my side. "They'll be fine." I checked my nearly indestructible watch—waterproof, freeze-proof, and shockproof. I loved it. "Well, actually, in about six minutes, they'll be running out of oxygen. So, I really do think we should get a move on."

At those words, all the clans picked up their belongings. Ruling by fear was not nice, but it was immensely effective. Fuck nice. My job came with a life expectancy that didn't clear thirty, and at twenty-two, I was already feeling that pressure.

It also helped that they knew I was protecting all of them as my own. I would make sure not a soul was harmed leaving the building. I may be a tad overbearing in that regard.

I waited as the rest of the clans exited through the wooden double doors with frosted glass panes. All the while, Hash stared daggers at me. Feeling his malevolent eyes on my back, I turned, raising a questioning eyebrow.

"I should have you arrested," he growled, scrunching his forehead.

I scoffed. "Good luck with that one," I taunted him, stepping onto the marble floor. I followed the echoing footsteps around the corner and into the harsh fluorescent light of the open lobby with marble paneling, then deviated from the path of the others, cutting to the side door, where I had the snipers waiting for me.

I took my first clean breath of the night air, chilly with the promise of rain. I sincerely hoped it would keep its word; I love the rain.

"So, that was quite the performance," Mark said, coming from my left. I stopped surveying the rooftops, turning my attention to him. I was not giving him the satisfaction of surprising me.

"Performance?" I questioned. "I was really quite okay with killing all of them."

He shifted his stance, the wind lapping at his thick dark curls, leather jacket, and jeans. He was as tan as a surfer god, with broad shoulders and deep brown eyes.

"You weren't really going to kill all those people?" he asked, assured of the answer.

I smiled cryptically and shrugged, "Would have depended on my mood."

Mark scoffed at that. I could tell his shifter blood was restless in the moonlight. His brown eyes gleamed with a light from within. He was second in command of the South Compasses Packs. Darren was the head dog down here, and I truly do mean dog in the most decadent sense of the word. Actually, that was an insult to pooches everywhere. Darren had the unique notoriety of having slept with the majority of the female population in our fair city. He had a daughter, Hannah, from his first marriage, but after his wife passed away, the manwhore was released.

"How's Hannah?" I asked, shifting the topic to Darren's real number-one priority.

He hesitated in his answer, avoiding eye contact and shrugging. "She's okay," he finally said. I wanted to ask why just okay, but my watch beeped at me.

"If you'll excuse me, I need to make good on my promise not to kill the snipers." With that, I took my leave. I might have rolled my hips exaggeratedly, but how long had it been since I had taken a lover? I groaned inwardly; too damn long. And shifters, their stamina was the stuff of legends. I did know, however, that trying to seduce Mark would be totally ineffective. He might not realize he was gay, but I certainly did. I still liked putting on a show, though.

"Olivia, wait," Grams said, speed walking to come even with me. "Need a lift?" she asked.

I smiled and nodded, not slowing my gait.

She nodded. "Around the corner at 6th street."

I nodded my thanks and continued on to free the weak, mortal assholes. I rolled my shoulders again, thinking that I needed a back rub from a tall, dark, handsome and stamina-driven nonexistent male. I sighed with disappointment before rolling open the sewer cage where I'd stashed them.

"Let's go, darlings," I said as the moonlight poured over their limp forms. Slowly, they dragged themselves up and ambled towards their freedom.

...

"You think that wise?" Grams asked in the back of her black limo.

I shrugged. "You will have to be more specific," I stated, rubbing my throbbing temples.

Grams held my emerald green eyes with her own slate blue ones. "Do you think it wise to intimidate the humans' ruling body of government? Or, perhaps we should discuss if you think it wise to have assumed that you spoke for all of the Supernaturals in that room? Or, more importantly, the kidnapping—"

"Enough," I interrupted, speaking quietly.

She flushed, angry with my behavior.

"What would you have me do," I asked, meeting her gaze, "let the humans' pathetic government dictate our actions? I did what I had to." I turned back to the window. "I do my job to keep us safe. If you want to blame someone, pick on the damn vampires."

The conversation was closed. She knew it, even if she didn't like it. I hadn't put her in this position for her inability to read people, and she knew me well enough to realize exactly how I operated.

Six years ago, when I was sixteen and clawing my way out of my own private hell, I found her managing a low-class, dirty, rat- and drug-infested whorehouse. She had the traits I needed: the ability to care for others without anger, an abundance of kindness and compassion.

I converted a mansion I had not-so-honestly inherited into a sanctuary for those like us and the children I managed to save.

Then I started killing humans and Supernaturals alike until Grams ended up as head of the Council for the Eastern United States. Her counterpart in the West gave his blessing to us and threw a few lucrative jobs our way, which was the only reason he was still alive.

Our rules stated that an Executioner could name and protect their choice for the Council and that was exactly what I had done. Anyone who wanted a change went through me, and no one ever managed to get that far; they couldn't compete with me. I was a genetically engineered killer, raised in Selena's own sick and twisted version of a boot camp. I had used all of my formidable skills to burn it and every living thing inside it, except Anna, to the ground.

Pushing those demons away for another day, I cracked my neck, peering out the heavily tinted and bulletproof glass window to the night outside.

I wasn't the only Executioner for this region, but I pulled a heavy caseload and was away more than I was home.

"How was Orlando?" Grams questioned, trying to reign in her frustration with me.

I turned from the window. "It went well. The usual vamp gone over the edge."

She nodded. "The children will be happy to see you," she stated.

I smiled at that, turning back to the window.

I loved the children. They were young, innocent, and full of potential. Potential to be better than me, to be more than I was. I turned my thoughts away from that dark alley and back to the night outside. I missed being on my own, driving in the dark reaches of small towns. The city was constantly moving, flashing, devoid of silence or stars.

"What's on the agenda for tomorrow?" I asked, adjusting my seat in the limo.

"The usual. We have a fairly full docket, and..." She hesitated before continuing, "Rose has been sick recently. I was hoping you might be able to pull a few shifts."

I sighed, slouching down in my seat.

"You're the best," she pushed on. "We make the most when you're in town." She adjusted her pastel purple suit, looking uncomfortable. "Besides, there have been requests for your particular skill set," she added, her chin held high.

I closed my eyes. My particular skill set. Yep.

"Alright," I said. "Have the schedule ready for me tomorrow."

The car slowed in front of the massive mansion. I loved this home, loved the thick Southern plantation-style pillars extending to the third floor. A Georgia mansion was how I thought of it. When I was trapped in hell, that's what I had promised myself as a safe haven.

I didn't want to push further into those memories, so I slammed the door to my mind as I slammed the car door and waited for Grams to come around the limo as it drove away.

"They should all be in bed by now," she said with warmth in her voice, "but you know how they are." She smiled, making her way up the three short steps.

Soft noise and light greeted us as the door pushed inward. I listened to the squeaking of furniture as bodies moved before the noise dimmed to nothing.

A skinny, eleven-year-old African American kid moved from the corner into my view.

"Hey," he said, leaning against the doorframe, arms crossed against his chest.

I smiled and inclined my head. "You staying out of trouble, Tommy?" I asked.

He shrugged, sparing a glance at Grams, who only shook her head and headed upstairs to bed with her cream heels clicking on the hardwood floors.

"Game?" he questioned, with a knowing smirk.

My smile grew. "Game on."

He exuded the innocence of a preteen, but I knew those were just his guards. In his short time on this planet he had survived and recovered from his own personal hell. Perhaps that's why Executioners don't live past thirty; we are really twice that age and our hearts just cannot handle any more.

I shook my head at that thought. Who the hell was I kidding? I lacked a heart.

...

Dawn light slipped past the plantation shutters as Tommy kicked my ass again in the racing game.

"Ugh! I am done," I said, putting my controller down, rubbing my burning eyes.

Tommy stretched, grinning like a fool from ear to ear on the flowery sofa. "Don't worry, Olie, I won't tell a soul." He mimed zipping his lips but was unable to complete the gesture as I smacked him in the face with a pillow.

He started giggling uncontrollably, holding his stomach, and I couldn't help but smile.

"Go to bed," I commanded, standing to stretch. My watch read 5:45 a.m. I groaned inwardly.

Crossing his arms, he attempted to deny my authority. It only took a raised eyebrow to persuade him to relent, but not before he had pulled me into a surprise hug before dashing up the stairs.

I smiled at his retreating form. He was doing better, thank all that is good in this world.

Pulling the throw off the back of the sofa, I snuggled in for a few hours of rest, sighing contentedly.

...

"Yo, Sleeping Beauty," a familiar voice called out, pulling me from my peaceful slumber.

"Kass," I responded unmoving, as her light weight rested on my back.

"What's up, my long-lost lover bug?" she asked, covering my body with hers.

Groaning, I demanded, "Time!"

"Time to get up and go get 'em," she stated, slapping my ass. I knew if I looked up at her Caribbean face, it would be split into a grin.

"I can kick your ass," I muttered into the pillow.

"Whatever, Suc-u-licious," she stated, pulling off the already too-small throw.

Opening my eyes, I saw Grams walk in, laughing. "Kass, you know she has never been a morning person." She was meticulously dressed as usual, in a soft pink pencil skirt and white blouse.

Kass's smile only widened, making her teeth seem impossibly white against her olive complexion.

I pulled my exhausted self into a sitting position. Bracing my head in my hands, I pushed my exhaustion and irritation into a braided cord in my mind. It was a trick I'd learned long ago in order to manage my inner turmoil. I did the same with all my emotions, tucking them deep within so I could push them out when needed.

Being a succubus, I carried great power in my emotions, my highest form of power. I could affect whole rooms if I did not exercise control. Most succubi and incubi leak a small amount of emotion; it is only natural. I did not. I attribute that to my hell and the bitch who created me, Selena. I pushed that particular braid of pain away deep into my core, exhaling.

"Let's go, Princess," I said, standing and dwarfing Kass. "I gotta learn the dances for..." I paused, turning to Grams.

"At least the next month," she stated.

Rolling my eyes, I pushed Kass into motion, but not before she sneaked a smile at Grams. "A whole month, I haven't sat that still in a long, long time," I muttered.

Grabbing a muffin from the deep burgundy bowl on the stone counter, I couldn't help but glance around the kitchen. I had kept the original cabinets, but refinished them with a soft white with dark brown handles.

Moving around the island to the ceramic sink, I filled a glass of water from the advanced filtration system, stretching my left hand above my head and leaning to pull out the crick in my side from sleeping on the couch.

"Quit stalling," Kass said, grabbing an apple from the stainless steel fridge and taking a crisp bite.

I dried my hands on the forest green kitchen towel before following her into the dance studio. It was one of my favorite rooms, spanning a quarter of the house's first floor with its light hardwood floor, framed by mirrors along three of the walls, not to mention the top-of-the-line sound system, easily controlled by voice recognition.

Swallowing the rest of my muffin down, I caught the clothing Kass tossed to me, chucking off my own travel-worn gear.

"That looks like it hurts," Kass commented as I slipped the bright pink top on.

"I know; could this color be more sick?" I asked, looking down at myself, disgusted.

"I was referring to the bullet wound on your shoulder," she said, not sharing my humor.

"Still not as painful as the color," I informed her, pursing my lips out.

She smiled warily, commanding the music to begin.

I loved this place and the release it promised. High-level mages had warded this room to prevent our influencing the rest of the house, or, in my case, the neighborhood.

A relaxed smile full of mischief crossed her face as she rolled her shoulders and relaxed into the music that was already pumping through the speakers. "Ready?"

I smiled back, cracking my magic open and drawing a braid out to wind around my limbs.

She swung her hips to the raging beat, her own magic intertwined with mine. As succubi, we made excellent dancers. Kitten was the dance club Grams and I owned that provided us enough revenue to keep up the home and meet the demands of raising our children, a few of whom were now at insanely expensive colleges.

Watching her in the mirror as the beat intensified, I absorbed each and every move without having to mimic her first. That was another kick-ass fact about being a succubus, although there were plenty of drawbacks. I shuddered, having seen the raw primal power our blood carried.

Pushing those thoughts away, I focused on Kass. At twenty-six, she was the best dancer at Kitten last I knew, before I'd left on my latest adventure. I assumed she still was; otherwise, there would be someone else here teaching me the latest routines. We updated our shows every month, for the simple fact we bored easily, and ran a different show Friday, Saturday, and Sunday. The dance group was made up mainly of succubi, although the last time I was here, there were a few vamps, shifters, and even one human.

Sweat drenched my clothing, plastering the obnoxious pink shirt to my back as we ran through the routine. It felt amazing to let my power out. I hadn't let it run this free since last month, I guessed. There was a tangible difference between forcing power at an opponent during a fight and reveling in it. I missed the freedom of it. I had been on my own so long, running from job to job, hiding from the nightmares that were robbing me of sleep. I needed to be here, to belong somewhere, and to know that what I did was more than just killing. I needed to believe I was creating some good in this awful world.

Kass tossed a towel at me, asking, "You good to go for tonight?"

I raised an eyebrow. "Tonight?" I asked disbelievingly.

"Yep, I have a hot date," she smirked, toweling off her sweat.

I shook my head. "What time?"

"Rehearsal starts at 8:30 p.m., with the show at 11:30. Just be sure to be there by 11:15 at the latest. I know how you're always on time," she stated sarcastically.

Throwing my sweaty towel at her, I skipped out of the room, gathering my clothing for a shower.

"Hey!" she admonished my retreating back.

Making my way to the second story where Grams's room was, I felt my thighs pull from the unaccustomed exercise. The wing where my old room was located was currently under construction to add a bathroom, update the plumbing and electrical, repaint the walls, refinish the floors—basically, everything.

Knocking tentatively, I heard Grams's voice coming from the lush study. As I pushed open the cream paneled double doors, she waved me into the bedroom, cradling the phone between her shoulder and ear.

"That is correct, Governor Hash," she stated sweetly. Even my ability to influence emotions completely dies on the phone. She was using good old-fashioned manipulation, a skill Grams had in spades.

I stopped in my tracks, wondering if I should stay and listen. I decided not to, mainly because I don't have the patience for his political double speak.

I walked through the enormous bedroom to the equally large bathroom. I eyed the oversized bathtub with jets, wishing feebly I had time to indulge in that pleasure right now. I simply didn't, so I started a steamy shower instead.

"Good God, Olivia," Grams scolded, entering the steaming bathroom a few minutes later. "Will you at least turn on a fan?"

Flipping the switch, she hurried out, mumbling something about sweating asses.

Sighing, I turned off my hot water reprieve, using the plush towel to clear a spot on the mirror before drying off my own body. I took stock of the image and didn't like what I saw. My usual waist-long strawberry blond hair had turned dishwater blond. The hollowness in my cheeks and under my eyes were reminders of my lack of sleep and regular meals, but it was the darkness in my eyes that had me most concerned. My eyes had always been a particular mix of blue and green, Grams used to call them sea eyes. Now I wasn't sure what color they were; darkness was all I saw.

I pushed those emotions down into my core, locking them away for another day, which I hoped would never come.

"Grams," I called out through the open door, "where's my duffle bag?"

"Being burned," she replied, levelly shifting papers.

"That's comical. What am I supposed to wear?" I asked, knowing full well everything was being washed.

Traveling from city to city, I never had much, just what I could fit into an army duffle bag that had seen better days, but that bag had been with me longer than anyone in my life. I'd be lying if I said I wasn't attached to it. I had never felt like I belonged, that I had a home, even now, but that bag kept me centered, kept me whole in a way brick and mortar could never do.

"I have a few things laid out for you when you decide to exit the sauna," she replied.

"Oh, you have got to be kidding me," I stated, eyeing her selections with distain. Her smile said she wasn't.

Chapter 2

The office was bathed in warm afternoon sunlight, making me pull at the itchy wool jacket for the millionth time as I wriggled in the plush chair in Grams's offices downtown, equally displeased with the pencil skirt she had me wearing. Who wore wool anymore? Ugh! Grams had proved a point, though—I needed to go shopping. I shrugged and wondered where in the world I would put my new outfits.

We moved from the offices into the conference room when too many people decided to air their grievances. Whether it was motivated by the rumors circulating about last night or just by the fact I was back in town, I didn't know or really care.

A young man sat at the other end of the mahogany table. He might have been the eighth or ninth; I was losing track as I ran my bare feet over the soft carpet. Gods, Grams had good taste in everything! The conference room wasn't sterile like all those other trendy rooms designed not to offend. Everything about it spoke of elegance and grace, from the soft peach walls to the lined bookshelves to the cream carpet I was enjoying.

"Thank you, Mr. Scott," Grams said, dismissing the man. "We will take your suggestions into account and let you know if we are able to incorporate them into our system."

Mr. Scott nodded and was about to rise from his chair when the door burst open, almost torn from its hinges. An incubus, wild with blood-red eyes, was dragged in, fighting against two other incubi. Mallory, a vampire I knew well, trailed behind, shielding the petite blond human the incubus was trying to reach.

I sprung from my seat, my earlier boredom and bare feet forgotten.

"Report," I demanded, putting myself between the riled incubus and Grams.

Mallory reached behind her and pulled the blond farther into the room. "She," Mallory stated, annoyed, "accidentally drew first blood."

"Fuck," I whispered. When drawn by another person, first blood from an incubus or succubus is a powerful amplifier of whatever our current emotions are. All rational thought flees, and the need to destroy spreads like wildfire through our bodies.

Luckily, training could diminish the urge and allow us to redirect the power into our fighting abilities. If training started early enough, first blood was never an issue.

"She was dancing with him," the incubus hissed. "Liar! Cheater! Bitch!" he screamed, lunging for her.

"Mallory, how fast can you get—"

She interrupted me with a hand. "Already called; ETA five minutes." I admired her calm demeanor.

I nodded. "Did you explain?" I asked, indicating the terrified human in our midst.

She shook her head.

I sighed, moving the girl into a seat away from the angry words being spouted in the corner. "Do you understand first blood?" I asked her as she wiped her tear-stained, petite face.

She nodded her platinum head, sniffling. "Good. Now, the vampires will bleed both you and him." Terror gripped her features. "It's the only way I know to take away the rage from first blood without killing one of you." I decided at that point not to mention that it wasn't a sure thing. I had been on cases where even the letting of blood had not extinguished the desire to destroy.

The fear was rolling off her in sickening waves. "What's your name?" I asked gently.

"D-Debbie," she stammered, casting a fearful glance over to where they were restraining the incubus.

I smiled. "Debbie, everything is going to be okay. I am very good at my job." I unwound a thick coil of power in my core, infusing it with compassion and contentment until I saw Debbie's shoulders relax in her chair.

I glanced at Mallory, who nodded, indicating the other vampires had arrived. Not just any vamp could drain living beings within an inch of their lives, only those with control above the rest. They needed a good thirty to forty undead years to perfect it, and even then, I had to intervene sometimes.

"All right," I said, standing. "Debbie, you come with me." She stood, ready to follow me out.

"No, Olivia," said Grams. "Please stay here. Everyone needs to see how to deal with this without someone dying needlessly."

I nodded. Besides Grams and me, two of her aides where present, watching with wide eyes. Being an aide to a political figure in the human world was night to the day of being an aide in the politics of the Supernatural world. Aside from their ability to fight to defend themselves and those around them, they were selected because Grams believed they would someday succeed her and have the courage to make the hard choices. Their names were Ali and Grant and they each belonged to minor clans. Ali was a descendant of Medusa, her blood too diluted for her to be considered a demigod, but with enough power for her not to be considered human. Grant had a more colorful background as a gypsy. Contrary to the stereotype, Grant could contact the dead as easily as breathing and place curses with terrifying results. They were both older than me, and I was fairly certain they had written me off upon meeting me.

I am not political, and whatever agendas they were pushing, I couldn't have cared less—unless, of course, they crossed one of our laws, and I had to put them down.

I turned back to Debbie. "Okay, let's sit back down," I said, smiling.

She didn't respond. She was turned away from me, intently watching the two vamps who had just entered the room. These dolls had apparently read too many vamp love stories, judging from their outfits. They were decked out in designer pants, dark sunglasses and, I'm fairly certain, silk button down shirts. I almost laughed out loud.

They shared a nod with Mallory, who looked underdressed for her vamp part in jeans and a tank top. But I was impressed that she wasn't being intimidated in the least.

"How did this happen?" Ali asked from behind me.

Mallory answered, "They were preparing for tonight at Kitten when we heard the crash. A case of glasses fell and broke. Best guess, it was an accident, which is why we brought them here instead of letting nature take its course."

"Smart move," the vamp with the longer brown hair said, removing his sunglasses to reveal piercing green eyes.

"Thanks, Morgan, your approval moves mountains," Mallory responded blandly.

He smiled at her and was about to say something else when the incubus in the corner started up again.

"Let's get this over with," I reminded them.

Morgan nodded and said, "Tate, you take the big boy. I'll have myself the lady."

He slid up with a practiced smoothness.

"Hi there," he said, looking down at Debbie. He only had a few inches on me. At five feet ten inches, I am tall for a female of any race.

He slid a finger down her bare arm, achieving the shiver he had been going for. "What's your name?" he asked gently.

"Debbie," she breathed out in awe.

Morgan smiled without showing his pointed teeth. "Debbie," he said, making her name sound like a promise, "can you sit for me?"

I couldn't deny it, up close, he was devilishly handsome. His green eyes danced as he made us all feel like we were imposing by being there. The pale vamp skin was a perfect contrast to his chestnut shoulder-length hair, but the kicker had to be his blood-red lips.

Debbie slid into the seat at his request, and he followed her down on one knee. Gently, he took her wrist into his own large hands, careful not to lose eye contact as he lowered his lips to her pulse beating there, placing a most tender kiss.

I rolled my shoulders; I really needed to get laid. He wasn't even touching me and I wanted him to sink his fangs into me as well.

"Please," Debbie whispered.

Morgan raised an eyebrow, seeking confirmation. Blood given freely was a monumental deal for some vampires. It seemed Morgan fit into that category.

"Yes, please," she repeated, just as softly.

A primal growl came from Morgan as he revealed his fangs and bit gently down on her soft flesh. I released the breath I didn't realize I had been holding. Debbie's head rolled forward and Morgan moved to support her body.

I slowly moved away from the pair, my eyes searching for the incubus. Tate was having a more difficult time subduing him, but he told the guards to move away as he continued his hypnotic talk. Was he actually sporting a Mohawk? I was thinking he was.

I watched the incubus try to break away from Tate's gaze, and then, as Tate took a deep breath and reached out, the incubus's eyes caught sight of Debbie and Morgan. The roar he let out was deafening.

"Protect her!" I yelled to Morgan as the incubus broke free and scrambled onto the table.

Sliding across the table on my ass, I sucked in a deep breath. He hit like a bull, knocking us both off the table, with me landing on top after our roll. Quickly, I sent my thickest ropes out, telling his limbs they were immobile. I had to admit it was a cheap trick, and it was usually seen through almost immediately. That, however, was with a rational individual, not a first-blood-driven beast. I would also admit that I kicked out more power than most. But don't worry, that will come back to bite me soon enough. There's a price for going against another's immediate desires, even when I have their best interests at heart.

I felt more than saw Tate behind me.

"Now," I whispered as he knelt next to me.

Sparing a glance, I saw the conflict on his sharply formed face. It wasn't blood freely given anymore. I pulled more power from my core, mimicking the contentment and security I felt with Morgan, leaving out the sexual attraction.

The incubus heaved a sigh, his limbs going weak.

Tate looked at me. I nodded in response as he took the limp wrist from me and waited, poised.

"Say it," I commanded.

As if in a dream, the words sounded from the incubus's mouth. "Freely given, it is freely given," he repeated, looking in Tate's eyes.

Tate flicked a final look towards me before drawing the wrist to his mouth, easing down his fangs so they entered the skin.

Again, I released the breath I'd been keeping in my chest. Checking my outfit, I realized I had torn the skirt clean up the side. Oops. I shrugged, meeting Grams's disapproving scowl.

Pulling the braids off the incubus's wrists, I watched carefully for any movement to buck Tate and me off. Finding none, I slowly, ever so gently eased off the contentment. He stirred, slurring a sentence I couldn't understand.

I waited, holding my breath again before pulling off the rest, leaving one strand out to ground myself. Once all my magic was pulled back into me, it would hurt like hell.

"Grams," I said, my voice sounding strained, "make sure even if they touch, there's no reaction. Otherwise, when he's strong enough, we'll be back in the same situation."

She nodded.

"Where are you going?" Grant asked from behind his glasses.

I smiled, staggering back a few paces.

"Shit," Grams said. "Everyone cover their eyes!" she yelled with authority.

Hitting the floor in between the bookshelves, I made sure Tate had covered the eyes of his feast before I pulled all my magic back in. The rebound effect was awful, golden light swarming into my closed eyes and igniting under my skin, making it raw. Concentrating only on my breathing, I braided the pain and magic into thicker and thicker cords, until I lost myself in the braids with no sense of self or pain.

Pulling in a ragged breath, I started to regain sensation in my limbs. Everything seemed fairly normal, nothing broken or severely bruised. My ears began to register sounds, although my eyes still refused to open.

"I assure you, Mr. Morgan, Olivia will be just fine. There is no need for medical attention," Grams said soothingly.

"I have a few questions I would like to ask her," said a voice I didn't instantly recognize.

"Yes, Mr. Tate, I do realize her ability to manipulate emotions raises many questions," Grams said diplomatically. "However, as you can see, she isn't in a position to answer you at this moment."

"Do you know how she did it?" Tate asked.

"No, Mr. Tate, I do not. Olivia..." She paused, unsure about how to proceed. "Olivia deals with people and circumstances most of us never have to worry about. How she was able to do what she did is not known to me."

"Will you have her call us once she is up and about?" Morgan asked, clipped.

"Yes," Grams assured him, "I most certainly will."

I heard the door closing and Grams letting out a long sigh.

Trying my eyes again, I found them more cooperative. Letting out a groan, I rolled to my side, attempting to sit up.

"One quiet day, Olie, is that too much to ask for?" she said, still staring at the door.

"Yes," I whispered hoarsely. "It always is."

I blinked rapidly until my vision returned to me, revealing Grant and Ali still sitting in their seats, looking a tad pale. I stumbled to an upright position and fell into the nearest chair, rubbing my temples.

"Did it work?" I asked hoarsely.

"Yes," Grams said, returning to her seat across the table. "He had no lingering effects of first blood."

I let a sigh out. "Good."

Lifting my head, I checked the time, 9 p.m. Unlike most organizations, we started our day around noon and finished around midnight, four days a week. It was a Friday, which was supposed to be our day off, canceled due to a high caseload and the meeting last night.

I had two hours before I had to be a Kitten, enough time for dinner and a shower.

"Can I get a car to the house?" I said, standing on wobbly legs. "I've gotta get ready to go to Kitten."

Grams nodded absentmindedly as Ali picked up the phone.

"Ten minutes," Ali reported, not looking at me.

I nodded, heading out and gaining stability as I went.

Outside, it had rained heavily, leaving the ground wet and the air fresh. I inhaled deeply as a black Explorer pulled to the curb. Speedy service.

"Where to, ma'am?" the driver asked as I situated myself in the back.

"To the manor," I answered. I didn't owe Tate and Morgan an explanation as to why and how I was able to manipulate emotions, but I knew Grams would ride my ass until I answered their questions. If I were lucky, it would just be to satisfy their curiosity. If I were unlucky, hell, I didn't want to think about that.

The twinkling lights of the manor came into view, bright pinpoints breaking through my dark thoughts, and I smiled at the intrusion. It was peaceful, tranquil, and undisturbed by the madness of the world outside.

"I'll need a ride to Kitten in about an hour," I said to the driver.

"Very good, ma'am; I will wait here," he replied. I was about to leave when a thought struck me.

"Um, do you want something to eat?" I asked. No one had ever waited on me, and while having a chauffeur was kick-ass, I had no idea what was expected of me.

Oh crap, I didn't even know his name. Fuck it.

"Hey, just park and come in. Oh, and what's your name?"

Five minutes later, the tall, lanky, chocolate-skinned driver and I were seated at the pine table consuming whole-wheat pasta and salads, and I knew his name.

"It's nothing exciting," I said to Jerry from across the table in the empty kitchen.

He smiled pearly white teeth that contrasted with his dark skin. He was older than me but had managed to keep the carefree nature of his twenties intact.

"Doesn't matter," he said, pointing his fork at me. "Although it is mighty odd you don't eat meat," he stated, returning to his meal.

I shrugged. "Never appealed to me."

"You ain't never had fried chicken?" he asked, leveling a fork knowingly at me.

I made a face. "Actually, I have. They make the same out of tofu."

He made his own pained face. "That just ain't right."

I leaned back in my chair, my stomach full, wanting nothing more than a soft bed for the night. I didn't have time for even a nap; hell, I didn't even have a bed at the moment. Pulling in my annoyance, I pushed away from the table.

"I need to get a few things before we leave," I said to Jerry.

He nodded, finishing his pasta. "I'll meet you outside."

True to form, I arrived late. Thankfully, I wasn't on first, which gave Gunther enough time for my makeup and hair for the "Return of the Kitten" routine.

He smiled, admiring his handiwork. "Good to have you back," he said. I grinned behind the half cat mask, making my way to the stage. Kitten was designed with a stage that could dominate the center of the room but could also be broken apart and moved as needed. It was currently in the middle of the room, and for a surprise entrance, I climbed into the lighting system, managing not to break an ankle in my high-heeled boots. I heard a few soft whistles and a "welcome home" or two from the techs as I made my way above center stage.

The announcer boomed loudly, "Ladies and gentlemen, we have a very special surprise for you tonight. The namesake of Kitten has returned home and..." The lights focused down as I swung myself onto the stage with a soft thump. "Here she is!"

The brilliant lights captured me along with the crowd letting out surprised gasps. I smiled slowly, seductively shaking my curled hair around my shoulders.

"Hello, dolls," I whispered alluringly into the earpiece, enjoying my sultry voice reverberating around the floor.

Enthusiastic applause greeted those two words and my smile widened. I couldn't lie, it was fantastic to be loved, even by these pleasure-seeking, overinflated moneybags.

My particular skill set, which Grams had alluded to, was the simple fact that my dancing was a natural aphrodisiac, so much so that those attending had to sign disclaimers releasing us from responsibility for the consequences of their actions after the show. Tonight was no different; if anything, the effect was more powerful after my extended absence.

After a few refrains, the others joined me as the stage began its slow circular motion, ensuring everyone got a fair view while they enjoyed their gourmet dinners. I felt the energy of my fellow dancers pulsing in my veins, mingling with my own power, sliding over my skin and amplifying every sensation. My skin was tender where the leather halter-top didn't cover and my breathing felt labored from more than just the exertion of dancing.

I lost myself in that energy's touch, all of us becoming one as I unbraided my power, slowly losing conscious awareness of my limbs, trusting they would still keep rhythm and dance.

Eventually, as the music stopped, I had to abandon the blissful escape of flowing through the music, and crashed back to reality, pulling in my braids of power. I hated the disappointment of that moment, but the show must go on. I exited with the rest of the dance crew below the stage and we worked our way back to the dressing rooms, changing makeup and costumes for the rest of the evening's routines.

I had minor parts in the other dances. Didn't mean I kicked out less power, just kicked it out less noticeably. We finished the sets, waved goodbye to the crowd, and retired to the dressing rooms. Checking my phone, I found a text message from Jerry, waiting out back to pick me up when ready.

I texted him back, *Give me 10, I smell.*

He responded, *Good lord take 20. I just got the Beast detailed.*

I laughed. He called his SUV "the Beast?" We clearly had things to discuss.

Leaving at 3 a.m. with wet hair wasn't the brightest idea, but I was tired and wanted to catch up on the sleep I'd missed the night before. Truthfully, I should have known that wouldn't be possible. There is no rest for the Supernatural, wicked or otherwise. As I exited out the back of Kitten, my hopes of a quiet evening dying as I saw Mark leaning against the Beast, talking with Jerry.

If I was lucky, he was just hitting on my driver, which was beyond fine with me. Just because I wasn't getting any didn't mean they shouldn't enjoy themselves.

I had just about convinced my delusional self that I was correct, seeing Jerry throw his head back, laughing full force at something Mark said while Mark sported an equally playful smile. I even gave myself a mental pat on the back when Jerry casually touched Mark's forearm and Mark leaned forward to hear him better, which he had no need to do. I actually stopped in my tracks, wondering if I should leave them alone a little longer.

As was customary in my life, the tender moment of love and joviality was soon disrupted. Darren jumped out of a limo that I hadn't noticed behind the SUV and demanded loudly, "Is she out yet?"

What the fuck was he doing here? My limbs grew cold and I groaned, hardly containing my desire to stomp my feet on Kitten's concrete steps, seeing my dreams of a fluffy bed dying a bloody death.

Mark pulled back from Jerry's window, equally annoyed and embarrassed, and even Jerry looked a little red. Oh hell, I had just met him, but I was fond of Jerry, and if he could bring tight-ass Mark around to enlightenment, I was going to help, not hinder.

"Over here, Blondie," I yelled, still annoyed as I began moving again. "What part of closed for business do you have trouble with?" I taunted. He was taller than Mark, but where Mark boasted the shoulders of a linebacker, Darren was lean with bleached-blond hair matching his store-bought tan.

He stormed over in his custom-fit suit. "I have been waiting all night for you."

Crossing my arms over my chest, I shifted my backpack, kicking a hip out. "Sorry, some of us have to work for a living, spoiled ass."

It was his turn to sport some frustrated red now.

"I don't have time for this," he said, grabbing my upper arm and turning away, pulling me behind him. That was a classic mistake. I had his arm pinned painfully behind him before he moved more than a step.

"No touching," I whispered in his ear as I pushed him forward and away from me, ready to lay steel down in this alley.

"Shit, Darren, back off," Mark warned, now fully recovered from his earlier embarrassment. "She doesn't know."

"And what, pray tell, should I know?" I asked, curious, but still annoyed.

"It's his daughter," Jerry answered, coming out of the car, pointing at Darren and shrugging. "She ain't right," he finished, as though that was enough of an explanation.

I uncrossed my arms, shifting my backpack. "You think?" I asked, not fully voicing the question if she was one of ours.

Jerry shrugged. "I've never met her, but from what they've been describing, can't hurt to check it out."

I sighed, making my decision and instantly regretting it. "Let's go."

Mark hung back, whispering with Darren before following Jerry and me to the SUV. I gave Jerry a hard look as I got into the backseat. He smiled widely, motioning Mark to take shotgun.

"I like Jerry. Fuck this up, Mark, and I'm not above removing a few key body parts," I warned, snuggling down in my seat.

Jerry glared at me in the rearview mirror. "Really?" he mouthed.

"Geez, just kidding," I said to relieve the tension in the air. I supposed I should have cut Mark some marginal sort of slack; at least he was finally venturing toward where his heart led.

"Do you want to know what we have observed?" Mark said as I went to put my ear buds in.

"Nope," I answered, moving my hair from the wet mark it had created on my black t-shirt, now regretting not drying it.

He raised an eyebrow, so I explained, "I'm going to enjoy my music while you and Jerry discuss whatever the hell you want, or nothing. Not interested." I hit play and shoved my ear buds in.

Mark opened his mouth to say something, but I saw Jerry's mouth moving and then Mark closing his own as he turned around to listen.

I closed my eyes, listening to Miranda Lambert, my favorite country artist. She was a woman after my own heart, without the Executioner job title, but with the unstable life and desire for revenge.

I sighed, letting my thoughts run wild. My control was renewed after dancing and I had no worries of leaking into their conversation. Darren's daughter being a succubus was wildly possible. I wondered how long Jerry had been employed as a driver to recognize signs of a succubus. I had never met his wife, but occasionally the power of a succubus went untapped, either because it was weak enough to go unnoticed or because events never exposed it, and those lucky souls blended into humankind, never knowing a minefield of power lurked inside them. Blend untapped succubus blood with the powerful shifter blood of Darren and it wouldn't be surprising at all that, at four years old, Hannah was starting to display unmanageable traits. I could only imagine how annoyed Darren must be, a genuine smile spreading across my face as I pictured his little angel's outbursts.

I pulled my focus back to the SUV, watching Jerry and Mark's conversation change as Mark gave the final direction and Jerry pulled into a long driveway leading to a correspondingly massive house. It was less Georgia mansion, more modern, with clean lines and chrome.

Pulling out my ear buds, I exited the SUV without waiting for Jerry and Mark, pulling in a clean breath in the predawn hours. It was quiet; I didn't feel any kick, no lingering emotions to denote an untrained child of our bloodline.

Darren exited the house, almost running towards us. "Took you three long enough to get here! I've been waiting."

I gave Mark an annoyed look. "He's scared, Olivia," he whispered.

I reigned in my annoyance, walking towards Darren. "She awake?" I asked, tucking away my mp3 player.

He flicked a glance toward Mark, running his hands through his disheveled hair. I took a new look at Darren, noticing the black bags under his eyes, which I had originally assumed to be from excessive drinking and partying, the wrinkled outfit, and the fear in those eyes. Mark was right. Darren was more than scared, he was terrified. True to form, I was only making things worse.

I didn't want to kill anyone tonight.

"Darren," I said softly, standing in front of him, easing my tense shoulders and relaxing my stance. "Take me to her, please."

He searched my eyes, noticing the change. "Olivia, she is everything to me," he pleaded, his eyes moist.

"I know," I said with a small smile and a gentle touch on his arm. "I will help her." That's me, making impossible promises I don't know if I could keep.

He nodded, turning to lead us inside the house. I turned to find Jerry still in the car. Oh, hell no. I shook my head, indicating he needed to get his ass over here.

Jogging to catch up with Mark and me, he gave a tentative smile. I ignored him.

If the outside was modern, the inside was ultra-modern, with a side of too-sterile-for-normal. That was all I had time to notice, as Darren raced up the stairs before I could take a second look. I jogged up after him, my calves and quads complaining thanks to the dancing earlier. I pushed on, starting to feel unsettled in the pit of my stomach.

Darren paused outside an open doorway. I pushed past him, sickened by the sight in front of me. Hannah was strapped down to a small hospital bed, an IV in one arm, a feeding tube in her mouth, and an oxygen mask generating her breathing.

Slowly, I made my way to her side. The last time I had seen her was two years ago, I guessed. She had been a normal, happy little troublemaker.

"When did her mother pass?" I asked, pausing at her side, my hands gripping the steel bed frame.

Without looking away from his dying daughter, Darren answered, "Right after her third birthday."

I nodded. "Is there a nurse on call right now?" I asked gently.

He tore his attention from Hannah, releasing a ragged breath as he answered, "Yes."

"Please call her in," I said, grinding the steel bed frame against my palms.

Darren left with Mark while Jerry waited in the hallway.

"Jerry," I called.

"Yes, Olie," he answered.

"I'm going to need to you run back to the manor and get clothing for at least a week for me and yourself." I turned to look at his shocked face. "I also need you to see Grams and have her arrange a replacement for me at Kitten."

He nodded. "Please go now," I said gently.

Without a word, he was gone. I heard the front door close a few moments later.

A minute after that, Darren and Mark arrived with a disheveled woman in a dark blue robe between them. "What can I help you with?" she asked me, rubbing sleep from her eyes.

"You are to stop all medication this instant," I said shocking her.

She recovered quickly. "I'm sorry, but unless you have a license to practice medicine, I do not take orders from you," she proclaimed smugly.

"You're fired," Darren said. "Pack your belongings. Mark will drive you home tonight."

She was stunned silent, and truthfully, so was I. I must be his last hope, I realized, and he was placing all his faith in me. No pressure. I took a long inhale.

"Darren," I said gently, "I might be able to change her mind." The threat of being fired, I was positive, had just helped my cause.

Not losing the scowl, he nodded, moving towards his daughter and reaching for her hand. "Don't," I whispered.

His gaze jerked to mine, shocked. I took another deep breath, coming to stand by his side. "Every emotion you feel right now will be transferred to her with your touch: your fear, your hopelessness, your guilt, everything."

He looked like a puppy I had just kicked. Pressing my hand to his, I offered, "I can help her," infusing into it all the hope I could muster. "But you have to listen to me." He nodded, a single tear slipping down his cheek.

The nurse stepped forward and demanded, "How do you know that?"

"Because she is exactly the same as me," I said, meeting her stare.

She scoffed, "She is a shifter, not a succubus," placing extra emphasis on that last word to indicate her disgust for my kind.

"Get out. You are not to be in this room without my supervision," I said. "As soon as her feeding tube and the breathing machine have been removed, your services will no longer be needed."

I nodded to Mark to remove her. Without hesitation, he took her arm, ignoring her squawking.

Turning back to Darren, I slipped his hands into my own. "She *is* a shifter, Darren. She just has an extra power, being part succubus," I said, worried he would view his daughter differently. Seeing no change in his worried gaze, I pushed on. "I've sent Jerry back for supplies. We need a room for him; I'll be staying here with her."

I wasn't sure he heard me, his face showing no reaction as he kept watching his pale, sleeping angel. Even her blond hair looked dingy. She was dying, I couldn't deny it.

"What did I do wrong?" he questioned, looking at me with a broken heart.

I squeezed his hand. "Nothing. You did the best you could." I sighed. "I'm guessing your late wife had latent power, and when she died, Hannah's own power came into full bloom. It's overwhelming when it happens like that, especially if you don't know what's happening. The sedatives she was on helped to give her extra time, but eventually, the continual dimming of our emotions leads to death, every single time."

Mark came back in the room, looking at us.

"Jerry will need a room prepared," Darren said softly, not looking away from Hannah. "Have the rollaway brought in for Olivia."

Mark nodded, heading out. I pulled my hand away from Darren. He finally looked at me, nodded once, and left.

I breathed a sigh of relief; I had my work cut out for me.

I checked my phone to find a text from Grams. *Trouble?*

I answered back, noting the time was after 5 a.m., *No worse than the usual. Coverage for Kitten?*

She responded, *Rose is better.*

Perfect, that was one item off my plate. My phone buzzed again, *Don't forget, Morgan and Tate both wish to speak with you. They called again inquiring after you.*

I had forgotten all about that. *One crisis at a time. Right now, they don't rate.*

I set the phone down as a maid came in with the bed. Setting my watch alarm for three hours, I landed on the thin mattress before she even finished unfolding it.

Chapter 3

The soft ping from my watch had me instantly alert and aware. Hannah's breathing still came from that awful machine, but with the drugs dissipating from her system, I could feel her emotions stirring slowly, as though underwater.

I pulled down the comforter and made a stumbling bathroom trip. Jerry had returned during my nap with my favorite duffle bag. Sorting through it, I saw that it was relatively untouched by Grams's cleaning. I changed into my favorite yoga pants and pulled my now-dry hair out of its braid, letting it fan around my shoulders in waves. Checking my jacket pocket, I found my mp3 player and scrolled through playlists, putting on my classical mix before breathing deeply and shaking out my limbs.

What I had to do next was critical: absorbing her emotions since her mother died, when everything began. I hated this part. I had so much of my own misery, I didn't want anyone else's. Pushing out a breath, punctuated by my nerves, I shook out my arms one more time.

Sitting cross-legged on the end of Hannah's bed, I picked up my phone and sent a text to Jerry. *You here?*

Yes, you need something?

Don't let anyone in until I text you, I responded, turning my phone to silent.

Have I mentioned I didn't want to do this? Trepidation formed a sickening lead weight in my empty stomach, but no time like the present to dive into crap that could kill me. I swallowed the fear, anxiety and insecurity that threatened to bubble up and choke me. I asked myself the same question I always did, *Was I willing to die for her?* The answer, predictably, was yes, so I began breathing deeply and centering myself, making sure my tightly woven core was quiet.

On my third exhale, I pushed my focus outside my body, hovering just above my skin in a perfect golden color. Fourth exhale, I formed a tendril of my consciousness into the whip I needed to break the bubble of Hannah's emotions. If I drew too large a hole, I wouldn't be able to contain it all, and she would feel the burden of the excess trying to get out, hampering my ability to keep her calm.

Fifth breath, I pulled my whip back, cracking it against her core, and thus began an onslaught of a year's worth of emotions that ripped toward my soul like a tornado. The first wisps were as dark as night, and once they made contact, I fought to maintain my ability to breathe.

Inky coils of tar coated my very existence with hopelessness so deep and vast that there was nothing else, a despair born of loneliness and the inability to understand why her mother left or why her father had such potent and volatile anger.

The ache cut a clear path across my chest, burning into my heart until tears spilled down my face.

Gritting my teeth, I fought against it all, braiding and coiling until my eyes ached from being clenched closed and my nails stabbed angry cuts into my palms. Still I pushed on, shaking my head and pulling in a clean breath, my tank top damp from the sweat pouring down my back.

Onward I pushed with no sense of time or release, seeing only darkness, until there was nothing left to pull. The silence weighed heavily and the air felt stagnant and overly warm. Behind my closed lids, I pushed everything I had pulled from Hannah into a metal ball, sealed the edges in fire, and dropped it into the pit of emotions that weren't mine. To my own ears, it landed with a loud clank. How many more could I pull from? How many more emotions that weren't mine could I absorb? I was worried I would tap out someday, be too full to help anyone else, but realistically, I wouldn't live that long. I pushed that thought away as well.

Dropping my chin to my chest, I felt around for my phone, opening my eyes slowly to ward against the rolling of my stomach and the dizziness in my head.

I texted Jerry, *I need the nurse.*

The door opened slowly and I didn't turn to look. "Get everything out of her," I commanded hoarsely. Crap, had I been screaming?

The nurse shook as she complied with my instructions. There was a form behind her, but I couldn't focus long enough to see who it was. Once she had completed the task, I pulled my energy from Hannah like a blanket being withdrawn from her sleeping form, and miraculously, her eyes opened.

I finally lost consciousness.

The emptiness was a welcome reprieve but it still couldn't drown out the voices around me.

"How?" Darren asked. "How?" he repeated, shock registering in his voice.

"Ain't my place to know," Jerry replied.

"It's been a full twenty-four hours and she hasn't moved at all," Mark stated, slightly worried.

"She'll be fine," Grams answered. "She did a draining pull; this is to be expected."

"Do you know how?" asked Darren.

I heard the rustling of fabric and the patter of tiny feet that could only be Hannah's. Gently, she pressed her tiny lips to my cheek, and then patted my head, a little roughly. "My Olie," she proclaimed.

I would have smiled if I'd had the ability.

"It's your brother, Darren. He's sending out a representative, given Hannah's sudden improvement and enhanced abilities," Mark warned.

"That selfish bastard," Darren said softly.

In the background, Hannah's baby talk sounded innocent and gentle.

I had never met Darren's brother Logan in person, thankfully. We traveled in the same circles occasionally when I worked security for Grams during political meetings and other such boring events. He was the head of the Shifter Nation for the entire United States. Why was he interested in Hannah? He was her uncle, so I understood the emotional attachment, but the representative did not bode well.

As succubi, we did not advertise our existence to either Supernaturals or humans, but those in certain circles knew who we were and what we did. Well, I should amend that—the majority simply thought of us as magically gifted strippers and/or whores. I was perfectly content with that undervaluation of our skills. Hannah's enhanced abilities rolled around in my brain as darkness descended yet again.

...

It wasn't the yelling or the thumping outside my makeshift sleeping quarters that did it. Hannah's soft sobs broke into my private darkness, forcing me out. I was on my side, facing the door and the empty medical bed, when my eyes finally did open to partial daylight.

I scratched my three-day-old hair, maybe four days old, who was really counting, anyways? Sitting up, I tried to get my body to start cooperating.

"Olie," Hannah screamed, her tiny feet pounding as she ran from behind into my arms.

I kissed her blond locks, inhaling jasmine. "Hi, baby girl," I croaked, looking for water.

Jerry came from my side, handing me a cup. "How long have I been out?" I asked, noting the strain and worry on his face, as the noise outside the door started up again.

"Three and half days," he answered, not looking at me.

"What's going on?" I asked.

He sat down next to me on the rollaway bed. "Hannah—" he started, then stopped as Hannah's head popped up, glaring at him.

"They say I'm wrong," she said, her bottom lip pouting out.

"Really?" I asked, stroking her hair. "Why is that?"

"Cause I make..." She screwed up her face, not sure of the words. "I make them all feel like me."

I nodded in understanding, holding her close. "There is nothing wrong with you. That is our greatest strength, being able to make people feel like we do, but we can't do it all the time." She pulled away to look at me. "That's why you will have a special teacher to help you."

She smiled, bouncing in my arms. "Really?"

"Yes, but right now, I think we need to deal with the commotion outside." I turned my attention towards the door.

"Jerry," I asked gently.

He grunted his response, worry clouding his normally carefree eyes, still staring at the door.

"Thank you," I whispered. I had known him for less than a week and he had stayed here with me, ignoring the risk to himself, keeping Hannah and me safe. I thought he might even deserve a raise.

He took a deep breath. "They gave the shifter representative the same explanation you gave them. He wants to take you and Hannah for testing in Chicago." Turning his attention to me, he added, "I wouldn't leave."

I smiled and sighed. "Why can't you be straight?" I demanded playfully. "Bi, maybe?" I teased.

He smiled as his carefree youth returned. "Sorry, darling."

"Oh well," I sighed dramatically. "Guess I better go deal with this representative."

I stood, stretching my stiff limbs.

"You sure you're alright?" Jerry asked as I reached the door.

"Eh, aside from needing a shower, right as rain." I smiled, opening the door.

Darren and Mark were doing an excellent job keeping two goons away from the door as another—the representative, I assumed—waited impatiently for his opening.

"Gentleman," I said, closing the door quietly behind me and crossing my arms defiantly over my chest, "your services are no longer needed."

I smiled, uncoiling long, thick braids of rope, the mental exercise feeling long overdue after three days of rest. Rolling my shoulders, I leaned a hip against the doorframe, looking for a fight.

Darren and Mark looked a little the worse for wear, but nothing that would leave a lasting mark.

"Who are you to make such decisions?" asked the representative, his waves of insecurity poorly hidden by his pathetic attempt at abusing his authority.

My smile widened, my confidence bolstered by the little angel awake and alive behind me. "Darling," I said, slowly moving past Mark, Darren and the goons, "I am the beginning, the middle, and, if you keep pushing, soon to be the end of your story."

He took a tentative step back, his shock of bleached blond hair rising a bit. Fear and violence were the only tools I kept with me. I leaned in close. "A little birdie said you wanted to take me and mine away for testing?" I hissed the last word out, my contempt and disgust pulsing in the air.

He paled, becoming flustered. "I am Steven, and I..." he stressed, pulling himself up straight, "was sent by Master Logan to assess the damage done by you, changing Hannah into a monster like you. She was sick and on her deathbed. You ruined her!" he hissed back, attempting to meet my hatred with his own.

Yep, that pushed me over the edge.

I pushed him over the railing to the floor below, enjoying the terror in his scream as I landed squarely on his chest, the cracking of his ribs bringing a smile to my face. The all-powerful Steven attempted to dislodge me, flailing as I looked down at him smugly, feeling his desperation to get away and his anger at his inability to do so.

"Get off of me, you whore!" he hissed at me. Slowly, sneering, I obliged.

"Tsk, tsk, Steven, that's no way to talk to your superior," I goaded him, smiling as he pushed into a sitting position, disgust, hatred and pain contorting his features.

I distantly heard the pounding on the stairs as the others took the less dramatic way down. I smiled, watching Steven writhing on the floor.

"Olivia," Mark said, keeping Darren behind him.

"Finish him," Darren said, deadly serious. The fucker had just said his daughter was scheduled to die.

I smiled, moving forward gladly.

One of the goons precariously stood between me and my kill.

"Easy," he said, holding his hands up in supplication as his buddy pulled Steven off the floor. "We didn't come here for this."

I tilted my head. "What did you come here for?" I asked, genuinely interested.

The man grimaced, his dark eyes looking slightly embarrassed. "In our official capacity, were to see Hannah and judge the effects of you being present around her."

"Why the testing?" I asked.

"Steven went a little off the reservation," he admitted, with a shrug.

I took a step forward and he held his ground uncertainly. Leaning forward, I whispered inches from his face, "If anyone Logan sends steps off the reservation again, your leader will be notified by their head on his front lawn." I leaned back, watching the sick look on his face.

He nodded once and moved to help his partner make a quick exit with Steven.

I really need to kill something, I thought, my fists clenching and unclenching at my sides.

Darren had gone back upstairs but Mark remained, watching me.

"You have issues," he stated.

I feigned shock, rolling my eyes as I moved past him upstairs to Hannah and Jerry.

"All clear," I said, knocking on the door.

Hannah rushed out, wrapping her arms around my knees.

"Olie, you stink," she proclaimed.

I laughed, heading to a shower.

Chapter 4

The steaming hot water helped burn off some of the irritation from my blood, but the core of it remained just under the surface, waiting to flare out at any slight misstep.

Jerry handed me my bag as I exited the bathroom in fresh jeans and a sea-green fitted t-shirt. "We gotta go," he stated, moving on.

I trusted him, but I seriously didn't like taking orders.

Sitting in the passenger seat, I kept my silence, knowing full well my irritation wasn't really at him and not wanting to burn this new bridge. Not many people tolerated me as long as Jerry already had, which spoke volumes for my nonexistent people skills.

So I sat and watched the countryside pull into view, the city replaced by a two-lane highway. Twenty minutes outside the city limits, I felt myself relax, my anger and fear for those I protected beginning to dim.

"Where are we headed?" I asked, shifting in my seat.

He spared me a glance. "Back to town," he answered, pulling a U-turn.

My face must have given me away. "Something pretty bad went down while we were protecting Hannah," he explained with a sigh. "I know you can handle the graphic gore, but for my own sake, I needed to take a drive."

"What are you?" I asked, worried he just might be able to read my mind.

He gave a halfhearted smile. "Good ol'-fashion magic dabbler."

I snorted. "Sounds dangerous."

He raised an eyebrow. "Hence why I am your driver."

I outright laughed.

...

An hour later, we were at the county morgue and I was grateful for the long drive. A stout man with blond hair and deeply embedded crow's feet met us at the door.

"Olivia?" he said with no emotion. He had to be ex-military, standing at parade rest, his eyes quickly assessing me before scanning the street behind me.

I nodded.

"Detective Mercer. Please follow me," he said, opening the door and holding it for us.

I raised an eyebrow at Jerry, feeling I had missed something. He shrugged, and I didn't see any glimmer of information kept from me.

Detective Mercer led us down a maze of barren and lonely concrete hallways until we finally arrived at a crowded, sterile morgue.

Mercer stopped at the first body, pulling the sheet back. A young woman stared back at me, her throat ripped out.

He moved silently to the next, keeping a close watch on me as he performed the same menial task, revealing a male teenager, also robbed of his throat. The next six were exactly the same.

"The show is over," I said tiredly. "Now's the part you tell."

The corners of Mercer's eyes clenched, the only sign I had riled him. "They were killed in their home and drained of blood by a vampire or vampires. You are now the new liaison between the Supernaturals and humans." He handed me a large file. "Fix it."

I warily accepted the thick manila folder he pressed against my chest, my aquamarine glare never leaving his own challenging, sun-bleached eyes. He looked away first. Turning, I looked to Jerry's shocked face.

I had to be honest, this was a blindside by Governor Hash and a very smart move on his part, but there really was only one way to get shit done.

I would take the job and I would "fix it," as Mercer so delicately put it. Then I'd assign it to someone who actually had a permanent address here in St. Ann.

"Are you my liaison?" I asked, not bothering to look at him as I perused the file in front of me.

He shifted uneasily, unbuttoning his tweed jacket and stuffing his hands in the matching pants, my question throwing him. "That is correct. My contact information is attached to the first file."

He walked us out, the added burden of the multiple homicide case files a lead weight around my neck. I had been back all of five days and already had more responsibility than I was comfortable with.

Fantastic.

I had Jerry drop me off at the manor and gave him the next three days off, considering he had missed the weekend with my three-and-a-half-day blackout.

I stood in front of the house in the dying afternoon light, wanting desperately to go in, throw my worries and cares away, snuggle up with the kids, and just be happy.

I missed them.

I missed being happy. It was an emotion I never really latched onto without them. Not surprising, given my history. Instead, I stood there with my eyes closed and my duffle bag at my feet, already knowing what my decision was and wishing I could change it.

Feeling the threat of hot tears, I knew I had to leave before they spilled down my cheeks. I picked a midsize car from the fleet at the manor and fled away from the one place I could be happy. I had work to do.

After a depressing drive, I stopped for a bottle of wine and French fries before heading to an overpriced hotel with an amazing view of the city.

Dropping my bag on the floor next to the bed, I hid a few key weapons around the room. Although I was registered under a false name in a luxury hotel, far from my dumpy motel comfort zone, it never hurts to be prepared.

Oh, and I had the Do Not Disturb sign hanging on the door, duh.

I drank straight from the warm wine bottle, spreading the files around on the desk. *Alright, little darlings, what are you going to tell me?*

I picked up the file of the daughter, the first body Mercer had shown me, thinking he might have reasons for a particular order.

She was twenty years old, attending college and home for the weekend. The listed cause of death was extensive loss of blood. There was an up-close picture of the wound on her neck. I turned it, studied it, and brilliantly concluded that I couldn't say what the fuck did it.

Next was her brother, eighteen, about to graduate high school, a wrestler and straight-A student. There was bruising around his left eye and rib cage. He had fought back before his throat was torn out, same as his sister's. Still no clues as to by what.

The mother was next, a forty-five-year-old biologist, relatively successful if her daughter's education was any indication. I compared the picture of her neck to the children's. The image was larger, allowing me to see four hardly evident scratch marks beginning at the base of her neck.

I meticulously went through the rest of the images: father, grandmother, grandfather, aunt and uncle. They were all the same, except for the mother. I held the picture of her wound apart; what made her different? If I was betting, I'd say she was the real target and everyone else, collateral damage. Who the fuck had she pissed off?

The files didn't give any personal information aside from the basics. I would need Mercer in order to move forward. I had a nagging suspicion he had planned it that way. Rummaging through the files, I found his number and dialed.

"Mercer," he answered, gruff and short.

"Olivia," I said, waiting for acknowledgement. Getting none, I simply plowed right on, "I need the financial workup on the mother, Jane, and the father as well. Also—" The line went dead; well, that was just rude.

Tapping the hotel pen against the files, I gave serious thought to finding him. He didn't seem the type to let this file gather dust while intentionally sabotaging me. That certainly didn't mean he wasn't, but typically, my instincts were dead on, literally. I'd give him the rest of the day before I started making his life interesting.

Checking my watch, I laughed. He wasn't the rude one, I was—it was 2 a.m. He, being a human, would be sleeping at this time of the night. Oops, guess I deserved that. Those four scratches bothered me. Did something rip out their jugulars? Where the fuck was all the blood? I pulled out the pictures, scouring all of them, looking for images that showed the carpet or furniture. Nothing. All I had were close-ups in the morgue. I was missing a large part of these files.

I looked down at my cell phone and debated, almost calling Mercer back. He apparently didn't like sharing. Moving to lie down on the couch, I took my wine but left the files, the information and pictures running through my mind. I was missing something, probably more than one something, and truthfully, I wasn't sure if it would be in Mercer's files or not.

I turned onto my side, sighing. Either way I had to resolve this. Human law enforcement thought it was a vampire. I wondered what the vampires thought of that. It was Wednesday—no, wait, Thursday morning, according to my phone. Mallory was off; I wondered what she was up to. No time like the present to find out.

I texted her, *You hear about the "vampire" murders?*

I waited all of three seconds before she responded, *Not vampires.*

How can you be sure? I texted back.

My phone almost jumped out of my hand, ringing.

"Are you fucking serious?" Mallory demanded.

"Typically," I responded, trying to hide my amusement at her.

"Do you have any idea of the fallout we are seeing because of the murders? There's holy water on every surface outside and I have people carrying stakes around the complex, and torches. Do you hear me?" She screamed, "TORCHES!"

Mallory, when not at Kitten, ran security for the Centennial House. She was just as pissed as me when the House came forward, announcing their presence to the public.

"You need me to run interference?" I asked hopefully.

"Fuck no!" she yelled again. "I have enough issues without a bloodthirsty Executioner darkening my doorstep. Figure out what the fuck killed those people, Ms. Liaison, and hurry up."

I didn't even have a chance to ask her how she knew about my added responsibility, as the line went dead. I stared at my suddenly silent phone, second time in one night. Guess my people skills were holding steady.

Sitting up, I pulled another long swig of wine, letting my feet rest on the coffee table.

Why the entire family? If the main target was the mother, why kill the rest? If I were the murderer, why would I do that? The first reason that came to mind was that they were all a part of something evil. Second was that I was worried one or more would come after me for revenge. Third, maybe I wanted to torture her by forcing her to watch everyone she loved die before her. I set the wine on the table, going back to the file, looking for the death order. Please let that be there, at least.

Times of death put the grandparents first, then three hours later, the husband/father. Three hours, what the hell?! It did not take three hours to drain a body, I could vouch for that firsthand, especially if a hungry vampire was doing the draining. An off-the-reservation vamp would have drained each of them quickly before moving on to the next. A human family of eight had little chance against the undead. Ugh! Again, the file was missing photos that would show if there were any signs of struggle beyond the son's bruises.

Back to the order, next were the aunt and uncle, both siblings to the mother. Strange, did they have spouses? If so, that was a loose end to tie up. After the aunt and uncle, the children were next, then finally the mother.

I scratched my nose and attempted to pull more wine, realizing sadly I was out. Crap, but I supposed I did need to get some sleep. I stretched and chucked the wine bottle into the garbage before stripping out of my clothing and crashing onto the bed. The green glow informed me the sun was about to rise at 4:30 a.m.

...

At 8 a.m., I was jerked awake by my nightmares, my sweat slick against my body, seeping into the white sheets beneath me. Shaking my damp locks, I stumbled into the shower.

When Mercer finally called back at 9 a.m., I was more than ready for an influx of information to my starving files.

"Morning, sunshine," I answered, cradling the phone with my shoulder as I laced up my boot.

He grunted, "Shouldn't you be sleeping?"

"Nah," I answered, strapping on my watch. "Sleeping is highly overrated. So, I have a few questions," I started, mentally organizing my list of questions.

"Meet me at the station," he said, hanging up, again.

Alright, while I will fully admit to having a whole nest of issues, he was just plain rude. I consoled myself with that fact while driving to the station.

"So, good looking," I said, setting my coffee on his desk, "what d'ya got for me?"

He didn't even look up, but studiously moved papers across his desk. Looking closer, I realized what the beautiful glossy photos were—crime scene pictures of the actual house. Score!

In the first photo, an immense red stain covered the baby blue carpeting, while the furniture was untouched. Up the stairs, I could see a body behind the railing with an arm casually draped over. The next picture was the body on the stairs, the daughter, also lying in a pool of her own blood, lifeless eyes clouded over in death, her throat ripped in half.

"Did they test those substances around the bodies?" I asked, reaching for the pictures over his shoulder.

Mercer looked up at me. "No."

Leaning closer, I took in the next picture, of the son, which confirmed what I had suspected. The room he was in had damaged plaster along one wall, furniture strewn about, and a bookcase overturned. He fought hard to live. As I looked into his empty, glassy eyes, I promised I would find the son of a bitch who snuffed out his entire family's existence.

"Do you want me to fail, Mercer?" I asked softly, close to his ear, my anger pushing against my shields.

His hands froze mid-shuffle, blood draining from his face.

"Why is my file missing these?" I whispered, moving closer and pulling a rope of confidence from my core to bolster my claims. I needed to know who the fuck this guy was playing for. If I had to break into the police station, I wasn't above it. Honestly, I wasn't above much when I was pissed off.

My phone buzzed, interrupting my interrogation.

"Olivia," I answered, straightening up quickly.

"Hey, it's Kass." Her tone had me moving away from Mercer.

"What?" I asked, wanting to get to the heart of the matter.

"I've been helping Hannah learn control and just overheard that Logan is going to be in town Saturday morning. Darren is livid. I don't know what Logan said, but Darren asked if I knew of any safe houses. Apparently, Logan owns this house and Darren is worried about Logan's goons trying to take Hannah," she finished quietly.

Ice moved through my veins. "Relocate Friday night. Do you know where?" I asked softly.

"Yeah, Olie, I know. You really think..." She paused before finding the courage to continue, "You think he would hurt his own niece for being one of us?"

"Absolutely," I answered. "I'll be over this afternoon. Isn't it a bit early for you?" I asked, checking my thick-banded watch.

"Um, yeah. Early start to the day and all that jazz," she answered unsteadily. Hannah's cry came from the background. "I gotta go, Olie."

I stared at my phone, wondering what in the three rings of hell was going on there. Shrugging, I turned back to Mercer. His color had returned; time to make it flee again.

As I took a few steps forward, he stood, stopping my progress. I gave him my wide-eyed, innocent look. "Don't," he warned, buttoning his black jacket and stuffing his hands into the navy blue pants. "Let's go."

"Where to?" I asked with fake enthusiasm.

He didn't answer me, walking away instead. This was not going well at all. Following him, I saw nothing but the blasé interior gray walls and yellow linoleum as we twisted through corridors, pressing open a metal door into the blinding morning light.

Squinting, I followed him around the squad cars, pristinely lined up and squeaky clean, to a rusty old pickup truck.

As I opening the door, it gave a warning creak. Sliding into the newly reupholstered seat, I gave his square profile a disbelieving look.

"What?" he asked, cranking the engine.

"Country much?" I asked as Hank Williams belted out on the stereo.

He grunted, leaving the parking lot and the police station with its steel gates behind.

Paranoia tapped my shoulder, pointing out that I was in a truck with a man I didn't know, traveling to an unknown destination with no one knowing where I was. That sounds like a brilliant plan, she taunted me. Those were some valid points. I mulled over whether I could take Mercer. It wouldn't even be close; it was much easier for me to drop bodies than it was for him.

That hesitation would undoubtedly give me the upper hand and get him killed. I leaned against the stiff new upholstery, feeling the gun in my back push back with reassurance, not to mention the hidden blades as well. I pushed paranoia back down and paid attention to the city outside the windows. The homes had become larger, newer, with landscaping that required a crew to maintain.

Mercer checked his paperwork, flipping open a manila envelope before pulling into the curved driveway of a home with tall wrought iron gates. I like the idea of gates, but these were easy to scale for a vamp and easier to bend for a shifter. The Manor had real wrought iron gates that could conduct electricity if needed, and I always thought it was needed.

The gates opened automatically as we approached, another huge no-no in security, although it did prove the family thought it had nothing to worry about. I was, of course, assuming this was the crime scene. The grumbling truck ceased its ranting as I slid out the side of the vehicle, taking in the austere face of the home, the intricate beauty of the burnt red door marred by the yellow police tape slashing across its face.

Mercer walked around his classic beast, leaving his file behind and picking up a briefcase from the truck bed.

I eyed his stiff gait and pondered the nonexistent conversation, my suspicions growing. Climbing up the pristine steps, I came up with a plan. Not the best of plans, but I was confident I could pull it off.

I followed Mercer into the home, closing and quietly locking the door behind me. He turned, raising an eyebrow, and I smiled a slow, sexy smile. "You have some explaining to do," I whispered.

He bravely moved within an inch of my face, his eyes giving nothing away. I smiled genuinely now—this could be fun. I moved my fingers to his button-down shirt, my eyes not leaving his face. "Mercer," I whispered.

He growled a reply, nuzzling my neck. I drew an exaggerated gasp, undoing the second button, my fingers stalling as I brushed the wiretap on his chest. "Don't stop," he said, a little too loudly.

I pulled his shirttails out of his pants, quickly undoing the rest of the buttons. "Take me now," I whispered roughly.

"Turn around," he growled, moving away to bang the table against the wall, nicely in line with the illusion that I was a succubus whore and his wiretap was destroyed in the process by my violent tendencies. I would almost be annoyed if I didn't find the situation ludicrous.

I gave a strangled cry. "More," I screamed.

He continued the assault on the table. "Come on baby, you can do better," I said with a sultry smile.

"Really?" he mouthed at me, rocking the table faster.

I made a strangled moan and started panting. Mercer was concentrating on the table and never saw me rip off the wiretap. "Fuck," he screamed, glaring at me. Then he remembered his part and kept his panting up.

I smiled, moving the tap outside, underneath his truck tire. Who even used these archaic things? Shouldn't it have been a high-tech pen? Guess I'd have to ask the guilty party on that and stop watching so much James Bond.

Mercer was waiting, arms crossed, when I stepped back in, not bothering to lock the door this time.

"What the fuck, Mercer?" I asked with equal measures of pissed off and slightly aroused.

"They made me wear it—" he started.

"Who?" I interrupted, shoving him back a step.

He ran a hand over his close-cropped blond hair. "Hash," he answered reluctantly. "He wants evidence to prove that you're dangerous."

I sighed. "You would do better with a video recorder."

He shrugged. "I took the gamble that you were smart enough to figure it out."

I rolled my eyes. "Well, that's just wonderful. Now what the fuck is going on with my file?"

He shrugged. "Hash told me to not disclose everything to you," he sighed. "When you asked me those questions this morning, I realized you were serious about catching the murderer, so I decided to help instead of hindering."

"Fantastic! I'd hate to kill you after our romance." I wasn't smiling.

Mercer didn't say a word. Smart man.

"What's in the suitcase?" I asked, changing the topic.

He opened it on the carpet, revealing an interesting chemistry set. "We are on our own with this. So we are going to have to test everything ourselves."

I nodded. "Guess we better get to work."

...

Four hours later, we were at a diner digesting our findings. It was all blood, and there was so much of it that if a vamp had committed the murders, they hadn't sampled a single drop, which just didn't make any sense. There wasn't a single fingerprint, anywhere. How the hell was that possible?

Mercer had seen the scratch marks on the mother also, but being the stoic detective he was, wasn't calling them claw marks, going with "suspicious lacerations."

Whatever.

If they were claw marks, that would mean vampires and shifters would be the most likely suspects. Granted, there were other Supes who had or grew claws, but the strength needed to subdue a family of eight shrunk the suspect pool to the largest of the races.

I rubbed my temples, eating my second piece of apple pie after consuming my meal of a greasy veggie quesadilla and a double order of fries. I had to get to Kass soon; it was already later than I had planned.

"How can you eat that," Mercer asked, pointing to my empty plate, "and look like that?" pointing at me.

I raised an eyebrow. "I'm fucking fantastic."

That got me a chuckle. The truth was, I blew through calories faster than a call girl went through condoms, and I was always a few short.

I checked my watch, 6 p.m. "Can you give me a lift back to my car?"

He nodded, finishing his own sandwich before we paid.

The truck ride back was as quiet as the first, but this time, it was from silent speculation, not from having an unknown eavesdropper.

"It feels personal. Did you notice the order of death?" I asked, turning towards him.

"Yep," he said, shifting in the driver's seat.

"Anything strike you as odd?" I pushed.

He gave me an uncomfortable glance as traffic began to move at the now-green light. "Let's not jump to conclusions quite yet." We pulled into the parking lot next to my car. "I have an appointment with the next of kin tomorrow at 10 a.m."

I nodded. "See you then." Getting out the truck, I headed to my own car, already late for Kass and Hannah. My subconscious was still kicking around the crime scene, so I didn't remember much of the drive.

I was hungry again, though.

Hannah met me at the door. "Hannah," I heard Kass ask in the background, "who is it?" There was a slight tendril of worry coating her words.

Hannah smiled, launching into my arms. I was twirling her as Kass came to the door. "Feed me," I growled, tickling Hannah to hear her bubbling laughter.

…

An hour later, we were all sitting down to chicken parmesan, homemade marinara noodles, and fresh-from-the-oven bread.

"Kass," I said between mouthfuls of pasta and bread, "I had no idea you could cook."

She gave Darren a sheepish smile that fueled a nagging suspicion in my gut. Kass knew the kitchen too well, was comfortable around the help, and kept dodging my questions. I didn't like what my instincts had to say about it all.

Scrubbed, teeth cleaned, and hair dried, Hannah was deep in slumber when I closed the book, *I Want to Be an Astronaut*, and sneaked out, closing the door partially.

I slunk down the stairs, pausing before turning left to enter the den, where I heard Kass and Darren talking. Eavesdropping isn't something I typically engage in, but I made an exception.

"Now isn't the best time," Kass's voice reached me.

"We cannot keep doing this. That woman saved my daughter's life." Darren's ice clinked in his glass. "I won't lie to her, Kass," he affirmed.

I turned the corner and saw that Kass had her head tucked underneath Darren's chin. He was gently rocking her, which ceased when he saw me.

Moving quickly away, Kass tried for an explanation. "Olie, this isn't what it looks like."

"Save it," I said, putting a hand up. "I want the next words out of your mouth to be the truth."

Darren pulled Kass close to him, exuding protection. I wouldn't have expected that from the glorified, self-proclaimed manwhore. I was reluctantly impressed.

"Same deal goes for you," I said, taking a seat in one of the insanely expensive and uncomfortable high-backed chairs, settling in for the long haul.

"Olie, I never expected this to happen," Kass began, pulling free of Darren's embrace to lean towards me.

"Um, I'm going to need a little more clarification," I said, trying to ease the tension and annoyance out of my voice.

Kass looked to Darren. He gave a small nod, and she took a long breath. "We have been seeing each other for three months," she said, returning her attention to me. "I didn't know, I swear," she said, tearing up.

"Didn't know what?" I asked, perplexed.

Kass and Darren shared another look. "About Hannah," she said, as though that would explain everything.

"You didn't know she was part succubus?" I clarified.

Kass nodded, tears in her exotic brown eyes. "I'm a little confused why you would," I said, adjusting as my ass went numb.

"But you knew instantly," said Darren, his surfer blond locks disheveled.

"Yeah, I can also identify most Supernaturals at a glance, along with at least two different ways to kill them; it's part of my job description," I said, shrugging and pulling a strand of my dingy blond hair to twirl around my index finger.

Kass shook her head, still upset, looking at her clasped hands.

"What is really going on here? You have never been so distraught about not being able to identify a Supernatural before." I planted both feet on the ground and moved forward in my chair, analyzing Kass.

She looked up with a remorseful expression, shrugging. "I'm pregnant," she whispered. "What if I fail my own child?"

I sat back hard in my chair, whoa. For a full-blown succubus to conceive was difficult if not damn near impossible. Silence stretched out as I contemplated this news. A baby, another shifter/succubus baby.

Kass looked at me expectantly. I smiled. "You'll be fine," I said, charging it with contentment. "You'll be an amazing mother and if your child blooms, you'll be the first to know and deal with it perfectly."

"How can you know? How long has it been since this happened?" she asked, fully sobbing now.

I moved off the chair onto my knees in front of her, still smiling. "Too long," I whispered. "You are never alone, Kass, you have me and an entire clan behind you."

She lifted her head. "You're not upset?"

I laughed. "No, I'm excited!"

She smiled and threw her arms around me, crying tears of joy. I returned her hug, mentally checking off all the things I needed Kass to get done before the baby arrived: a will, a power of attorney, medical instructions, living arrangements, etc.

"We are getting married, Olie," Kass whispered into my ear.

Okay, now I was mildly upset. "Married?" I asked. Oh, marriage had a whole host of problems for me and I desperately wanted to talk her out of it, but the hope and love in her eyes killed the arguments before they ever reached my lips.

"Wow, that's a lot to take in," I said, easing back into the uncomfortable chair.

"What's wrong with marriage, Olivia?" asked Darren, his earlier joy replaced by concern.

"It makes my job complicated. Hannah and Kass are my top priority if something should happen, but being married puts the responsibility for both of them squarely on your shoulders, and I..." I looked away from my clasped hands to him. "I am the Executioner if anything happens to them."

Darren shifted uncomfortably and Kass's olive skin paled. "You mean like what almost happened with Hannah?" she asked.

"No," I said, trying to stay diplomatic. "That was beyond his control and understanding. I don't punish for what others don't know. However, now that you are both aware what Hannah is, there are policies in place that must be followed." I rubbed the back of my neck. I had written those policies when I was eighteen, the first legal document I put into effect with my hand-chosen leader. "Some of those items are not going to make sense, but each exists for a very specific reason and must be adhered to."

"Or what?" asked Darren.

It was my turn to shift uncomfortably. "The law has been amended since its inception to allow for wiggle room, but the end result is the same: If you fail to protect them, I assume responsibility for all the succubi in the house and relieve you of your head."

Spreading my hands wide, I said, "So you see why I'm concerned." I met Darren's stormy brown eyes. "I don't really want to kill you."

They both let go of the breaths they were holding. Yep, I have that effect on people. The title Executioner should pretty much explain it.

"That's a relief," Darren said, sitting back into the sofa. "I would never do anything to harm Kass or Hannah or..." he smiled at Kass, placing his hand over her stomach, "the new baby." He returned his attention back to me. "I understand your position, and while I am sure I will make mistakes, I will do everything in my power to keep them safe."

His demeanor may have seemed relaxed, but there was no mistaking the determination or sheer will power he was kicking out in protecting his family.

I nodded. "First order of business: you need to acquire a home not in your brother's name. Until that time, we will put you up in a safe house. Be ready to move Friday night. Second, you will all be assigned new cell phones." I stood up, stretching. "I'm not taking any chances."

Kass and Darren stood as well, walking me out. Darren started to say, "This house and all assets of representatives of the Clan belong to the Clan. I..." He paused, correcting himself, "We"—he smiled lovingly at Kass—"will undoubtedly catch grief for this breech of protocol."

I nodded. "I can see that, but—"

Darren raised his hand, stopping me. "I understand, Olivia. The first priority must be my family, and if something does happen to me, I wouldn't want them homeless," he said, taking my concerns seriously.

I nodded, reaching the door. "I'm glad we're in agreement about that."

"Olie," Kass said, taking my hands. "One more thing..."

I was mentally screaming, *what now?*

"Will you be my bridesmaid?" she asked hopefully.

My mouth opened and I squeaked. Then I closed it and tried a second time. "What? Kass, you have so many friends..." I trailed off, then found the words, "...who would be far more qualified in the girlie arena."

She rolled her eyes. "Yeah, that's why I'm not asking you to be my maid of honor. Just think about it, okay?" she said, opening the door. "It would mean a great deal to both of us."

I walked through the door, glancing at the happy couple, shocked out of my comfort zone. "Yeah, I will." I sighed. "So this means I'm back on as the replacement at Kitten?"

She smiled. "Yep. Good news is, the doctor cleared me for another week or so, since my body is already used to the constant dancing."

I nodded, making my way to the car. "Bye!" Kass yelled from the door. I lifted my hand in farewell, still not sure how I felt about everything.

Chapter 5

The really awesome and kick-ass feature about having a driver was the chance to process everything that had just happened without having to also concentrate on my surroundings. Less than two weeks of being spoiled by Jerry and, already, I considered him vital to my survival in the city. I sure could have used him that night.

I sighed, switching the radio to the local country station, smiling as I thought about Mercer listening to the same. Rolling my shoulders, I shifted my mind back to the murders.

There were so many unanswered questions, and I wasn't much of a stealthy detective. I was more the kind of girl who started pounding on doors and getting into dirty laundry while potential suspects were hog-tied. Part of my job as the Executioner was to determine complete guilt before I killed. Did I need it personally? Nope, sure didn't. However, running around murdering anyone I had a slight dislike for did not boost morale. It was a fine line, leading by fear.

Kass and Darren seemed so happy, overjoyed by the new addition and the survival of Hannah. I was jealous of their life; while they certainly had challenges to overcome, they would do it together, fight by each other's side, and raise two little angels.

For only a moment, I let my mind question if I had to be this way, a violent, short-tempered dancer. What else would I be? Normal? Could I have a steady, uneventful job with no threat on my life and coworkers who were not mortally terrified of me?

I laughed to myself. Nope, couldn't do it. I liked the excitement, the thrill of the chase, and the taking of lives. Something in my makeup was critically wrong, I understood that. But I had used it constructively, protecting those I loved.

My phone rang and I dug into my cross-body purse for it while trying my best to also pay attention to the road. It was a number I didn't recognize, but I answered, "What?"

"You have been dodging us, Olivia," said a voice I didn't instantly recognize.

"You are definitely going to have to be more specific than that."

The voice sighed. "You know, the manipulation of emotions to give blood freely at the Supernatural Council meeting," Tate said, as I now recognized the voice.

"Oh yeah, about that, I've been slightly preoccupied," I answered, completely missing the black SUV until it rammed my driver's side, effectively ending the call with Tate. The door crumpled into my body with my ribs taking the hit. Pain laced through my left leg and I knew without looking that it would have a huge, bloody gash. Fuck. The intensity of first blood boiled beneath the surface as the precious essence gushed out of my body.

Before the SUV had finished pushing my car, I redirected my blood lust into action, reaching for my gun and throwing myself into the backseat. My breathing was labored as my ribs screamed at the effort. Reaching deep for reserves of strength, I grabbed the strap of my purse and slung it around my head. I slipped onto my stomach, wincing as my ribs yelled at me yet again, and was out the backseat passenger side door and under my demolished car before my attackers got out to look for me.

I belly crawled, each and every movement driving sheer, blinding pain to my nerves from my ribs. I silently screamed at myself not to whimper, not to make a sound. The attackers finding an empty car would only grant me a few minutes' reprieve. At least that's how it went when I had been tricked by the same move myself. No one expected a person just rammed to possess enough mental stamina to block the pain and be able to move. Thanks to Selena, I could function just fine.

Finally, underneath the SUV on the driver's side, I stopped a moment to listen as the shooting pain in my left side caused me to pant in short, shallow breaths.

"Where the fuck did she go?" I heard, along with the searching of the car.

Perfect. The SUV was still running with the driver's door open. I exhaled another painful breath, climbing in as quietly as possible, leveling my gun at Steven in the passenger seat.

I really should have seen this one coming. First blood pounded in my temples, dimming my vision temporarily. My control was tested and maintained, as demonstrated by the fact I didn't shoot him on sight.

Instinctively, he held his hands up. I should have listened to Darren and killed him earlier. Throwing the SUV into reverse, I squealed the tires, pulling a 180 and probably ruining the transmission as I shoved it forcefully into drive. I kept the gun trained on Steven the entire time.

"Don't even dream of doing anything but sitting there and looking idiotic," I hissed between labored breaths. I really wanted to shoot him. Taking my eyes off him for a moment, I made a hard right into traffic, serenaded by screaming horns.

"I don't think so," he said, using the momentary slowing in the turn to jump from the moving vehicle. Fuck, I really should have shot him first. Was I ever going to learn? Pushing my head against the headrest, I drove dangerously to my hotel, parking the SUV in the local river first.

Glad I didn't have to obtain a new key card from the front desk in my current condition, I slammed my room door closed behind me. My cell was gone and I had no transportation. I heaved a sigh, ripping my shirt off and assessing the blackening bruises on my left side and sickly looking purple at my ribs. Taking a deep breath, I probed, seeing if anything was broken. It hurt like hell and I had to sit when my vision tunneled, threatening to end my rudimentary first aid. But my luck held; all ribs accounted for.

Throwing my ruined clothing away, I climbed into bed naked. I would heal faster than a human, but not as quickly as a shifter or a vampire. The sting of first blood would fester for days in my system and I would be crankier than usual. Great.

I drifted to sleep quickly, dreaming of the ways I was going to kill Steven. I had underestimated him. It wouldn't happen again.

My watch alarm woke me up at 9 a.m. My body was demanding more rest, but I had to deny it. The scalding hot shower helped loosen up my left side, but it was still sporting ugly yellow bruises that only renewed my plans to kill Steven. What I had seen last night as a gash on my left leg was now a thin scab running its length, but it still caused some discomfort as I got ready to face the day.

Dressed in my working leathers, I called the manor from a coffee shop five blocks away from my hotel.

"Grams," I said.

"Olie," she responded distractedly.

"First, I need a car, preferably Jerry, sent to the address I texted you yesterday, with an extra phone and gun. Second, call Kass and tell her plans have been moved up. Third, no shifters are to be trusted, with the exception of Darren," I finished, leaving no room for argument.

"Understood," Grams said. "Are you—"

I hung up on her; she was going to ask if I was okay. I sighed, drinking my overpriced coffee. What did she expect me to say? Yep, I'm great, had a hit taken out on me, sporting some gnarly bruises, and now potentially have a whole new list of people I need to kill. Yep, I am fucking fabulous.

I was trapped in a deep, dark pit of self-loathing, one I knew all too well. I had long ago given up on ever climbing to my freedom, instead flourishing in the distraction of throwing myself into one life-threatening situation after another.

If I were honest, brutally honest, I'd admit I was looking forward to the day when the knife was true, a bullet my last sensation. Death was my next big life move, not marriage and kids. How fucked was that? The sick part was that I felt sure I deserved to never be happy. Not after everything I had done, not after the blood that coated my blades, not after the decisions I had made. I wasn't destined for happiness, and it wasn't destined for me.

I wanted to push those emotions down deep, but I didn't have the energy or a reason to. Instead, they lingered just beneath my skin, sealed from the outside world but raging inside. I took another sip of coffee as "The Beast" pulled up. I wanted to smile but didn't have it in me.

Opening the passenger door, I gave Jerry directions to the police station. I still had a date with Mercer.

Thankfully, Jerry wisely didn't say a word more than to acknowledge my directions. Either Grams had warned him or he had picked up on my obvious body language. I had a tentative relationship with him at best, and given my current mood, I could ruin the entire thing in an instant. It had been a long time since I'd had companionship on my treks. Did it really matter? In a few days or weeks, I would likely be gone again for who knew how long, and forgotten—except, of course, for my legendary itch to kill.

As we pulled into the rain-dampened parking lot, I turned to Jerry. "In or out?" I asked.

"Out," he responded, playing with the radio. I stood there a moment, debating if I should say anything else. I wanted to say I was sorry for my misery and dragging him down. That it was probably best if he got himself out of this now. I closed the door instead, zipped my jacket, and added a few notches to my self-hatred, forcing my emotions within the boundaries of my skin.

At 9:45 a.m. I sat at Mercer's desk, waiting and staring at my bruised hands holding my warm coffee. I could feel my emotions cooling, leaving me with a sick, empty feeling. I already missed the misery; feeling something was better than sinking into the empty pit of desolation that was closing me off.

At 10:00 a.m., Mercer interrupted my brooding by stealing my coffee. I raised an eyebrow at him.

"Fee for parking your ass where it doesn't belong," he said, sporting a dark blue jacket and matching pants that set his platinum blond hair off nicely.

I almost smiled, but it came off as a smirk.

"Let's go," he commanded, moving away from the desk.

I moved along after him, stuffing my now empty hands in my jacket pockets, feeling my restlessness on a new level. Mercer was a peculiar hard ass, and yes, I really mean that in the physical and literal sense. While he projected the ultimate soldier, ready to carry out any order quickly and efficiently, I couldn't shake the notion that he had majorly pissed off his superiors by following his own moral code. After all, he was currently saddled with this case and with me.

The police station was decorated worse than most public schools, fluorescent lighting complemented by equally glaring linoleum and never-ending hallways. We finally arrived at the correct door.

Mercer ushered me into a conference room with a well-dressed man and woman sitting at the table.

"Mrs. Hatcher, Mr. Lowery," Mercer greeted them, "thank you for coming down here today under these circumstances."

"Whatever we can do to help, Mr. Mercer," said Mrs. Hatcher. Her dark brown hair was styled in an adorable, perfect bob. Pearls around her neck contrasted nicely with a black scoop neck dress. Her white-tipped nails tapped rhythmically on the faux wood table.

"Yes, Mr. Mercer, how can we help?" Mr. Lowery spread his large and slightly chubby hands wide, his balding head reflecting the light and his glasses reflecting Mercer's face. He was also well dressed, in a black pinstripe suit and navy tie.

Mercer opened his file. "Is there anything you can tell us that would shed light on why your spouses were targeted?" he said, diving into the heart of the matter.

So they were the husband and wife of the aunt and uncle found dead in the house. They both said no. Mercer tried again. "Did you notice anything suspicious, any unusual behavior from your spouses?"

Again, nothing useful.

"What was the relationship like between Jane and her son?" I asked.

They both shared a look before Mrs. Hatcher answered, "It was fairly rocky up until about a month ago. Then, suddenly, he was the perfect child. Did everything Jane said with no complaints, back talk, or problems with the law."

"I think something she was working on helped," added Mr. Lowery.

"What did she do?" Mercer asked.

They both shrugged. "She was very secretive, just said it was vital for everyone's safety," answered Mrs. Hatcher.

"We never gave it much thought, honestly," said Mr. Lowery. "We never imagined..." His voice trailed off as he lowered his head. He never imagined someone would reach out and claim the lives of those he loved. Mrs. Hatcher reached over and squeezed his hand.

"If we are done, Detective?" she asked, equally upset.

Mercer nodded, getting up to hold the door for them.

I settled back against the black plush chair, thinking.

Mercer came back, collecting his paperwork.

"So," I said in an annoyed tone, standing up into his personal zone, "Where did Jane work at?"

Mercer shrugged. "Back to digging. This case isn't going to be easy."

With that, he was gone.

I made my way back to the Beast and Jerry, unsure of what my next move would be as I climbed into the passenger seat again.

"Where to now?" Jerry asked, turning down the volume on the station he was listening to.

I shrugged, not making eye contact.

"Well, in that case," he said, pulling out of the police station and towards the busy city, "I have an idea."

I didn't bother to ask where; I didn't really care. I had time to kill, a red tape nightmare preventing me from properly doing my job, and a sick, sinking feeling in my gut.

I watched the horizon with an empty mind as my subconscious worked on problems even it couldn't figure out.

When we pulled into a mall, I asked, "Lunch?"

Jerry smiled. "Absolutely, then we are going to update that horrific wardrobe."

I looked at him, taken off guard. "Shopping? Really?"

"Yes," he answered, coming around the SUV to help me out. "Now, my dear, let's go. I've been given full permission by Grams to buy anything I see fit."

I laughed, closing the passenger door, hiding my hands in my jacket pockets from the chilly wind. "Anything?" I asked, wanting to push this issue.

"Anything for you," he amended, adjusting his suit jacket.

I raised an eyebrow. "Come on, I'm sure we can find something for your trouble of playing personal shopper today."

He linked his arm with my own as we walked uphill to the cream and green building.

We had just settled with our salads and pizza when a leather-clad group of demigods walked past our table. I smiled at the leader, a tall Norse offspring with flowing blond hair, chiseled features, and the body of a Viking warrior.

I watched playfully as Jerry observed, star-struck. Finally regaining his composure, he pointed his salad fork at me, claiming, "Looking that good should just be illegal."

I smiled. "Demigods."

"Huh, how do you know?" he asked.

I rolled my eyes. "Because they're that good looking."

He laughed before we both dug into our food. Truthfully, it was a little more complicated than just the look. Certain beings gave me feelings; over the years, I had identified which gave what. It was my trusty sixth sense, so to speak. I never delved too deeply into it, but it was handy when I needed to know if wood or metal would be a better weapon.

As we finished our meal, Jerry took my arm again. "Let's get you dressed, my dear."

I gave him a weak smile.

After a barrage of lingerie shops, where Jerry completely disregarded my opinion that I didn't need anything special or fancy in that area, I was finally able to get actual clothing from him in the form of jeans and cotton t-shirts. I'm not a complicated person.

I was perfectly content to leave at that point, but Jerry cryptically shook his head. "I have been given specific instructions that you are to have formal wear as well." His smile was evil, and I told him so.

But I couldn't resist his boyish charm and joy at having a living dress-up doll and unlimited spending.

In a store that was ridiculously overpriced, I fell in love with a pink chiffon dress. Running my fingers over the soft fabric, I dismissed it as foolish to spend that much.

Jerry had other opinions. "Oh, no you don't, my dear," he said, pulling my size off the rack and heading for the fitting rooms.

"Jerry, it really is too expensive," I said, trailing along behind him like a lost puppy.

He pushed me into the fitting room and threw in another four dresses, giving me the "oh, please" look.

"Let's get on with my fashion show," he said, settling into a chair in the hallway.

I laughed, shaking my head, saving the blush pink dress for last.

The first of the dresses was a deep purple strapless top transitioning into neon blue with a low waist and dark purple beads as highlights. I exited the dressing room with my hands on my hips.

"No freaking way," I said.

"But Olie, you look amazing." He turned me around.

I moved my feet as far apart as I could, which was only about a foot. "Just how do you expect me to chase after the bad guys like this?"

"There may someday be an occasion when you won't need to chase bad guys," he tried.

I huffed and went back to his other selections. We ended up leaving with the pink dress and two black ones, one long and the other cocktail length. He didn't let me see the total, probably worried I would change my mind. And probably right.

I wandered, window shopping at the salon next door, pulling a dull-blond lock of my own for inspection. As I let out a discontented sigh, Jerry picked just that moment to notice my dawdling.

He smiled, pulling me into the salon. A bored-looking, pink-haired, overweight pixie greeted us. No, I do not mean an actual supernatural pixie, but she had the typical storybook tiny frame and delicate features.

"Do you have an appointment?" she asked.

"No, do you have any openings?" Jerry asked, smiling brightly.

She looked down at her book, flipping a page with her turquoise nails. "Possibly. Give me a second," she said, picking up the phone.

Jerry and I moved a step back. My stomach grumbled. He laughed. "After this, dinner, possibly at the same pizza place." I smiled at that.

"Sir," the pixie said, "Ray will see you."

Jerry smiled like a fool and pushed me ahead of him. I plopped down in the chair and the flamboyantly gay man with thinning hair asked me, "What can I do for you, darling?"

I smiled. "Surprise me."

That earned me raised eyebrows from both him and Jerry.

A starving hour later, we emerged back into the food court. Jerry was staring again.

"What?" I asked, debating how many slices of pizza I wanted.

He turned back to the menu, his smile widening, if that was even possible at that point.

I shrugged and played with my now shoulder-length, deep red with highlights of purple hair, littered with pixie-like layers pointing out at random angles. It was better than anything I ever could have described. That man had talent.

Well fed and well dressed, we headed back to the Beast, passing the demigods again. The Thor look-alike was pulling a long drag on a smoke and I couldn't help but take a second look. He smiled, nodding approvingly at me.

"Nice hair, Kitten," he complimented.

"Thanks," I said, passing him. "Nice ass."

The thunder of laughter followed Jerry and me to the car where we proceeded, under his careful direction, to load everything in a manner I didn't understand, but which he claimed would keep everything important from wrinkling.

I sighed, arranging and rearranging as directed, until a slowly rising feeling of discomfort made me look down the parking lot towards the townhomes beyond it. A creeping behind my eyes distorted my vision slightly; I shook my head, hoping to dislodge it. My feet began moving of their own accord.

"Olie, Olie!" Jerry screamed as I walked into the oncoming traffic circling the mall's parking lot.

I turned, finding my vision leaving me completely. I ran, seeing only the horror movie in my head that forced me into action. Dimly, I was aware of Jerry starting the Beast to follow as I jumped the wall between the homes and the mall. I spun in a circle, trying desperately to latch onto the screams or the scent of blood.

In my mind's eye, I held her by her tan throat, disgusted by her pathetic attempt to plead for her life and those of the half-blood brood she called children. Not wanting to waste time, I lowered my fangs, sinking them bone-deep into her flesh before shredding her jugular. She babbled endlessly as I made my way to the children's room. She had been intelligent enough to have a separate lock on their door, but it made no difference. I was the dominant life form in these pathetically small living quarters.

In my real body, I fell to my knees, unable to move, unable to help as I watched their executions. Each was the same as their mother's, throats torn from their delicate frames. I willed myself to move, screamed inside my head, and thought I heard it echo in my deaf ears.

He chuckled in my mind—he, I screamed at myself, was a male. The fucker might be making me helplessly watch his murders, but I was in his head, and I would find out who the sick fuck was. He felt me turning from helplessness and pulled quickly away, leaving me with a dim vision of a parking lot and stairs directly in front of me.

Like a drunk who had lost motor function, I crawled up the stairs, using the handrail for support. At some point, Jerry arrived. "Call for help," I whispered.

He did as instructed as I finally reached the top, listening to Jerry scream at the 911 operator that he didn't know what happened.

"Murders," I whispered as I touched the beat-up brass doorknob, cold against my feverish skin. I again wanted to whimper, but swallowed instead, pushing the knob slowly.

I heard Jerry's intake of breath and rapid-fire instructions to the operator again. Apparently, this time he wasn't receiving any talkback.

I felt more than heard the little gasps for life. Running into the children's room, I saw three forms lying still, while a fourth was struggling, a teenage girl.

I floundered for something to stop the bleeding, tearing off my shirt and pulling her upright against me in an attempt to stop her racing heart from pumping her life force out onto the pale brown carpet. The air was thick with fear, her own mixed with it, having watched her siblings die in front of her with no skills to save them.

The tears flowed down without my noticing as I soothed her damaged soul, knowing she would never make it. Her skin felt deathly cold under my fingers, a cold I knew all too well. It was all I could do to ease her transition. Pushing my own wrecked emotions down deep, I pulled contentment and joy, wrapping it around her limbs. Her erratic movements stopped and her breathing evened out while her blood soaked my t-shirt and ran down my stomach to slither off my leather pants.

Still I held her, promising over and over I would get the son of a bitch and make him pay dearly.

It felt like hours later when I felt Jerry pulling me away as the paramedic put her small body into a black coroner bag. I heard what I thought was my name yelled somewhere outside.

Mercer rushed in. "Olivia," he repeated. My eyes refused to leave the small bags lining up to leave.

"Get her out of here," he told Jerry, who began leading me out.

"I'm sorry, ma'am, but I need to collect your clothing," said an investigator.

Both Jerry and Mercer went to tell the guy to screw off, but I waved them off, depositing everything but my underwear into the bags the investigator had labeled.

"Thank you, ma'am," he said, careful to keep eye contact.

"How the fuck do I get her out now?" Jerry asked. "Wait—Mercer, watch her. I have new clothing in the car."

Mercer nodded, wrapping his black blazer around my shoulders. I shivered involuntary. Mistaking it for cold, Mercer rubbed my shoulders. "Kid, come back to me," he whispered.

I pulled my gaze from the bag to his pale blue eyes. "I felt him, Mercer," I said, grabbing my biceps, shaking. "I felt the sick fuck rip their throats out. He enjoyed it, called them half-bloods." I shook my head, my breathing irregular, looking back to the small bags. "These aren't murders, Mercer," I said, returning to his eyes. "This is genocide."

Mercer's hands stilled on my forearms, dark alarm crossing his eyes as Jerry returned with soft jeans and a pink V-neck. "We'll get this fucker," Mercer said to me.

I searched his eyes, not finding any hint of deceit or false bravado. I nodded. "Call me if you find anything. I'll do the same," I said, turning into Jerry's embrace.

"Take care, kid," he said, so softly I thought I imagined it.

The police had efficiently set up a barricade where the neighbors waited. An older woman with the same eyes as the dead woman cried into a policeman's shoulder. Another woman, younger than the first, just let the tears fall, patting the older woman's back with her hand. Family, I thought quietly. My eyes landed on the demigod from the mall. He raised a dark blond eyebrow. I shook my head, pushing closer to Jerry.

Jerry firmly buckled me into the Beast and went around to the driver's side. I stared at my hands, seeing the blood I had already washed off. It was my fault. I was out shopping while they were being hunted and eliminated. *What were they?* I asked myself, bowing my head into my hands. Every indicator said human, plain old basic human. What made them so special that they needed their throats torn out?

I let the darkness close over me, drowning out all other emotions, as I watched their deaths play out over and over again.

Hours later, as I assumed by the night sky out the window at Jerry's small but comfortable home, I buried the memories, having replayed them and tormented myself enough. I hadn't gotten a look at him in any mirror or reflective surface, nothing. Not a scrap of seeing through his eyes gave me any idea how he had been able to manipulate me, either.

Jerry placed a cup of coffee in front of me, sitting across the table in his pale yellow and green kitchen. I took a sip, shaking my head.

"I can't see anything that helps us know who did this or how he would be able to manipulate my vision." I rubbed my temples, feeling overwhelmed.

Jerry cleared this throat, his vision lost to the brown surface of the coffee. When he finally gained the courage to meet my eyes, he said, "I have an idea on that."

I set my cup down and crossed my arms over my pink shirt, waiting for him to elaborate.

He held his hands up in surrender. "Before you go jumping to conclusions, I had nothing to do with it, nor did I even know it was actually possible."

I relaxed my arms into my lap, noticing the softness of the denim, giving him the benefit of the doubt. He leaned his dark, lean frame forward, pushing his usually immaculate suit against the whitewashed table. "This is old magic," he said, using his pointer finger to tap the table, adding emphasis to his revelation.

I didn't tamper with magic, aside from what was naturally gifted to me. "What's the difference between old and new?" I asked.

Jerry blew out a breath, leaning back against the white chair. "You got a few decades?" he asked seriously.

"No. What are the main features that make you think this is old magic?"

"Well for one," he said, leaning forward and bracing his elbows on the table, "it ain't been seen in a century."

I braced my elbows on the table, mirroring his stance. "How is it that, on occasion, you are a well-spoken individual, while on others, your grammar leaves much to be desired?" I asked, honestly interested in a break from the turmoil in my head.

He smiled and made a wide, carefree gesture, brushing pretend dust from his shoulder. "It's all about presentation. Sometimes, I need the aura of a well-educated man. Other times, a hood rat be betta."

I smiled, leaning back against the chair. "Very true."

"Now," he said, leaning forward conspiratorially, "back to this being older magic than my granddad." He cast a look behind me and my back stiffened, waiting for the attack, relaxing only when he turned his gaze back to mine. "There are ancient stories of mortals walking in the realms of the gods, learning and bringing back that knowledge to the people. That is the first and last time it is ever mentioned. So for this fucker to be able to do it to you, he has to be old and powerful..." He paused on that word, searching my eyes with an uncomfortable intenseness. "So do not think you can handle him alone," he stated slowly.

I rolled my eyes. "Thanks, got it," I said sarcastically. Before he was able to scold me again, the kitchen door opened.

I reached in my boot for one of my hidden daggers. Jerry, on the other hand, without looking at the open door, just waved Mark in from the rain, expecting him. Oh geez, how much had I missed? I had been out of the loop for only a few days, wasn't it?

I shook that out of my head, focusing back on the matter at hand. I raised a now red eyebrow at Jerry, silently asking if Mark could be trusted.

He nodded, getting back to his explanation. "The second reason is that it is a very high level of magic, which takes, oh, maybe a century to master before the wielder is no longer frying the subject's eye sockets."

I sat back hard against the chair, crossing my arms over my chest. Fantastic, not only did I have a psycho on my hands, I had a well-educated mage psycho. The key was to figure out what the similarities were between the two families, and that was Mercer's court, not mine.

Mark opened the fridge, grabbing a beer and sitting to my left at the table. "Interesting day at work?" he asked Jerry.

Jerry now raised his own eyebrow, silently inquiring if I trusted Mark enough to share the day's events. I nodded. "It's either from you or on the news, I would guess," I said, shrugging and rubbing my temple.

Jerry relayed the events that led to my being in his kitchen, while I checked my cell phone. There was nothing from Mercer, but I did need to share with him what Jerry had said.

The thing that is killing is old magic, and experienced. Be careful, I sent, grabbing my own beer from the fridge and sitting back at the table.

Jerry went to the drawer next to the sink, pulling out takeout menus. "Well darlings, what will it be?"

We finally decided on Chinese. I ordered the chicken lettuce wraps without chicken. Jerry was properly scolded on the phone for that request. He pulled the phone away, glaring at me.

"What?" I said, pretending innocence. "I like the sauce!"

Jerry made an annoyed sound after hanging up the phone. "Oh," he said, turning from the kitchen drawer, "whoever is getting into your head has your blood. That is the only way to make the connection."

I nodded. "That list has to be very small. I can start there tomorrow and work backwards."

After dinner and a report from Mark that Kass, Darren, and Hannah had been successful moved into the safe house and Darren had an offer in on another home not far from our manor, I took my leave.

Jerry let me drive the Beast to my hotel, partially to conceal where I was staying and partially to allow him and Mark to have some time together. Besides, I still hadn't come clean with the details of my own personal hit squad and I didn't relish getting either of them involved. Steven was mine.

Pulling out of the older, quiet neighborhood, I took a few side streets and turns I didn't need to in order to ensure no one was following me.

A lonely night bellman helped me with my numerous purchases. I tipped him and closed my door, wanting a shower to forget this day, but knowing full well my night would be short and terror-driven.

I pulled the new pink V-neck over my head, tossing it on the couch, followed by my boots and jeans. Reaching a hand to release my bra clasps, I stopped dead in my tracks, shocked at the undead sitting on my bed.

"What the fuck?" I spat, mildly humiliated in my underwear, and annoyed that Tate had found me.

Eventually, his brown eyes made it back to my own darkening green ones. "We need to talk," he said softly, the attraction plain on his face.

I scowled, crossing my arms over bare skin, watching his eyes track back down for a moment. He cleared his throat. "We heard what happened."

I sighed, walking towards the bathrooom. "You are going to need to clarify which incident you're talking about," I said, starting the hot water for a shower. "And furthermore, you can either wait until I get a shower or talk to me while I'm in it," I said, stripping out of my undergarments, leaving the door partially cracked. "It's been a long fucking day," I whispered to myself, stepping into the tub and drawing the curtain, glad it was only transparent to my shoulders before becoming a solid white.

"Why is that?" Tate asked, his voice coming from just outside the bathroom.

Damn vamp hearing; I forgot how annoyingly impressive it was. I sighed, letting the hot water run rampant over my body. The bruises from the hit and run had healed along with the cut. I slammed my hand against the tiled shower stall; that's how my blood became available to the general public. I just left that vehicle in the fucking street. Idiot!

"Are you alright?" Tate said, now in the bathroom with me.

Rubbing my hand and checking if I had cracked any tiles, I glared at him until he resumed his previous post outside the bathroom.

"I take it back. I don't care what incident you were referring to. What did you need to talk about?" I asked, the exhaustion perfectly evident in my voice.

"The letting you had Morgan and me assist with," he replied.

Had to give it to the man, his political tact was spotless.

"I didn't force him against his wishes," I said, referring to the young man he had pulled from. I shampooed my hair, washing the blood and dirt out, sad to see some of the dye leaving with it.

Tate moved uncomfortably against the open threshold. I sighed, turning off the water and pulling a thick, plush hotel towel around me before also wrapping up my damp hair. True to form, the place was a sauna.

"Tate," I said quietly, opening the door. "I swear I did not force him. I only helped get through the rage of first blood to help him calm down. If he didn't want you to drain him, I couldn't have made him say that he did."

His eyes again took their sweet time finding my face. Crossing my arms with irritation, I kicked a hip out against the door fame, noticing the yellow cast in Tate's eyes.

"Holy fuck, when was the last time you fed?" I asked, now very worried.

I watched Tate's fangs descend. "Not since that day," he said around his enlarged teeth. "I was worried."

"Fuck, Tate, how old are you?" I said, moving to sit on the bed and holding out my wrist. "Let's go, you idiot."

He moved silently next to me, kneeling and greedily inhaling my scent through his now even more advanced senses. Succubus blood was powerful; freely given to a vampire, it was doubly so. I was feeling a tad sorry about putting him off now that I saw how seriously he had taken the matter.

I closed my eyes to squish the sensations he was building in me, which was a terrible idea, as it only made them more alive. From my wrist, I felt his gentle lips move along my forearm to my elbow, and give a gentle nip at my shoulder.

That earned him a yip from me and I could feel him smiling against my neck. "Are you certain you are telling me the truth?" he whispered against my neck.

"Yes, Tate," I said, fighting to keep my voice and heartbeat even. The last thing I needed was to kick out seduction pheromones and end up in bed with him. Not that I wasn't tempted to. The extended life of vampires led to an amazing skill set in the bedroom, as I'd had the pleasure to experience firsthand. But one of my cardinal rules was to not sleep with those I worked with. Tate, being the head of one of the Houses here, where I was bound to spend time, unfortunately counted as a coworker.

I felt him push the towel off my damp hair. "Tate," I warned, "I will withdraw my offer."

That was all the encouragement he needed. Gently, I felt his fangs pierce my skin, one landing perfectly in my jugular, while the other was slightly off. Asshole, I thought to myself. He knew exactly how to prolong this. A clean bite into my jugular with both fangs would be a quick feeding. He had essentially doubled his time at my neck. Asshole.

One thing vamp books have correct is how amazingly pleasurable a bite feels. It was a prelude to seduction or a heightened sexual experience, which

I was not thinking about. I felt my pulse escalate while my breathing was a little too close to panting for my liking. It probably had something to do with the fact Tate now had me pinned under him on the bed, my calves against the comforter, while my toes brushing the carpet fibers as I flexed them.

He twisted ever so slightly, causing my back to arch and a whimper to escape my lips. Dammit, now I was panting.

Pulling his fangs out but keeping them drawn, Tate bit his lip, pressing his blood against the wound in my neck to stop the bleeding. I didn't expect to feel his forehead against my own. I opened my eyes wide into his brown and yellow tinted gaze.

"Olivia..." My name on his lips was a promise, one I desperately wanted to have him fulfill. I was so dangerously close to saying yes.

"What about the other incident?" he asked.

I clenched my eyes closed, feeling all the heat and desire shut down faster than I could pull it in. I pushed against his chest, and, thankfully, he moved to sit next to me.

I sighed, running my hands through my tangled hair, bracing my forearms on my knees. From those few moments of intimacy, I wanted to let him in, but I didn't. "Nothing you need to worry about," I answered as I stood and rummaged through my bags for something to wear, confident that answer applied to whatever he was talking about.

He leaned back, legs spread apart, hands situated behind him. Hot asshole. His eyes, still glowing, watched me too closely.

"It did not sound like nothing," he responded, clearly having no intention of leaving.

Huffing, I dressed under the towel into black yoga pants and a turquoise tank top with new undergarments.

"It will be nothing," I answered levelly, turning back to him with my arms crossed, thankful his eyes had returned to being only a lovely shade of brown.

"Your vehicle was totaled," he said, still showing no signs of leaving.

I sighed, returning to the now vented bathroom to comb my hair, not knowing what else to say to Tate. Yes, I was almost killed. Yes, I know who one of the men was. No, I'm trying not to start an internal species issue.

Hair combed, teeth brushed, I exited the bathroom to find Tate leisurely lying on my bed with his hands behind his head.

I took one look at him and rolled my eyes. "I'm going to bed," I announced, not remotely caring he was trying to throw my game. Let him try. It would take more than one sexy-ass vamp to screw with me.

He raised a questioning eyebrow. "Alone," I clarified, throwing back the covers and snuggling in.

I was far more exhausted than I admitted to myself; once my head hit the pillow, I was out. I never heard Tate leave. I expected my dreams to be the same awful nightmares as the ones haunting my waking hours. I was surprised when the sunlight snuck between the curtains, waking me up. I couldn't remember the last time I had slept an entire night.

Some time in the middle of the night, I had lost my bra and pants, which was more typical of how I slept. What I wasn't expecting was to see a shirtless vampire next m in bed.

I'm not going to lie, I really wanted to pull down the covers too see if he had anything else on under the sheet. Well, at least that explained why I hadn't heard him leave.

The view was amazing. While I initially wouldn't have called Tate my "type," I was suddenly learning how wrong I was. His lean exterior hid the chiseled, sculpted chest and perfectly formed abs. His arms were still behind his head, emphasizing his bulging biceps.

A lazy smile graced his lips, and I knew I was in trouble. "Are you enjoying the view?" he asked with his eyes closed.

Cocky asshole. "Nope," I said, hopping out of bed. "I was debating if I should kill you for not leaving." I crossed my arms over my chest, remembering, as his eyes opened, I wasn't wearing any pants.

His tongue peeked out, running over his bottom lip before his eyes made it back to my own gaze. "Damn it, Tate," I scolded, "I work with you." I dashed to the bathroom, feeling my self-control fading fast.

When I exited cautiously, Tate was, thankfully, dressed and in the other room. Quickly, I grabbed my clothing, moving out of his sight to get dressed. After losing my working leathers, jeans would have to do, with a jacket over my white shirt to hide my guns and silver knives.

Coming back into view, he said, "Sorry, Olie, it's been a long time since I woke up to the smell of desire." He gave me the strangest look.

What the hell do I say to that? I opted for nothing, noticing his interest in my files strewn on the table.

"I'd like to help with these," he said, indicating the murders.

I sighed, sitting next to him. "I'd like that, too."

"What do you need?" he asked gently, moving the photos across the table.

I ran a hand through my red hair, pulling it up. "I need to know how they're connected. The killer thinks they're abominations, evil, and must be eliminated. If I knew why, what trait they shared and which member had it, I might be able to protect others."

He nodded. "Can you get me DNA samples?"

"I can," I answered. No, Mercer would never, ever give me what I wanted. That didn't mean I didn't have other methods. Besides, working within the system had proven ineffective and gotten another family killed.

I was done playing the Governor's game.

Tate pushed away from the table, standing, his earlier attraction forgotten. I really wished I could do the same. Desire pushed against my self-control, straining to make it past my skin and into the air where he would undoubtedly sense it again.

At the door, he paused, turning to look at me again, strangely. "I saved my number in your phone. Call me once you have what we need," he said.

I nodded, leaning against the doorframe. His hand reached out to cup my cheek while his lips touched briefly on my forehead. "This isn't done, Olivia."

"Nothing ever is," I said, closing the door. That's a complication I really didn't need, attraction to a Master vampire.

Rolling my shoulders, I pulled my phone from my purse, answering Jerry's text, *What time you be here?*

45 minutes, I answered.

Chapter 6

After making sure that Jerry had Mercer thoroughly distracted and away from his office, I crawled into the dusty ventilation shaft of the morgue. I had already persuaded the security guard to shut off the security cameras, and, yes, it was possible that I'd used my fists.

Dropping down into cold storage, I set the backpack on the ground, getting to work. Cold storage was exactly as it sounded: table after table of dead bodies. No one was here this early. Apparently, the budget cuts had eliminated the morning shift, so only swing and graveyard were left. That provided me with an opportunity to steal what I needed.

While I had no problem dismembering a living body, doing so to a dead body was slightly unnerving. I pushed down my breakfast that wanted to make an appearance, threading my emotions into a slow and easy braid to keep my mind off the fingers and blood I was taking.

My phone vibrated, but I ignored it. The sooner I got the samples to Tate, the sooner I would know what the hell was going on.

Leaving the same way I had entered was my best escape route. Balancing precariously on the occupied table, I stretched my body, my fingers grasping the edge of the vent before I pulled myself up. Using my physical abilities felt great after neglecting them for a few days. Perhaps, if I had time, I would even go for a run, the kind in which I wasn't being chased or chasing something. That sounded divine.

Once I had jogged a few blocks away from the morgue, I checked my phone. It was Kass with a reminder that Logan would be in town tonight. Fantastic. I groaned. I needed to wrap up the hit on me with a hit on one of his own. I couldn't wait to see his face when I delivered Steven's head on a plate.

I texted Jerry, *Ready*.

We had already agreed on the pickup location. Now I just had to wait until he got rid of Mercer and picked me up. I probably had at least an hour, which was why ten minutes later, I was highly suspicious when the Beast drove up and Jerry rolled the driver's window down.

Cautiously, I crept from the shadows of the alley. I was mortified when Mercer leaned forward and said, "Let's go, thieving beauty," before sitting back just as quickly.

Throwing caution to the wind, I stomped to the Beast and jumped in the backseat.

"Jerry, what the fuck?" I hissed.

"He was on to me in the first ten minutes," Jerry answered without much interest.

"I'm not giving the samples back," I said, daring him to try anything.

Mercer didn't bother turning around in his seat. "Didn't think you would. Turn left here," he directed Jerry.

"How do you know where we're going?" I asked, since I hadn't texted or called Tate to let him know I had been successful.

"If you think you're the first one Tate approached to obtain those samples, you are mistaken," he said. "But you are far more capable of breaking into the morgue than anyone else. Plus, I won't lose my job."

I sat back hard against the seat, pulling my silence around me like a protective cloak. It had only been an information-gathering mission to Tate. I scolded myself for thinking it could have been anything else, and I was grateful I hadn't given in to my desires. At least self-denial was good for something.

Jerry looked at me in the rearview mirror. "You okay, Olie?"

"Just fine," I said, turning my attention outside my window.

It took an hour to reach the lab and Tate; good thing I had packed dry ice in my satchel. I didn't bother saying a word as I threw the backpack at him in the underground bunker. It was in the middle of deserted farm country, far enough from the city to guarantee privacy, but close enough for Gunner, the resident forensic lab geek, to get to town if he needed to.

The inside the of the lab was spotless, with stainless steel work tables and machines I didn't even want to understand whirling, stirring and beeping as results were being processed. Gunner was a sight to behold: overweight, he waddled more than walked, mumbling to himself and giving the rest of us cautious, brief glances. He didn't like us in his domain. I couldn't blame him. Hell, I felt the same way.

He tried to get us to leave, but Tate flatly refused. Gunner, motivated by Tate's undead nonverbal threat, decided not to broach the subject again.

I sat against the wall, out of the way, mentally berating myself for falling so easily into Tate's trap. I was an idiot, even if we might learn something valuable here.

Jerry, Tate and Mercer wisely kept their distance from me, banding together close to the door.

"That was fast," Tate said to Mercer, leaning against a metal table, his hands casually in his black pants pockets, while his dark blue shirt contrasted nicely with his light Mohawk and eyes. Bastard, I mentally berated.

Mercer cast an uncertain glance my way before returning to his conversation. "After the attack on the second family and Olivia, it seemed apparent I was being railroaded at work when my requests for a rush job went unanswered."

Tate was staring at me. "You were attacked again?" he asked. I ignored him.

Jerry and Mercer only knew of the mental hijack, while Tate only knew of the physical attack. Personally, I didn't need them in my business, and all of the above was exclusively my business.

"What was the first attack?" Mercer asked.

Tate answered, "Someone turned her car into an accordion and left her bleeding out."

"Damn it," Jerry cursed.

I sighed. "Yeah, I know, not my brightest moment."

"That opens up who could have gotten a hold of your blood to the entire city!" he reminded me.

"I am aware of that," I said. "I didn't have much of a choice. It was either run or get my head blown off by some very upset gentleman."

Tate's eyes had started to take on a yellow sheen. "What was the other incident?" he asked, still staring eerily at me.

Mercer answered steadily, "Yesterday, the murderer hijacked Olivia's mind and made her watch his slaughter leading her to the scene too late."

I rapped my head against the concrete wall, watching Gunner cast a terrified glance my way. He should be scared—I was a walking time bomb. If Steven didn't get me, the unknown killer would certainly destroy my sanity.

"So-so," Gunner started, stuttering. "Just to clarify...you...you have two sep-separate bad guys trying to eliminate you?"

I gave Gunner a genuine smile. "That would about sum it up, this week," I answered.

Gunner nodded, his pasty cheeks turning bright pink as he got back to the work in front of him, carefully cataloging the samples I had brought.

I liked Gunner. He had a simple nature and he didn't enjoy us being here, interfering in his work. "So Gunner, how long will this take?"

He cast a furtive glance at the three men behind him. "More time than your love life and death threats could warrant conversation."

I threw my head back and laughed heartily, standing up from the concrete wall. "Now, that is highly doubtful." I stretched, standing.

Gunner cracked a small smile, trying not to notice me stretching. "I'll call Tate once I finish," he said, returning to his work.

As I climbed the stairs out of the bunker, Tate was hot on my ass. "Keep your hands to yourself," I mumbled quietly, knowing he could hear me. "And quit checking out my ass," I hissed.

Mercer and Jerry climbed quietly into the Beast, leaving me alone with Tate. What the hell?

"Drive back with me," Tate requested quietly.

"Need another hit?" I asked tapping my neck.

He moved faster than I could track, pinning me against his ridiculous yellow sports car, whispering softly, "If I wanted it, I would have it."

Have I mentioned he's a cocky asshole?

Shoving him away, I got into the bumblebee car, not saying a word. Tate was pushing me, and he was well aware of it. From staying the night uninvited to attempting to incite me into fighting him, he was being a button-pushing ass.

The gray interior of the car smelled new, and I had to admit the seats weren't awful to sit in. Tate started the engine and I understood why people called it purring, but it was annoyingly loud.

I was aware of his sly cautious peeks as we made the hour drive back. I may have wanted to ask what the hell he wanted, but I kept my silence. Based on his silence, he may have finally caught up with the fact that I killed for a living.

I thrummed my fingers against the door armrest as my stomach decided to growl loudly. Tate pushed a few buttons on his steering wheel and Jerry's voice came over the speakers. Cute trick.

"It appears Olivia is in need of sustenance," he declared.

"Did you ask her where she wants to eat?" Mercer asked.

Silence met that question, followed by Jerry's laughter.

"She isn't talking to you, is she?" Jerry asked, and I smiled. "Oh, you've really pissed her off now. I highly suggest you pull out all the stops and get us all some amazing sustenance," Jerry said, disconnecting the call.

Tate gave me an irritated glance; I raised one eyebrow at him, accepting the challenge.

His grumbling was music to my ears; I was ever so glad to share my irritation. After a few more clicks on the steering wheel, another voice came over the speakers, one I did not recognize, nor could I place the language. Whatever was said, though, gave Tate a smug smile as he zoomed in and out of traffic into a questionable neighborhood.

"Should I bring my guns?" I asked earnestly.

He scoffed, parking in the small lot and coming around to open my door. "Madam," he said with regal elegance.

I rolled my eyes at him, crossing my arms and turning to face him. "Right this way," he motioned, offering an arm. I took it as Jerry and Mercer exited the Beast. Jerry buttoned his black coat, giving me a look, asking if I was serious. I shrugged, staring pointedly at Tate.

Chapter 7

Thirty minutes later, I was singing his praises. Seated in a maroon, open booth in a quiet, romantic Italian restaurant, I was on my third piece of four-cheese pizza.

Tate had his arm resting leisurely on the back of my seat, admiring his handiwork. My eyes had rolled back in my head as I moaned with pure bliss. He chuckled before taking another sip of what I assumed was blood.

I didn't care. I was too engrossed in the explosion of tastes occurring in my mouth. Jerry and Mercer were equally enthralled, although Mercer was having a harder time relaxing amidst such a high vampire population. I wasn't sure if he knew what was around him or if his instincts were kicking in.

I felt relatively safe in the company of a Master vampire and with guns hidden under my jacket. While the bullets wouldn't kill the vamps, they would give us time for an escape.

Leaning back, stuffed, I sighed contentedly.

All I wanted to do was curl up and sleep. Here would be fine; I wasn't picky. But I had a full afternoon and night ahead of me. Tate took care of our bill while we waited for him in the shade outside.

"Well, Olivia," he said, taking my arm again, walking to the car, "what do you say to some quality time together?"

I stopped midway to the vehicles. "Look, Tate, knock it off. I'm going to get to the bottom of these murders, even if you don't try to seduce me." I leaned forward, brushing his ear with my lips, "I appreciate your help, but I know you're not really interested."

As he stood back, a sheepish smile graced his lips. "I'm that transparent?" he said, spreading his hands and shrugging.

I shook my head and headed to the Beast. "Call me once you hear from Gunner," I answered, getting in the backseat as Mercer and Jerry got in the front.

"Men," I complained, trying not to notice the pang my heart gave at that complaint.

Jerry smiled behind his aviator sunglasses. "Tell me about it."

Mercer scoffed, looking out the window, pretending not to hear us.

"You want a rundown of your agenda for the rest of the day?" Jerry asked in his efficient voice.

"No," I grumbled. "I would really love a nap."

...

There was no nap. Instead, we dropped off Mercer with his promise he would call if he succeeded in getting around the blocks in the investigation. There was something going on with the children, I just didn't have a clue what. One battle at a time, I reminded myself. We now had an undead helper finding out everything illegally and a detective trying to find out everything legally.

We had to catch a break.

At Kitten, I signed a heap of paperwork, reviewed the dances, interviewed a new line cook, and slept in the offices until it was time to learn the new Latin routine, undoubtedly my favorite style of dance, not to mention my love of the outfits. Our costumes were sheer silk belly dancing scarves tied cleverly to hide the matching undergarments with the traditional rows of coins embroidered to the fabric. We jingled like it was Christmas.

That's how Kass found me, shaking my ass to see how much noise I could make. Yeah, at times, I was like a four-year-old.

Laughing, she sat me down, putting layers upon layers of makeup on.

"You going out as Kitten?" she asked.

"Nope, not tonight, just Olie," I answered, smiling and trying to keep my good mood. I wanted to be tearing apart information on who was killing and why, but there was no new information for me to work on. Honestly, I was just hoping to get out of entertaining the shifter leader who had arrived today.

"How is everything going?" I asked tentatively.

Kass shrugged, her eyes shining as she blinked rapidly. "Logan and Darren got into a huge fight," she said, coming to sit in the chair next to me. I swiveled my chair to face her. "He accused Darren of neglecting his responsibilities to the clan by picking me over them." She sniffled.

"What did Darren say?" I asked softly, wondering if the accusations from his brother would prompt a change of heart in him.

"He said, yes, he was. He was choosing his family over the clan, and if Logan had a problem with that, they could part ways right then without further communication." She sobbed quietly. I placed a hand on her back, letting her cry into her hands.

Darren had made the right choice, at great heartache and peril to himself. Why Logan couldn't understand the concept of family being more than a clan, but an underlying bond of beings who would never abandon or stop fighting for each other, I could never understand. I respected the terrible decision that Darren had been forced to make, and was proud of how easily he had made it.

Kass reined her emotions in with a deep breath. "I feel awful, causing that rift," she whispered, wiping away the tears with the tissue I gave her.

"Kass, it's not your fault. Hannah is a succ. Whether or not Darren and you fell in love, he would be making the same choices he is now. "

She nodded. "You're right." She tried for a smile.

"Thank you, Olivia. I've been telling her the same thing," Darren said, coming into the room.

I smiled at him. "How's the house hunting going?"

Kass brightened at that. "Amazing. We found this great home—needs a little work, but it's perfect and close to the manor." She smiled as Darren walked behind her, brushing a kiss against her forehead and placing his hands gently on her shoulders.

I smiled. "You'll have to show it to me soon," I said and mentally added, when my life settles down, which really had no chance of ever occurring.

Kass squeezed Darren's hand on her shoulder and a pang of jealousy raged through me before I clamped down on it with my iron will. I wanted to be cherished like that, to have no greater worries than family rivalries. Pushing a slow breath out, I reminded myself that the reason it was her only problem was because of me killing anything that came remotely near her and my kind.

I forced a smile, standing. "I'll see you guys out there."

"Oh, Olie," Kass said, calling after me, "I almost forgot. We are trial running warded mage bracelets to see if they can block some of our powers. We wanted to try it with you tonight, since you have the strongest reach, so let it out," she said with a smile.

...

The music pulsed through my veins until my heart kept beat with it. My breathing became heavy and labored from the constant movement of my hips, sweat dripping down my back to be absorbed into the sheer silk above my ass. I loved every second of it.

My power swelled and rose, twirling around my body and those dancing with me. I hadn't caught a glance of Kass, but I assumed it was only because our stage hadn't circled to her yet.

Our second outfit was a golden glitter sequined mess with a halter top and a perfect skirt that flowed with every twist, turn, and booty-shaking move. Smiling, I lost myself in the music, the sense of beauty I found in every perfectly executed move, and the release I felt in my muscles, along with my relaxed control.

I never did see Kass, but I did see the majestic demigod from the mall. He gave a small wave, which I acknowledged with a smirk and slight head tilt, much to the annoyance of his date. I can't lie, I did smile a little wider at that.

When Shakira sang of the She Wolf in the closet, I took Kass's words to heart and took the lead, pulling out all the stops as I ended on my knees, thrusting my hips and running a hand along my side. The tension in the air thickened as I pulled myself back into the other dancers.

The bracelets were good as gold; no one rushed the stage in a fit of passion, but the effects of the dance were still evident from gaping mouths and panting breaths. After more testing, I could see implementing this full time.

Backstage, I realized I had forgotten how nice it was to have the semblance of a normal routine. I saw familiar faces and caught up with the latest gossip. Traveling as often as I did, TV characters became more reliable for social interaction than actual people.

After showering and drying my now short hair, I went out back in the new pink dress Jerry and I had picked out, with cowboy boots and a few key bling pieces of jewelry.

Outside I was greeted by Jerry's catcalls. Laughing, I turned around and gave a curtsy. He was impeccably dressed as usual, in a black suit and tie.

"Mama, you really need to stop hiding behind those yoga pants," he said, taking my bag from me as we walked towards the Beast.

I smiled at Mark next to the Beast. "Awe-inspiring performance as usual, Olie," he complimented, greeting me regally.

"I didn't know you were a fan, Mark," I said, sliding into the backseat. He smiled, shaking his head and talking with Jerry outside as I checked my lipstick in the rearview mirror, leaning forward over the center console.

Settling back down, I checked my phone in my small matching clutch, also a purchase made with Jerry. *Heading out to dance. Please hurry; I can't drink!*

I laughed at Kass's text as Jerry and Mark got into the Beast.

"So where to?" I asked, shockingly bright.

Jerry and Mark exchanged a look. "Oh, no," I said, "we are not going to Flame."

Jerry cringed. "We aren't excited about it either, but Lorraine, Logan's fiancée, heard about the re-opening."

"There is a reason Flame went up in flames," I grumbled from the backseat, slouching against the leather interior.

"I couldn't agree more," Mark stated, sharing a look with Jerry.

Jerry sighed. "Will you two at least try to make the best of this, please?"

I kept my mouth shut, not about to make promises I knew damn well I wouldn't be keeping. "At least there is alcohol in a pretentious, mix-species club," I admitted with a shrug.

"Now, was that so hard?" Jerry asked, staring holes into Mark.

...

Three hours later, I had lost count of how many margaritas I had consumed. Lethal tendrils of anger and death hovering around Kass and me were the only reason we weren't engulfed by people at the small table we had been shoved to.

"I think we should leave," I said again, shifting uncomfortably at the table. Jerry and Mark had already given up on this hellhole and were guarding the Beast, which was actually necessary. Lorraine and her friend Wanda were on the dance floor, which really resembled more of a brawl waiting to happen than actual dancing. My disgust for this place might have biased my opinion, since dancing was my occupation—when I wasn't killing.

Lorraine blended into this club perfectly: a size-2, delicate woman with an Asian cast to her features, a sculpted ass, and fake boobs. I was fairly certain she was not wearing anything under the silver, skin-tight fabric she called a dress. The four-inch heels did nothing but make me concerned about her future back issues.

Wanda, on the other hand, was nothing like I expected. Plump, short, with platinum hair and an awful tan, she was trying desperately to belong in a world that didn't give a shit about her. I genuinely felt bad for her obvious lack of self-esteem and the fact her best friend didn't mind dragging her into all kinds of uncomfortable situations. I was personally ready to beat some asses just because of the looks and shoves she was receiving.

And where were the darling fiancé and husbands to these three? Oh, nowhere special, just in the uncrowded smoking area in the back, where Kass could not be. I refused to leave her. Have I mentioned they had been there the entire time? My only impression of Logan was of a dark blond head of hair and the shoulders of a linebacker, while I didn't even get a glimpse of Wanda's husband.

I wanted to pound my head against the table again. Kass checked her phone for the hundredth time, it seemed, sighing dejectedly.

"Hopefully, it means he's working things out with this brother," I suggested helpfully. She gave me a thin smile.

"I hope so," she responded, taking another sip of her water.

I ordered another margarita as my stomach grumbled. Kass gave me a look, apparently having heard my stomach's complaint. "What?" I grunted. "Some of us didn't get dinner."

She smiled, rolling her eyes. "I forgot," she said, clicking the side of her phone to check for any messages.

I smiled and paid the waitress for my drink, noticing she needed to eat more to support her enormous boobs.

Kass's efforts were finally rewarded when her phone pinged at her. "They're leaving," she explained. "Said they'll meet us outside."

I let out a long sigh of relief. "Guess we have to get the bimbos."

She gave a small smile. "At least we're leaving."

"Agreed," I said, slamming my drink before we made our painful way to the dance floor.

My threatening aura must have dimmed, or the men were now too drunk to pick up on it, as more than a few tried to press against me as I made my attempt to find the girls. I had left Kass at the sidelines for this exact reason. Twisting and occasionally pushing, I finally found them both hip deep with someone who was not their fiancé or husband on their asses. Huh, call me old-fashioned, but I didn't think that was appropriate. The tall, dark-haired beauty raised his head from nuzzling Lorraine's neck and I cursed violently—vampires. I spared a glance at the light-haired, younger, shorter one on Wanda's neck, also a vampire. Fuck me.

I must have said that out loud. The dark-haired one raised an eyebrow, smiling slowly and carnally. Wanda chose that moment to raise her head awkwardly, pulling away from the blondie behind her.

"Hi," she slurred, "we leaving?"

"Yup," I said evenly.

The blondie pulled her back, muttering sweet nothings, I'm sure.

"Hey," I said to him, breaking his attention from his latest conquest, or should I say possible feeding? Oh, no, I hadn't thought of that. We were so in deep shit. I pointed to my ring finger on my left hand, indicating a wedding ring, and then pointed to Wanda, who was completely oblivious.

His face fell dejectedly and he pulled her closer to him. "You're married?" he asked. I glanced at the dark-haired one, who was listening intently. Lying to vampires about not being mated was high on their list of things not to do. They valued the bond between two mates second only to blood being freely given. The reason was simple enough: clans have always been governed by a mated pair. To disturb the relationship was to break apart the clan, guaranteeing Masterless vampires (which was dangerous for everyone) and eternal death.

If they both had led these vamps on and lied, followed by letting the boys feed from them, I was so in the shit. I wanted to take it outside where my hearing wasn't so hampered by the pounding music, but that would mean running into the husband and fiancé, and I really didn't need to complicate this situation.

Wanda gave a halfhearted shrug, to which blondie tightened his grip, his eyes flashing amber. I sighed. "Did you feed?" I asked him.

He nodded, not breaking eye contact with Wanda. Turning to the dark-haired one, I nodded silently, asking the same question. His face turned into stone as he pushed Lorraine away from him, nodding. I raked a hand through my burgundy hair. Part of me wanted to walk away and say, fuck it, deal out punishment as you see fit, but I knew that would only cause problems for Kass. As much as I disliked these two right now, I had to fix it.

"Your Master?" I asked, moving the girls next to me.

"Who the fuck are you?" the light-haired one asked.

"Olivia, Executioner of the Council," I answered, keeping my hands loose at my sides.

He backed up slightly; evidently, he had heard of me. Turning my attention back to the dark-haired one, I asked again. "Master?"

His eyes roved over me, and damn if my heart didn't flutter slightly. That was a first. I tried to control it so he wouldn't hear it. His lip curled up slightly before his look reached my eyes, and he indicated I should come closer with his index finger, pushing Lorraine out from between us.

With a smirk at his dramatics, I closed the short distance between our bodies. Brushing the hair from my ear, he leaned closer, whispering, "Tate." Damn if I didn't get goose bumps from that word. Whether it was from his breath or Tate's name, I didn't care to find out.

My shoulder sagged slightly as I answered him, "I accept the punishment for their actions, only to be delivered by your Master."

Tall and dark pulled back, a genuine smile on his lips now as he sized me up and nodded. I sighed again. "Let me get them to my friend for safekeeping," I requested.

He nodded. Turning away, I grabbed both of them, roughly propelling them in front of me into the crowd, which moved very quickly. Pissed off and deadly had made a return appearance.

Kass raised an eyebrow at their treatment. Not releasing either of them, I leaned towards her and whispered, "They let two vamps feed from them under the assumption they were single."

Kass pulled back stiffly, her eyes wide as she mouthed my name. I nodded. "I took punishment."

She closed her eyes, shaking her head before she angrily looked at Lorraine and Wanda. "Let's go," she said, treating them equally as roughly. Terrified by Kass's response, they said nothing, letting her drag them away.

I felt tall and dark behind me before he slipped his arms around my waist, dropping his lips to my ear to whisper, "Had you not called our Master's involvement, I gladly would have taken you for myself as punishment." His emphasis on that last word made me smile, and I leaned into him, swaying gently to the music. His fangs raked temptingly against my skin. "Care to reconsider?" he asked huskily, responding to my movements.

Turning to face him, I laced our legs together, earning me a groan of pleasure. "In a different life, I would have gladly surrendered to your punishment," I whispered, letting my mouth graze his neck. "But since I let Tate feed from me the night before last, you should probably tell him."

His entire body stiffened at that information. He wheeled me around to the back, past security and upstairs to a plush, black and red waiting area. What was it about black and red that all vampires loved?

Tall and dark didn't wait, but instead burst through the double doors lined with security.

Tate was engrossed with the female on his lap, but was conscious enough to notice our entrance. "We have a problem," tall and dark announced.

"Really, Blake, that's what I pay you for," Tate answered, not looking up.

Blake shuffled at the insult. "It's not his fault. I evoked punishment by his Master," I said.

At my voice, Tate stood, dropping his entertainment. "Olivia," he said breathlessly.

"Hello again," I said to his devilish smile.

"What was the offense?" he asked Blake, not taking his eyes off me. The fucker was enjoying this way too much.

"Two of her female companions portrayed themselves as single and allowed me and Jackson to feed from them," he answered stiffly.

He laughed, throwing his head back, ignoring the woman pulling her clothing on angrily. "Oh, Olie, this is too wonderful."

I grumbled, crossing my arms. "In their—or, really, my—defense, I don't believe they had been briefed on vampire protocol."

Tate just kept on smiling at me. The tinted glass window behind him would have given him a perfect view, if he had been paying attention.

"Bullshit," Blake coughed from behind me.

"You disagree, Blake?" Tate asked.

"They both were informed of what was expected once we fed from them. Neither gave a fight nor disagreed with those terms," he stated in almost military fashion.

I sighed, throwing my arms up. "Alright, Tate, fine, you have me dead to rights. I'll abide by the rules set forth, but remind you of my right not to be forced into anything I don't agree too," I stated.

"Oh, Olie," Tate said, sitting down and steepling his fingers, "what would the fun of that be?"

"I am certain you will think of something," I said, wanting to also sit, but I was in his domain in front of his people. I was already in shit; I didn't need to disrespect him to make this worse.

"Would you like to sit, Olie?" Tate asked politely.

"Yes, thank you," I said, coming around and sitting on the maroon couch.

Leaning forward, Tate had a wicked look I didn't like. "Olivia, you being submissive is something I will have fantasies about."

I raised an eyebrow, not willing to hint at anything.

"Jackson, what would you like?" he asked the vampire behind me somewhere, his gaze holding mine.

"I want a chance to feed from the Kitten," he demanded.

Tate raised an eyebrow, silently asking if I could deliver. Standing, I turned to him. "Now a good time?"

He eyed me warily. "Where is she?"

I smiled. "You're looking at her."

Jackson scoffed. "Bullshit," he said, echoing Blake's earlier words.

I sighed tiredly. "What would prove to you I am the Kitten?" I asked, crossing my arms.

Tate answered. "Seduce him."

Turning, I looked at him skeptically. "That's not a difficult challenge," I countered, feeling I was getting off easy.

Tate settled back. "I think you will find it is. You see, Jackson has a particular fetish for pleasantly round women, which is why he was smitten with your friend."

The fucker had been watching. I sighed. "Music?" I asked

Blake hit a few buttons on a wall panel and the music from the club was blasted through the small office. Jackson still had his arms crossed defensively against his chest. "You want to stand or sit?" I asked him.

He shrugged and again Tate chimed in, "Standing. And, Olivia, do be a dear and lose the clothing. Jackson is a newer vampire, and I would hate to ruin that lovely dress."

The fucker was really enjoying this. I wondered if he realized I danced half naked most of the time, so this wasn't going to affect me at all.

"Done," I countered. "I will lose it before he feeds."

Tate nodded, motioning I should get started. I wished he were forcing me on Blake. That I could get behind; this was going to take some acting.

But the sooner it was over, the sooner I could leave. I tuned out everything, including the awful music blasting through the club, except for the beat, which I could work with. Rolling my shoulders, I shook out my arms, placing my hands on Jackson's crossed arms, giving him a small smile behind hooded lids, gently pushing his arms down.

He was compliant, and I hadn't even broken out with the real source of my power yet, playing off his earlier emotions while dancing with Wanda. Smiling wider, I curled my hips close to his in the pattern I was working off of.

Running my hands over his abdomen, I slinked down, trailing my hands over his hips and down to his quads. Turning, I pushed my hips up against his before trailing my hands slowly up my legs. Once my head was against his shoulder, I dropped my energy into the room as pure desire, attraction, and a painful need, washing over everything.

Blake gripped the love seat in front of him while Tate's fangs lengthened. I felt Jackson's response from behind me.

"Convinced yet?" I asked him, tipping my head back.

"Yes," he growled.

"Will you unzip me?" I asked softly, pulling away, much to his dismay, as his fingers dug into my hips. I toned down the emotions I was pushing off and Jackson took one hand off my hip to unzip me with vamp speed. I would be lucky if it was still in one piece after this. The pink beauty made no sound as it hit the floor.

Tate was staring in open admiration, the amber shining behind his almost black eyes, while Blake slowly licked his bottom lip.

Tilting my head to the side, I felt Jackson's fangs press against my neck before he bit down. Cringing, I pulled the rest of my emotions in. I had forgotten how awful new vamp bites were.

He moaned behind me, drawing in more and biting down harder. I schooled my features, braiding the pain into my core while biting down hard on my bottom lip.

Someone touched my cheek and I opened my eyes to find Blake talking to Jackson. "Enough. Bite your lip or tongue and close her wounds."

Numbly, I felt Jackson nod as his fangs left my neck; I sagged with relief when I felt his blood healing the deep puncture wounds.

Jackson left the room, staggering; succubus blood was powerful. Blake led me back to the love seat, gently sitting me down.

"Never been bit by a newbie?" asked Tate, still smiling.

"I have," I cringed, rubbing my neck. "It's just been a while."

Fatigue settled over my limbs and I leaned my head against the armrest. Had feeding two of the undead depleted my reserves that quickly? No, I had fed more than that before and been perfectly fine. It was something else. The tension in my temples made my stomach clench with fear.

"Tate," I whispered.

"Yes, Olivia, do you need a rest now before your next performance?" he asked with humor in his voice.

"It's him," I said, equally as soft.

It took him only a moment to realize who I was speaking about. "I can't move," I whispered, terrified.

"Olie, what do you see?" he asked, kneeling before me with his hands on my bare knees.

"Nothing. Bite me," I asked, my voice shaking. "Hurry," I begged.

Tate lowered his mouth to my knee, not attempting to draw any blood as he bit down. I let the toxins overwhelm my senses and found I could move again. Pushing him away, I ran out the office, down the stairs, and flung the back door open, leaping into the alley.

There I paused, which was enough time for Tate and Blake to catch up. Turning in a semicircle, I felt the pull again behind me and took off running with everything I had.

"What do you see, Olie?" Tate asked again, not even straining—damn vamp speed. I focused on the second vision, causing me to crash into garbage cans.

"Glass roof," I said between my labored breaths. "It's a gallery of some kind, blue walls." I darted out into traffic to horns and screeching tires, fighting the heaviness that wanted to take over. Please let me get there in time, I repeated over and over. I didn't want to help another soul cross over. I couldn't stand to fail yet again.

Down a dark industrial street, I turned abruptly, knowing we were close. "There!" I screamed, pointing to the light in the top floor of a commercial renovation building with huge glass windows on the roof. Without another word, Blake wrapped his arm around my naked waist and propelled us airborne.

Tate landed softly on the roof next to us. "What's the plan?" He asked.

I didn't waste a moment answering as I pushed ahead full force into the triangular glass ceiling, shielding my face with my forearms. The glass gave way, slicing my shoulders and shins as I turned on my side for the fifteen-foot drop. Rolling away from the glass, I heard the screams from down a blue hallway. Not waiting for the other two, I sprinted ahead, fighting the exhaustion that bloomed in my muscles.

Fatigue caught up with me and I slammed my shoulder into a wall, turning and finding an enormous wolf shifter in mid-form throwing around the patrons of the gallery. Lowering my center of gravity, I slammed into his black and silver midsection, taking us both down.

Mid-form made this fucker tall with the head of an overly large and aggressive wolf, combined with a hairy, almost human body. It was a form that drove fear into most. The stench emanating from him had me wrinkling my nose as we rolled onto the orange floor tiles.

There is only one sure way to kill a shifter, beheading, and, no, I did not have a large sword hidden in my bra, nor did I have a magic bra or panties that would turn into a sword. All this I contemplated as I blasted punch after punch into his face that caved as I hit it, leaving my hand covered in dirt and worms.

What the fuck, a dead shifter? How the fuck do I kill this? I groaned.

I must have said that last part out loud because Tate's voice answered, "Keep it busy, Olivia, while we get everyone out of here."

Yeah, right, that sounded like a perfect plan as the thing threw me over his head, slamming my back into the metal beamed ceiling. Catching my ankle on my trip down, he held me upside down.

The mangled jaw tried to form words I couldn't understand as I used my other leg to kick brutally into its neck, hoping the bone there would crumble as easily as the face. I was rewarded for my effort, as bone and dried muscle disintegrated against my kicks. It was then I realized I had also lost my shoes somewhere while running to get here, and now had bugs clinging to my toes. Eww.

I didn't have much time for that thought before big and ugly spun me, adding some force behind his throw into a painting protected with glass. I cringed as I felt the slivers pierce my exposed back before I landed hard on my knees, driving more shards into my abused flesh.

"Hang on, Olivia," I heard Blake call out.

"Don't have anywhere else to go," I yelled back as nasty sent a punishing kick to my stomach. I wanted to braid the pain away, but it was so intense I feared blacking out, so I pushed it away and staggered to my feet, feeling glass cutting the delicate flesh and watching the empty eye sockets track me.

We were facing off with a table and chairs between us. Without any other option, I grabbed a chair, slamming it against the creeper's head, which flew off with a sick crunch.

My hopes of that killing it died when it stumbled, arms outstretched, still able to track me. Grabbing another chair, I slammed it with all my force into a knee, hobbling creepy further, and then treated the other to the same. When it was unable to do more than crawl, I finally breathed a sigh of relief.

"Olivia," Tate said, "move now." He held a burning bottle of something in his hands. Not needing to be told twice, I booked it over to him, limping heavily.

Tate let it fly, igniting the dried corpse into a brilliant display of flames. Breathing deeply, I turned to Blake.

"Geez, you're a mess," he said, as though I hadn't just gone six rounds with an undead shifter.

"Yeah, well some ass made me get undressed," I said, pulling shards of glass from my knees, tensing when Blake pulled a few out of my back.

"The good news is that your lovely dress is still in one piece," Tate said, looking me over, "unlike you at the moment."

Sirens wailed in the distance. "We need to leave," Blake said. I nodded, not wanting to surrender the rest of my minimal clothing to the police.

Blake picked me up carefully and walked to the balcony. He and Tate jumped the hundred-foot drop easily. I attempted to stay conscious, but my adrenalin was depleted, and with the heavy pull of oblivion still clinging to me, I gave in to the welcoming blackness.

Chapter 8

I was warm when I woke up. Something soft brushed against my cheek.

"She's waking up," I heard a faraway voice say.

"Stay still, Olie, we're almost done." I thought I heard Kass along with the distinctive clink of glass hitting a metal tray, accompanied by the smell of sanitization.

I must have passed out again, for when I next awoke, the sun was blocked out by heavy curtains, and a warm body was pressed up against my own.

"Kass?" I whispered.

The warm body next to me shifted as I blinked rapidly, trying to regain my sight.

"Easy there, Olie," said Blake.

"Blake?" I asked, finally getting my vision to come together.

He brushed a lock of hair behind my ear. "How do you feel?"

"Like I've been drugged," I grunted.

He smiled, caressing my cheek. "That's to be expected."

"Where am I?" I asked, not bothering to move from his touch.

"My place," he answered. "We needed to keep a twenty-four-hour watch on you to be sure the fucker doesn't try and attack again."

I sighed, rolling to my back. "Yeah, all that crap," I said, my moment of peaceful contentment broken. "Bathroom?" I asked, sitting up to a head rush.

I felt Blake's hand stabilizing me on the small of my back, while he used the other to point to a door to the left.

"Leave the door open, Olie, so I can hear if you need me," he said sternly.

"Alright," I answered, relieving my overly full bladder. Looking down, I didn't recognize the shirt I was in. "Did you change me?" I asked.

"No, Kass did," he said, pulling on what sounded like pants. Well, at least one of us was dressed. "Your clothing was brought over this morning and is being cleaned now."

I yawned. Why did everyone feel the need to wash my clothing? I got around to it enough. "Are there other clothing options if I shower?" I asked, flushing the toilet and washing my hands.

"My wardrobe is at your disposal," Blake answered, leaning against the doorframe in only a faded a pair of blue jeans. If I thought Tate had looked good, I would gladly eat those words for the beauty in front of me. Broad shoulders tapered into a well-defined stomach with two beautiful groves on his hips disappearing into the denim. He could unquestionably work part time as a WWF wrestler. I now needed a cold shower.

Turning around, I opened the glass shower doors to start the shower.

"Do you need any help?" Blake asked, clearly noting my interest.

"I think I got it. You mind a little privacy?" I asked raising an eyebrow.

"Don't need it," he answered.

I sighed. Vampires were notorious for being the playboys of the undead world. Suave and powerful, they thrived on one conquest after the next.

He must have sensed my mood shift. "You alright?" he asked, concerned, reaching out to my shoulder.

"Yep, just tired," I answered, which was the truth. I was too tired to play his game, too tired to pretend I wasn't in a miserably foul mood after what had happened. While we may have saved one group and killed an undead shifter, there was still a puppet master pulling the strings, and if he could raise one undead, I was certain he could raise another. It was just a matter of time.

"I'll be in the bedroom if you need me," he said, turning and leaving. Well, that was unexpected but not unwelcome.

In the shower, I took stock of my injuries. Most of the slices had turned to just scratches, and, while they itched, I was able to walk without a horrendous limp. I was grateful they hadn't tried to give me vamp blood. Vampires healed the quickest of all the undead and for humans their blood was a powerful drug and remedy. For succubi it would heal any outward injury, but the effects on our internal organs could kill us.

Shifters healed slower than vampires, but were equally dangerous in battle. What they lacked in vamp speed, they more than made up for in brute strength. I supposed it made sense that shifters were being reanimated. When vampires were killed, they turned to dust; there was nothing to reanimate. Humans would be too weak, and most of the other races of Supernaturals tended to cremate their dead.

Drying off, I recognized the clothing sitting on the toilet as the outfit I had worn when Tate visited and stayed the night uninvited. I certainly hoped they were clean. Towel drying my hair, I went into the bedroom to find Blake leafing through a file.

"Are you hungry?" he asked with a knowing smile, as my stomach announced its demands.

"What do you have there?" I asked, curiosity putting my stomach on hold.

He came around the bed, still a shirtless wonder, and propelled me towards the door. "Eat and then we can discuss what was found."

I had to climb down three levels of Blake's monstrosity of a home and follow my nose to the overwhelming aromas to arrive at the kitchen, which I instantly fell in love with. I swear he had copied a cooking show, with his stainless steel appliances and large island. There were rich blue accents in places, it was definitely a man's kitchen, no hint of female involvement at all.

I came in behind Jerry, eating at the island. He turned mid-bite to rush me in a hug. "Thank all that is holy, you're alright." Putting me at arm's length, he scolded, "Don't you ever take on an undead shifter again. What the hell is wrong with you?"

I shrugged out of his grasp, reaching for a grilled cheese sandwich. "What would you have me do? Sit by and watch it murder again?"

"Olivia, do you have any idea how powerful they are?" Jerry asked.

I sighed, saved from answering when Tate waltzed in. "Olie, good to see you up and about. Nice work with the undead shifter," he said, joining Jerry and me at the island.

Jerry grumbled something under his breath. Much as I liked Jerry's protective nature, fighting and killing things was what I did, a vital part of who I was.

A heavyset, dark-skinned woman entered the kitchen. From her attire, I assumed she was housekeeping. "You need something to drink?" she asked me.

"Milk?" I asked. While I would have loved a stiff drink, I didn't think that would be in my body's best interests.

She delivered me the glass and a plate for the sandwich I had almost devoured, putting another on the plate. "Thanks," I said with a smile between bites. Jerry and Tate continued to fight silently, trading looks and gestures that I was not paying attention to.

At that moment, Mercer walked in the kitchen as well. "What are you doing here?" I asked, shocked.

He raised an eyebrow. "Can't I be concerned?"

I rolled my eyes. "Try again."

He pulled on his brown suit jacket. "There have been some major developments from Tate's side of things you are going to want to see."

I nodded, picking up my sandwich to follow him. "You're going to want to finish that," he said.

I greedily ate the last bites, chugging my milk, before following him up to the second floor and into a large conference room.

Stacked upon the table, almost to my waist, was file after beautiful manila file pertaining to the case. "Finally," I breathed, opening the first ones, grateful to understand what the hell was going on with these murders.

I was lost in dates, facts, dollar amount, eyewitness accounts (not really sure how Gunner managed that), family history, medical information, schooling, employment, unemployment. I finally had to ask for a whiteboard to sort through everything. Mercer had already completed his own whiteboard and was waiting to see if I arrived at the same conclusions he did.

The sun sank low in the sky and the moon shone before I realized I was starving again. Tracking downstairs, I was hoping for some additional grilled cheese, hope that faded when I realized the clock above the stove read 2:30 a.m. While creatures of the night like me were still awake, the human help had probably turned in for the night. Unsuccessful in my search, I was taking inventory of the refrigerator when Blake walked in.

"What are you looking for?" he asked, now fully clothed in a light blue pullover that did painfully beautiful things to his dark hair and cobalt eyes.

"Gold," I answered with a shrug.

He shook his head, smiling. "Why do I bother?" he asked. Coming around, he pulled out leftover pasta.

"No meat?" he asked.

"Correct," I confirmed.

He shook his head, pulling a white plate down, and dishing some out. It smelled amazing and my stomach growled yet again. He raised an eyebrow. "Really didn't think Jerry was telling the truth about you being a vegetarian."

"Well, he was," I said, following the plate to the microwave where it couldn't heat fast enough.

Handing me a fork, Blake leaned against the island, watching me.

"What?" I asked, still watching the plate turn round.

He ran a hand over his face. "Nothing," he said.

I shrugged, finding my subconscious doing summersaults over all the information I had pumped in. There was one brilliantly bright, obvious connection: the targeted families had children who went to the same school. It just seemed too easy. The teenage boy who had defensive wounds and the teenage girl I helped to the other side both went there—same grade, even. It was a bright, obvious connection that my gut didn't trust, or rather didn't think was the whole story. The art gallery was having a fundraiser for the very same Thurgood Marshall High School.

Pouring over the financials had revealed a few items out of place, things that Gunner couldn't run down and confirm. Once I finished my exhaustive list of items, I needed to track them down.

Their medical history was sparse, and I couldn't help feeling something was missing there as I chewed on the fork thoughtfully. Maybe they had a nurse at the school who could offer some assistance.

I yawned and stretched when the microwave finally announced it was done with my food. Blake placed it on a placemat on the island and sat down next to me.

"I think if I stare long enough, I will see the gears in your head turning," he said, settling himself tiredly.

I nodded. "Probably." I devoured my plate and felt my own exhaustion settle in.

"Where am I sleeping tonight?" I asked, rubbing my temples.

"Same place as this morning," he answered in a sultry voice, "my bedroom."

I raised an eyebrow at that. "Really? I would have thought you had a guest room or two in this insane mansion."

He smiled. "You like the place?" he asked.

I gave him a dubious look. "Yeah, it's gorgeous, like you don't know that?"

He shrugged. "Can't say I ever get tired of hearing it."

I smiled at him, setting my plate in the sink. "Bed?" I asked.

He nodded, groaning. "But don't tell anyone we went to bed this early. I do have an image to maintain," he said, straightening up.

I laughed. "The image of the master partier? Out till 6 a.m. with a different girl every night? I wouldn't dream of ruining your game," I said, making my way upstairs.

"I know, I'm being domesticated now. Different night with the same girl," he said, following behind me.

"How boring for you. I can always stay with Tate if you need to go sow your wild oats," I said seriously.

"Why? Do you want Tate to watch you?" he asked, slightly aggressive, jogging to come even with me on the stairs.

"No, but I also don't want to deal with a horny vamp," I said, giving him a slight push teasingly.

He leaned in close as we reached his door. "Care to help with that problem?"

I smiled, forcing my eyes away from his perfectly formed mouth to his mischievous blue eyes. "Nope," I said, entering his room ahead of him.

Blake scooped me up with his lighting fast speed and strength, depositing me on the bed. I may have let out a schoolgirl squeal before I remembered myself.

"Blake, get off," I chided with a hint of laughter as he pinned my arms on the bed, that being the only contact between my overly warm body and his overly tempting, broad-shouldered physique. I gave a half-hearted tug to free my wrists, fighting back a grin. Blake smiled mischievously down at me. My body warmed at the close contact and my heartbeat sped up. What was it about this vampire that sent my common sense off the deep end?

Leaning down, he gently brushed my nose with his own soft skin, whispering, "Don't forget..." He shifted his attention to my mouth, the warmth from his breath increasing my breathing. "You..." My heartbeat increased. "Owe..." His lips brushed the corner of my mouth as electricity shot straight to my groin. "Me."

I closed my eyes, waiting for a kiss that never came. Instead, Blake moved off me, moving slowly and predatorily to the other side of the bed, undressing. I tracked him with my eyes rolling to my stomach, letting out a sigh as he stripped out of his light blue sweater, revealing the hardened flesh underneath.

"Olie," he said, drawing my attention away from his god-like body. "If you continue to look and smell that way, I will lose my ability to control myself."

I smiled, walking on my knees on the bed to him. "Control is highly overrated."

His eyes glowed amber, exciting my already heated libido. "No," he stated, turning away. "If you won't stop, I will have to have someone else watch you. I will not put you in jeopardy with all that is happening."

I stopped short, settling my weight on my calves. "Oh."

It had never occurred to me that Blake would be concerned about my mental status, nor had it occurred to me that the monster hijacking my brain could and would do it during sex. Those thoughts instantly killed my frisky mood as I moved off the bed, feeling sick.

Rejection never felt very good, no matter what the reasons were. "Olie," Blake said gently as I gathered my bed clothing, keeping my back to him. I heard him move around the bed, gently touching my arm, turning me. "Olie, look at me." I did, but I certainly didn't like it. "It's not for lack of wanting, but I would never forgive myself if my desires caused you pain or discomfort." His blue eyes gleamed devilishly as he amended, "Except for the good pain." He leaned in close and kissed my cheek, lingering before pushing me towards the bathroom. "Go change."

I did as he said, taking care of my bathroom necessities, leaving the door cracked. When I came out, he was already in bed, reading a book. Sliding in next to him, I stayed on my side of the king bed, letting a deep sigh out as I slipped into sleep.

Chapter 9

It was dark and cold. I wasn't breathing, yet I wasn't scared, either. I knew this place, knew these sensations. I had stayed here a long time before moving on. I had stayed to watch my pack to be sure they were safe and guarded. This time, I had been called back, summoned from the Beyond by a great evil.

I sucked in a breath as the scene unfolded before me. The darkened woods felt old and alive as the wind disturbed the tree branches with a voice I could almost hear, if I stayed ever so still. I couldn't feel the warmth of the fire that was casting shadows into the small clearing, nor could I hear the person in front of me or make out any form other than a thick shadowy blob of pure hatred.

Turning to my left, I saw the hazy outline of a lion, his head reaching to my shoulder. A slow throbbing began and the lion gained clarity and structure, turning to look at me with eerie caramel eyes, flecked with hints of darker brown. His mane darkened into blackness, while his body was striped with black and light-brown fur. Unafraid, I brushed my hand over the softness of his fur, letting my hand settle on his back.

"It is evil," he rumbled.

I nodded, removing my hand and turning back towards the darkness in front of me. While the forest contained its own magic, the darkness from the blob radiated evil, death, and decay. I was scared.

"Can you see him?" I whispered.

The lion shook his head, the movement transferring to his shoulders as a man stood next to me with the same caramel colored eyes and light brown hair. His nakedness didn't offend or excite me; it was as though all my emotions had been removed, even to my own senses.

The man turned to the blob, shaking his head and his shoulder-length hair, dipping to hide his face as he lowered his head, growling softly.

"You must stop him," he commanded.

I nodded. "I will always try."

He looked at me sharply. "That is why the other called to you and why I must do the same." He turned his attention to the shadowy figure, the muscles in his jaw flexing menacingly. "I can only fight for so long. He will claim me like the rest. You are my only hope, Executioner." He said my title with authority and I felt the binding form between us.

He turned towards me and I nodded, feeling his pain as he tipped his massive head back, roaring at the pitch-black night sky.

"Who are you?" I asked, softly afraid of breaking the spell.

He turned towards me, his jaw clenched, red rimming those beautiful caramel depths as he lost the fight for control. I noticed the long scar from his shoulder to stomach, the slash on his throat, which still looked raw, and the tattoo of a lion baring his teeth on his right thigh.

Suddenly he reached out, clamping his powerful hands to my upper arms. Instantly, I felt the tug that was ripping away pieces of his soul. He had suffered in silence, I noted dimly as a scream of pure pain ripped through my throat, leaving me breathless as I looked back into his eyes, feeling the struggle to regain his identity.

I clamped my own hands on his upper arms as well. "Fight it," I hissed through my clenched teeth, focusing on braiding the pain. But I couldn't, it wasn't mine, and, while I understood he needed me to feel it, I couldn't control it.

"Do not let him win," I hissed, trying to push my strength into him. It bounced back as his black pupils turned red, the color spreading into his entire eye sockets.

I felt him slipping. I watched only the hazy form I had seen at first return. His eyes went blood red, and I was holding onto air.

From the fire pit, I heard the roar as my blood ran cold and my heart stopped beating. The lion returned to life as the walking dead, his eyes hollow red orbs. His voice echoed inside of me as he lost all control, belonging now to the evil being in front of me. My breathing was ragged and my tears fell heavily as I tried to force my way to the blob. Screaming, I clawed the air, unable to move, unable to manipulate anything, but fighting nevertheless.

In slow motion, the blob turned blood-red eyes toward me. Looking for some cause of the disturbance I was creating, but finding nothing, it smiled an evil, toothy grin and turned back to its latest conquest.

I was slammed back into my body, drawing a shuddering breath, finding Blake latched onto my wrist as Tate pinned me down.

Lifting my head, my eyes made contact with Blake's as he released my wrist, closing the bite marks. I was on the ground in Blake's room, watching him pant, which was odd for a vampire.

Tate had deep cuts on his face that were healing as he moved off me.

"What the fuck was that?" Tate asked, touching his face gingerly.

I shuddered as I remembered. "I was wrong," I said, my voice scratchy from what must have been screaming. "It's not the killer who's contacting me. It's the shifters." I sat up, noticing my shirt was drenched in sweat.

Touching my face, I found my tears were real as I blew out a shaky breath, sitting up. "It was awful," I said, shaking my head and trying to get my emotions in check. "I need to talk with Logan. I'm hoping he will be able to identify the shifter I saw reanimated."

Blake moved into my line of vision. "Olivia, biting you isn't breaking the bond anymore, neither is hitting you." He settled back on his heels. "Cutting you was next on our list."

I nodded. "The one he called was more powerful than the others. I think whoever is calling them is gaining strength."

Blake touched my face. "We cannot protect you anymore."

I laced my fingers with his. "I understand," I said, nodding and pulling myself up on shaky legs.

Tate supported me to the bed, sitting next to me, his silence unnerving as he and Blake traded a look. Blake crossed his arms, standing in front of me.

"Olivia," Tate began. "You stopped breathing."

I nodded as he continued, "Is this really worth your life?"

Shocked, I turned to Tate, saying, "Innocent people are dying, families are being eliminated all because of some psycho's belief that he's the ruling life form. Yes, it is unequivocally worth my life," I finished, feeling steadier. Softening my voice, I continued, "If you and Blake no longer wish to help, since it's a shifter matter, I understand." I looked at Blake. Vampires and shifters could coexist peacefully, they just typically didn't. Neither clan was overly joyous to help the other.

Tate sighed, a very human action, and I returned my attention to him. "I'll have to speak with Morgan," he said.

I nodded as he moved away, dialing his phone.

"Regardless of the decision, I want you to stay here, Olivia," Blake said, regarding me with no humor.

"Are you sure it's worth it?" I asked, mirroring Tate's questions with dismal humor.

"You're worth it," he said, his eyes never leaving mine.

I nodded, giving him a slight smile, off balance at his words.

"I'm going to shower," I said, standing up.

Blake nodded, walking me to the bathroom and firmly closing the door behind me. Undressing, I slipped into the hot water, letting my tears flow as the heat seared my body.

When I finally emerged from the steam, I found the room empty. Dressing quickly in jeans and a royal blue shirt, I texted Jerry, stating I needed to talk to him.

He responded that he was already downstairs. Glowering at my phone, I raced to the conference room, finding it deserted. Next I tried the kitchen, which had donuts and toast that I greedily scarfed, but still no Jerry.

I was rounding a corner when I heard voices, which I followed to a formal living room.

Tate, Morgan, and Blake were perched on a couch together, while across the room, Darren and a man I assumed was Logan were looking equally uncomfortable. Jerry and Mark were leaning against the doorframe as I entered.

"Olie!" Jerry exclaimed, embracing me in a hug.

"I'm okay, Jerry," I said, pulling back, noticing his sleep-deprived worry. "I need your help, though. I need all information on how the undead can contact the Executioner. I'm hoping Grams has some information on that."

He nodded, heading out, pulling out his phone. Mark touched my back and I turned toward him. "Glad you're in one piece," he said, and I gave him a small smile before he followed Jerry out.

I turned to the rest, hands on my hips, ready to give a hard-ass, play-nice speech, when my gaze locked on Logan and all the air left my lungs.

I stood there, feeling my heart pounding painfully in my chest before I was able to think about speaking. "How is this possible?" I whispered, shaking my head and clenching my eyes closed, certain I was imagining it.

Again, I looked at him, and he stood, dressed in a navy business suit and matching light blue shirt. He took a step away from the couch towards me, mildly uncomfortable as he extended his hand. "Olivia, I'm Logan. Thank you for agreeing to meet with me." I ignored his comment and his hand, stepping into his personal space, inhaling the soft scent of the woodlands as I tipped his chin up, checking his neck for the raw scar from my dream.

Touching his unblemished neck, I dimly noted that Blake had stood up, a restraining hand from Tate keeping him from intervening.

Logan's skin was warm against my chilled fingers as I backed away from him, wrapping my arms around my waist. Blake sat back down as I blew out a breath.

My heart thudded in my chest as I pulled another breath in, deeply gathering my thoughts. "Who do you look like?" I asked softly.

Logan spared a glance to Darren behind him, shifting his weight uncertainly and stowing his hands in his pockets.

Closing my eyes, I tried to sound a little less crazy. "Who do you look like that is dead?" I asked again.

Logan replied stiffly, "My grandfather."

I nodded.

"Olivia," Morgan stated leisurely, positioning against the side of the plush couch, "we haven't brought him up to date yet."

I scowled, about to smart off, when Morgan continued, "We were just discussing the debt his fiancée owes."

"Morgan," I said, my voice deadly low. "I took that debt."

"Did you now?" he said, examining his cuticles, feigning disinterest.

It was not a good day for Morgan to play games with me. After that dream and the deaths I had been witnessing, thrown together with not having killed anything in over a week, he was treading on very thin ice.

I ground my teeth. "You are testing my self-control."

Darren looked properly worried, sitting forward. "Olie, what happened?" he asked, genuinely concerned.

Blake answered for me, his power play pushing my last nerves. "She dreamt of the killer reanimating a shifter who apparently might be your grandfather."

I blew out a breath, looking back to Logan and the eerie similarities between him and his grandfather. His expression was guarded as he sat next to Darren, regarding me warily. "Why did you check my neck?" he asked softly. While he was playing the same power games as the vamps, I didn't doubt he could take out a Master vampire for a second. One doesn't acquire power in our world without being able to kill one's enemies.

"He had a slash," I said, my eyes clouding with memories. "A scar across his chest, and a lion tattoo on his thigh," I ended, blinking back to the scene before me: vampire and shifter pitted against each other.

Logan shared a look with Darren before pulling out his phone and texting. Texting was smarter than an actual phone conversation, as the vamps would be able to hear both sides of the conversation.

Setting his phone back in his jacket pocket, he looked back at me and nodded. "I'll have someone check his grave site."

A shudder raked through my body as I remembered how ancient the trees were. "We need to know who knew about the site, as well. From what I saw, it had magic of its own that was violated."

Logan looked at me, surprised. I shrugged before turning as Jerry came in flustered, looking to the shifter and vampire annoyances behind me.

"You're not going to like this," Jerry stated.

"Worse than the pissing contest behind me?" I asked, rolling my eyes.

Morgan cleared his throat, a pointless act, since he didn't breathe, while Darren coughed, covering up the unexpected laugh at my comment.

Jerry glanced at the men behind me, uncertainty flashing on his features. Adjusting his tie nervously, he composed himself as his dark eyes returned to my own. "This might be better outside." I nodded, following him out. Jerry, wise to the ways of vampire and shifter hearing, texted the information to my phone.

The Executioner can be called upon when there is corruption or deceit in the dead's own race. They will reach out to the Executioner in an attempt to right the wrong done to them.

I stared into Jerry's dark depths, a sinking feeling nestling in my chest. I turned back into the room. The vampires were staring daggers at the two shifters, who had their attention on me. Although it was reassuring to know that leaving my blood on the street after the hit and run, while stupid, was not the cause of this current turmoil, I now had to deal with corruption in the packs, which is not in my job description. Rubbing my temples, I sighed. It didn't matter, I needed to get whoever it was off the streets and end the killing.

"Logan, we really need that list, please," I said softly, not liking the tension in the room.

"Blake," I started, equally as softly, "can you give me a lift?"

Blake spared a look at the vampires on either side of him before answering, "Gladly."

I nodded. "Jerry, get Logan and Darren home safely and get that list to me ASAP," I said, deleting Jerry's text and striding to the kitchen for more food.

Stuffing another donut into my mouth, I turned to find Blake and Logan behind me, each looking slightly uncomfortable.

"What?" I asked, ungraciously around a mouthful.

Blake's light blue eyes met my own, annoyed, before I turned to Logan's caramel-colored eyes with a raised eyebrow. He took a deep breath before beginning.

"Can you please tell me what happened at Flame?" Logan said peacefully, settling on a bar stool next to me, his body language screaming repressed anger.

I took another look at Blake, who shrugged, moving behind me to the kitchen cabinets.

I swallowed my bite, my mouth feeling uncomfortably dry. I pinched the bridge of my nose before adjusting on the island stool. I did not want to have this conversation. I am a fantastic killer, but I am horrible at tact.

"Logan," I said, speaking his name as I drew my eyes back to his, "are you certain you want the truth? I don't sugar coat."

"I didn't ask you to sugar coat it," he demanded. "I asked you politely to tell me what happened. I fail to see the difficulty in that request."

I turned, holding my donut up as I stood. "You are so painfully correct." Turning to Blake, I grinned evilly from ear to ear. "Blake, darling, would you be so kind as to tell him in detail how his fiancée broke supernatural rules?"

Blake grinned widely, his fangs descended. "I would be honored, Olivia."

Blake came around, resting his hands on my shoulders as he brushed a delicate kiss against my cheekbone. With a sinking feeling, I belatedly realized this may not have been my best idea, but the demand for revenge in my chest pushed that nagging conscience away.

Logan nodded, shifting his weight in his seat, attempting to contain the frustration twitching in his jaw.

Blake began with what I was certain was a devilish grin as I moved to get a drink of milk.

"Lorraine was divine, dancing seductively..." I let Blake's voice trail out of my consciousness, not wanting to hear how alluring he found Logan's fiancée. Not that it mattered; hopefully there would be nothing but mind-blowing sex happening between us.

Heaving a sigh, I turned around to see Logan's jaw begin ticking as Blake described the orgasmic experience of taking her blood. I had to admit, he was a great storyteller.

Logan closed his eyes, clenching his fists. "I wasn't aware," he said, meeting my own eyes again.

I grimaced with understanding. A painful truth was better coming from someone you cared about than someone who would use it as a point of contention. I could subdue his anger, braid it down, even absorb it, but just because I had the ability, didn't mean I needed to exercise it on him.

"While we are on the subject of truths, fair warning: Steven and I have a few issues to work out," I said, taking another bite of donut.

Logan's shoulders readjusted as he also reached for one. "I heard," he said.

I smiled, chocolate frosting dotting my teeth. "Enjoy fishing your SUV from the river?"

Logan chewed thoughtfully. "Maybe I didn't hear about this, actually."

Raising an eyebrow, I continued around my next chocolate-covered, sprinkled bite, "You didn't know he tried to take me out in a T-bone accident?"

Logan ate the rest of his plain donut in one bite before answering angrily, "No."

"Well, you know now," I said, raising my glass of milk at him in a mock toast. "I will deal with him. It's personal now."

He nodded. "Can I ask a favor, Olivia?"

I raised an eyebrow, finishing off my milk. "You do mean another favor, correct?" I said with a smile to lessen the insult, pretty sure it had the opposite effect.

He raked a hand through his hair, similar to Darren. "Yes, another. Let me deal with Steven."

I groaned, picking up another donut. "That's asking too much," I said to the island, startling him by turning back quickly, donut forgotten. "Unless ... On one condition."

He nodded, and I leaned in close.

"No more grief to Kass and Darren, and I won't kill Steven," I stated, leaving out that I still reserved the right to beat the everlasting hell out of him.

His eyes darkened before returning to their normal color. He stood, adjusting his suit jacket, shaking his head. "You don't understand what you're asking of me." He hesitated, leaning closer to me. "You don't understand what you have asked of me thus far."

I sighed, looking up at him, shrugging. "That's your decision."

He gave me a long look before leaving. I didn't understand what was happening behind his gaze, and I didn't care.

"So, wanna go on a goose chase today?" I asked Blake with false excitement, rubbing my hands together.

Blake raised an eyebrow, still smiling. "Why not?"

Making our way back to the living room, I found Tate alone, sitting on the same sofa where we had left him. "What's wrong?" I asked, unnerved by his stillness and sheer lack of emotion.

Tate leaned back, staring at something off in the distance. "The Vampire Council has been alerted to what is occurring here," he said, bringing his attention to me before standing. "Since we are the test subjects for our coming out, they find our..." He hesitated, trying to find the right word, settling on, "developments very entertaining."

I cringed. Politics were annoying; vampire politics tempted me to an even earlier grave. Tate was the Master of the Centennial House, and from the sound of it, their revealing themselves was not on his to-do list, but the Vampire Council ran all the Houses across the world, no matter Tate's disapproval of their decision.

I blew out a breath, forcing a confidence I didn't really feel. "No worries; we'll figure this out."

Tate nodded, his attention turning back to his own thoughts. Blake tugged my hand, pulling me away from his dismal Master. He kept my hand, pulling me close in the hallway, his slow smile showing just the tips of his fangs. My eyes were consumed by that view.

Gently, he pushed a gun into the back of my pants, his fingers running over the delicate flesh, before slipping my favorite throwing dagger into my back pocket, letting his hands graze my panty line.

"How did you get those?" I asked huskily.

"You were out of it for a while. I had to get your affairs in order," he said, moving away, leading me to the garage and his own version of a beast.

I laughed as he clicked the garage door open. Boys and their toys.

"So, my fair lady, where are we headed?" Blake asked, sliding behind the wheel.

Nestling my head against the plush leather, I exhaled verbally, organizing a to-do list. "Well, my dear driver, I need to head to Thurgood Marshall High School and interview the teachers and nurse. I also need to follow up with Kass to be sure everything is going smoothly. And I need to catch up with Mercer on the investigation. Oh, and I probably need to figure out if this connection with the undead goes both ways."

Blake tapped the steering wheel, backing out of the garage. "How about we hit up Mercer at the police station first?"

I nodded, mentally organizing all the things I needed to ask him.

Chapter 10

The police station was silent as we parked and headed in. This time, I had the forethought to stop for coffee for myself and Mercer.

Finding Mercer's desk empty, Blake and I perched on the edge, trying not to scare the other occupants of the police station. At least, I was trying not to scare them. Blake may have been smiling so widely they all got a shot of his extended canines. Giving him a playful shove, I raised an eyebrow as I leaned towards him. "Quit it," I whispered.

Blake feigned innocence, moving his attention to something behind me. Turning, I offered Mercer his coffee, which he ignored. Standing up, I turned to face him, setting his coffee on an empty space on his cluttered desk. Mercer was angry. Aside from the hot scent I was picking up, he had yet to make eye contact with me.

"Mercer?" I tried softly, as he sat down forcefully in his chair.

He finally raised his light eyes to my own. "What's wrong?" I asked, gently leaning toward him as Blake twisted around to watch him.

His lips pulled away from his teeth in a snarl. Slamming his hands on the desk, he catapulted towards me. "What's wrong?" he hissed, looking disgustedly at Blake, then at me.

"Did you think you could manipulate me that easily?" he hissed, pressing his finger just under my collarbone. "I know what you are, demon. You're not welcome here anymore."

I felt my heart constrict, gripped by a cold frost. Closing my eyes, I turned away from him, walking out of the police station. Blake stayed to growl something nasty at Mercer, I'm sure, but I didn't even bother. I had defended myself until I was blue in the face. Once they called me demon, they never came back around, but more importantly, I didn't want or need him. I sighed, shoving my hands in my pockets as Blake unlocked the SUV, grumbling.

Blake drove in silence for a few minutes before saying anything. "He's wrong, Olivia,"

Resting the back of my head against his leather headrest, I answered, "It doesn't matter, Blake. He has made his decision." I shrugged. Mercer was meaningless, but it was an important lesson. I was letting others too close. My guards had been fractured, where, I couldn't recall, but now more than ever, I needed to bolster them.

I needed to keep anyone and everyone away from my emotions; anyone with access to them was dangerous to me. I had learned how to control my own turmoil long ago, but the damage others could wreak on me, that was where the real danger lay.

"You are not a demon," he repeated, as if it were important I believed that.

I gave him a small smile, reaching out to pat his forearm. "It doesn't matter, Blake. This isn't new; it never will be." I sighed, turning my attention back to the road. I just wished it wouldn't sting so badly, but that's what happens when I let my guard down. Foolish, foolish me.

The simple truth was that I didn't know if being a succubus was being a demon. All the lore I had ever encountered claimed we were soul suckers that could twist and take the soul of a human. Thus far, with all the horrible things I had seen and done, that had not made my list of abilities. If this case was teaching me anything, it was that to take the soul of another being took a hatred and evilness that I had yet to acquire. Give it time, though; a few more people turning on me, and I might change my tune.

Blake blew out a breath he didn't need before asking, "Where to now?"

I squinted at the midday sun, exhaling my own breath, "You wouldn't happen to know where Thurgood Marshall is located?"

Blake pulled over, shifting the SUV into park before using the large touch-screen console. "I do not. However, I can find it."

I smiled. "Well, ain't you fresh and modern for an old fella," I said, trying my best Southern accent on.

His look was priceless, and I couldn't help but throw my head back, laughing, which seemed to make him happy as he smiled, selecting the correct settings before pulling back onto the road, his GPS guiding us.

Chapter 11

Two hours later, we pulled into the elite, private, and difficult-to-get-into Thurgood Marshall High School. Without Blake's ability to glamour the guards, I would have had to hog-tie them just to make it past the first set of gates. Having a partner was turning out to be handy, but dangerous for my underworked emotions if Mercer was any indication.

Walking up the stone steps of the castle-like structure, I tried to organize a plan of attack here. "Principal first?" I asked with a half shrug.

Blake shook his head. "Who do you want to talk with first? The principal will probably shut us down and have us escorted out forcefully."

I thought about that as we continued up the stairs to the large, ornately carved wooden doors. Blake held the door open for me as I answered. "The nurse, I am hoping, will have information regarding their medical history. Speaking of which, did Gunner find anything from the samples?" I asked as we headed down the long hallway lined with lockers.

Blake shook his head. "I'm not sure."

The nurse's office was conveniently vacant of students, and Blake didn't need to glamour her in order to gain her cooperation.

Probably due to Blake's gorgeous smile, this plump, middle-aged nurse was willing to divulge all sorts of private and personal information with a gentle nudge. Apparently HIPPA didn't apply to Supernaturals. I'd have to remember that for future reference.

"You didn't notice anything strange or out of the ordinary about the students in question?" Blake asked, leaning forward in his seat, batting those brilliant baby blue eyes.

I kept back, trying to be invisible, as Blake continued the seduction of information.

She tilted her head, tapping a finger against her chin. "The only thing they all had in common, to my knowledge, was that they all needed blood work and physicals for a new program Mr. Davis was organizing."

"Is Mr. Davis available this afternoon?" Blake asked seamlessly.

She twisted her fingers hesitantly. "Lauren?" Blake prompted temptingly as her shoulders relaxed and she tilted her head to the side dreamily.

She smiled. He hadn't used glamour once. Amazing, I had seriously underestimated his skills.

She peeked up at him through lowered lashes, blushing at his suave smile.

"He took some time off, but I might know his home address," Lauren said, biting on her bottom lip.

Blake balanced an elbow on her desk mirroring her enamored expression. "What would it take to get said address?" he whispered.

Blushing again, she sent a gaze my way, her face falling, remembering I was still there. Standing up quickly, I pulled my phone out. "Call," I said abruptly, fleeing the room to give him privacy.

I sighed against the closed door, moving away from it once the soft moaning began. I didn't want to hear any of that.

I was sitting in the waiting room, as far as I could get from the closed door, when Blake emerged, wiping his mouth. Cringing, I stood and headed to the door. Blake's hand on my arm turned me towards him.

"What?" I asked briskly.

"I didn't sleep with her." His blue eyes bore into my own.

I blinked, a few choice responses flooding my brain. "It's none of my business." I turned to open the door. He turned me again.

My irritation spiked. I let it flow into his hand. "Shit," he said, pulling back and staring at his hand.

I crossed my arms across my chest. "Why is it so important that I know this?"

He glanced at his hand then back to me, stepping closer. "It is," he said, with heavy emphasis on both words.

I shook my head, exiting the nurse's waiting room and heading for the SUV. I left it at that, but he didn't.

"What was that?" he asked, sparing a glance my way.

"You mean what you felt?" I asked to his nod. "My emotions, I didn't bother to hold them in." I shrugged. "It usually doesn't hurt."

He shook his head. "It didn't. It was just ... different." He flexed his large hand against the steering wheel before asking, "Can you do that with all your emotions?"

"Yes," I answered, regarding him warily. I had a sinking feeling where this was going.

"Man, sex with you must be amazing," he said, giving me a boyish grin.

I rolled my eyes. Yep, that's exactly where I thought it was going.

"What?" he asked as I turned to look out my window.

"Nothing, Blake."

"Shit, Olivia, I didn't mean—" he started before I interrupted him.

"You didn't mean to imply that the only reason anyone ever sleeps with me is due to enhanced sensations?"

"Shit," he said again, going silent.

"Being the Kitten makes me a trophy fuck as well." I was attempting at humor, but my words rang painfully true.

Blake huffed a response.

I was staring out at the landscape when Blake's cell phone went off. He cast me a look before hitting a button on his steering wheel, sending Mallory's angry voice into the SUV's speakers.

"Get your ass over here now, Blake. If I have to deal with these malicious, sick, and demented protestors any longer, I am going to kill them all." She over pronounced each word, making it drip with venom.

Blake rested his head against the headrest as we moved onto the freeway. "Mallory, I am with Olivia attempting to hunt down the beast responsible for the killings. Can this wait?"

"No," she hissed before hanging up.

Blake exited the highway and got back on going the other direction, pounding the steering wheel with an intensity that had me taking a peek at the muscles in his clenching jaw.

I reached over and tapped his hand. "Do you want some help with your anger?" I asked.

"No, I am not an out-of-control shifter." He growled at me.

I smiled, running my eyes over the flexing muscle in his bicep. "No, you are not," I answered.

An hour later, we were at the Centennial Compound. I meant that in the exact definition of the word "compound." It was an old castle they had restored on the outskirts of town, complete with a moat and exterior guard wall. We parked in the modern and out-of-place parking lot, walking to the elaborately carved wooden gates.

Blake stalked quickly downstairs into the basement and I jogged to keep up with his long strides. The guards let me pass since I was with the head of security, but I did receive a few looks. Barreling through a steel door, I bumped into his back, squeaking slightly. He kept blocking the door with his massive frame as Mallory yelled at him.

"Do you have any idea what I have been putting up with all fucking day?" she yelled. "Those fucking religious fanatics have been throwing holy water on our people! Attacking them with silver! Where the fuck have you been?"

I felt the tension in Blake as he blocked the doorway, radiating out in waves. He had declined my help, so I kept my hands to myself, but his blocking the door was annoying. They must have been staring at each other for at least three minutes before I called out, "Hi, Mal."

Blake moved to let me by. "Olivia," Mallory said with her back to me. Her voice sounded soft and I could imagine why. I moved behind her and wrapped my arms around her waist, drawing in the pain, frustration, and the fear that she might fail to keep her people safe. I stayed that way until I felt her shoulders relax against me.

"Thanks," she whispered, before pulling away.

I staggered slightly, leaning against the desk with a million high-tech gadgets, the screens displaying the mess of protestors outside.

Blake had finally entered the room, sitting behind me.

"What do you want me to do?" Blake asked, the anger and hostility dripping from each word.

"Fix it," Mallory growled, massaging her temples.

"How?" Blake asked, standing and throwing a keyboard against the wall. "How the fuck am I supposed to fix it?"

"I don't know, but you are the fucking head of security. FIX IT!" Malory finished, screaming the last words.

Fangs extended from Blake's gums, followed by Mal's in a wet, sucking sound. I smartly backed away so I was no longer in between the two. I liked both of them, but they wouldn't be paying attention to the collateral damage, which included me and the high-tech gizmos here.

Turning away from the staring and hissing contest, I took in the rest of the room. It was larger than I had initially thought, a long room, leading down into a tiered auditorium of sorts. Each level had vamps behind computer screens, busily monitoring the exterior and interior of the compound.

Stepping down to the second level, I sat next to a dark-haired petite vamp with a pencil skirt and button-down blouse.

We both cringed when we heard Tate start screaming.

"Is there any way you can get the names and addresses of the protestors?" I asked.

She raised an eyebrow, said nothing, continuing to type on her computer. I hoped she was doing as I asked. I shifted my view to the massive screen in front of us, watching the anger and hatred pour out of the protestors as they screamed and yelled. The worst had to be the small children in their midst. Protective ran heavy in my nature, even of children who were not mine.

I drummed my fingers on the desk, only half listening to the breaking of furniture behind us.

"Do you have a plan?" the petite vampire asked, breaking her silence.

"I have the beginnings of one. Can you also find out their jobs, churches, and where their children go to school, please?" I asked as nicely as possible, which for me was something.

"Only if you get them to stop breaking things," she replied.

I nodded, turning back to the noise and standing with a sigh. "I have an idea," I stated louder than needed; they did have enhanced hearing, after all.

They all stopped in various crouched positions around the room. Mal raised an eyebrow, so I added, "No, it doesn't involve killing anyone." Unfortunately.

Tate straightened out first, adjusting his black button-down shirt into his olive green slacks. "Olivia, how nice to see you," he greeted, recovering quickly.

I gave him a rueful smile, climbing out of the pit to survey the damage. The sofa seemed intact, so I carefully perched on it.

Mallory tossed her hair over a shoulder before coming to sit next to me, glaring at Tate and Blake the entire time. "So, before any of this can be implemented, there needs to be an intelligence gathering session, which I believe one of your employees is working on. "

Blake, his black hair disheveled, moved to right a chair that had somehow survived the trip across the room, taking a seat in it.

Tate remained standing, clearly a power move, but I wasn't going to point that out. I did have a shred of common sense.

"So, the greatest problem I can see is not that the protestors are harming your housemates, but the fact that the feeling of safety in your House has been compromised," I surmised.

Tate growled, avoiding eye contact with me.

"I'll take that as a—" With that, he turned toward me, his eyes highlighted in amber.

"Hey, Tate, I get it," I said, easing the situation back down, or at least attempting to. "If these protestors showed up outside my gates, they wouldn't live to see the next night."

Tate adjusted his sleeves again, looking away. He hated to be vulnerable; we had that in common. "So," I continued, "the best way to stop the protestors is to show them exactly how vulnerable they really are."

"I thought there was no killing involved," Blake muttered. He'd earned the glare I leveled at him.

"No killing, just following. Learn their patterns, attend their churches, befriend their neighbors, have a reason to be at their kids' schools, meet their family members. Ingrain respectable vampires into their lives." They were listening and thinking. "If that doesn't work, we can kill them," I said a shrug.

"Do it," Tate said before leaving.

I nodded and smiled. "Then can we go see the professor?" I asked Blake as my phone started playing Ricky Martin's Shake Your Bon Bon.

Growling, I answered. "I need your help," Kass hissed quietly.

"What?" I asked, instantly on alert, standing as I readied for action.

"Lorraine isn't showing up at the Lion Ball tonight," Kass finished, with a sense of urgency I didn't understand as I sat back down.

"Okay," I said, waiting a breath for her to continue. When she didn't, I asked, "Do you need me to make her?"

"No," Kass answered hastily, "I want you to put on a fancy dress and get your ass down there tonight."

"Kass—" I started, rubbing the bridge of my nose.

"Olivia, get dressed and get down there," she hissed before hanging up.

Heaving a sigh, I spared a look at Mal. "Can I borrow some clothing?"

...

I was primped, polished, and dressed in a to-die-for navy blue dress that hugged me in all the right places. Blake ran his roving eyes over me again as I exited the car.

Raising an eyebrow at him, I said, "Don't worry. I still have weapons hidden."

He smiled at me. "I expect nothing less from you. You have the address to get a cab back to my place?"

I nodded, closing the door and strutting to the entrance. The guard at the top of the marble stairs graciously waved me in when I explained I was late for my date, Logan. He was human; otherwise, I doubt I would have been allowed in.

I scanned the room, my gaze settling on Darren first, bent low over a table, discussing something passionately with his brother. I made my way over, gently resting a hand on Logan's as I sat, pulling the anger and irritation I felt rumbling beneath the surface. Not wanting to create gossip, I smiled warmly at Darren, who greeted me, relieved.

"I don't need a date," Logan hissed at me.

I straightened his tie before murmuring, "You certainly do not; what you need is someone to help mask your personal problems while you deal with business." I held his gaze longer then was recommended for a shifter, but I wanted him to know this was business.

I snagged a glass of champagne, taking a sip before continuing. "Since you can't be trusted to handle your personal shit, consider me your built-in self-control."

He watched me warily. I smiled at people passing our table, making a wide berth around the angry Alpha shifter.

Kass reappeared at that moment. "Olie, thank goodness," she said, sitting down next to Darren.

"Thank you for coming," Darren added, nodding.

"Of course," I answered, skimming Logan's hand again, pulling more crap out. If the asshole thought this was easy for me, he had another thing coming. If he weren't Darren's brother, I would have left him here to rot as the packs vied for a more stable leader. As it stood, I was apparently now invested in Logan staying the head of the shifters.

I fucking hate politics.

Suppressing my annoyance, I took in the lavish ballroom with a copper-domed ceiling and intricate marble flooring, complete with a second floor boasting a gold railing. This wasn't an environment I could see shifters being at ease in. They were more of a biker bar crowd, from my experience.

"Who picked the venue?" I asked, as Logan took a shot of alcohol before the waiter could set it down.

"Guess," Kass said from across the circular table.

Scowling, I pushed away the glass from Logan. "You're not making my job easier."

Settling back, he kicked out his long legs, lacing his hands across his abdomen. "How goes the case?" he asked. I took a sip of champagne.

I scanned the crowd absentmindedly. "We have a few leads. Hopefully, something will pan out. Did you check on your family plot?" I asked, returning my attention to him.

Sitting forward, he pulled my chair closer to his own. "Yes, and you are correct, the body of my grandfather is missing. I've forwarded the list to Grams of those allowed in and those with enough power to get in."

Nodding, I blew out a breath. "I was afraid of that."

"No additional murders have been reported?" he asked.

Shaking my head, I answered, "Not that I am aware of, but I have lost my connection to the police."

Logan raised an eyebrow. "Look at you, making friends."

I shrugged. "It's better they're not involved, anyway. This is a matter for us."

He nodded, tracking something over my left shoulder. I turned and smiled at a breathtaking blond in a stunning red dress. She and her date looked terribly out of place; I pushed out confidence and ease.

"Hello," she greeted, nodding at me.

I smiled, extending my hand as they came to stand between Logan and me, even though we were still very close together.

"Hi, I'm Olivia. We were just finishing discussing some sensitive business, but please let me scoot down so you both can grab a seat," I said, sliding down two chairs around the large table.

Logan followed my movements, his darkening eyes making me worry he was too pissed to pull this off. The fucker shouldn't be drunk, unless he was really trying. A shifter's quick metabolism made it almost impossible to get inebriated.

The woman nodded, smiling as she sat and exchanged pleasantries with Logan, which I tuned out, focusing on Kass. She shrugged, hiding a smile as my eyes glazed over.

Fucking politics.

The rest of the evening passed much the same way. I was overjoyed when dinner was served, but slightly disappointed when the only things I could eat were the over-steamed veggies and buns.

Huffing a sigh, I tried to pick around the bacon potatoes.

Logan leaned over, grabbing a bite off my plate. Pushing it toward him, I said, "You can have the rest; I don't eat meat."

He looked as though I had grown a second head. I shrugged, picking at his steamed veggies in turn.

"That can't be healthy," he said around a mouthful of meat.

"Neither is how much I drink," I said, taking another inventory of the room. I kept smiling in response to the curious glances we kept getting. I probably needed to come up with a cover story on why Lorraine was not here. Telling people she was a worthless slut would not be in keeping with tonight's theme of keeping the lion shifter head of the packs.

"There is dissension in my packs," Logan rumbled close to my ear.

"I'm aware," I said gently. Leading wasn't easy. Nothing was simple, and someone was always unhappy. Always.

"Do you need help in handling it?" I asked, poaching the rest of his veggies.

He sighed, switching plates with me as we huddled together, talking softly. "I'm trying to avoid a blood bath."

"You're a shifter. It's in your nature."

"And what do you know about our natures?" he asked, almost suggestively.

"Enough," I answered, pushing away the plate and leaning against the uncomfortable bamboo chair, forcing myself not to cross my arms.

The parade of people picked up now that Logan's shoulders had relaxed and he cracked what appeared to be a rare smile.

Twirling my straw in my third or perhaps sixth drink, I decided I was sufficiently liquored up to ask Logan to dance at the next lull in visitors, which was looking to be about now.

Leaning over, I nudged his arm resting on the table. "Wanna dance?" I asked hopefully. Dancing would recharge my control and expend the annoyance I had sucked from him.

"I don't dance," he informed me.

I huffed as Darren cleared his throat. "With all Olivia has done, a dance wouldn't hurt," he said, glaring at his older brother. My heart warmed at Darren, trying to make my life easier by provoking the sibling he was already having a hard time with.

"We were just on our way to the dance floor," Kass said, snatching Darren's hand.

Reluctantly, Logan stood, following my lead onto the sparsely occupied dance floor. The ballroom was richly decorated, with a painted ceiling depicting a Centaur in battle. Smiling, I hesitantly reached for Logan and was shocked as he gently drew me close with calloused hands, resting a massive right hand on my hip while his left hand took my right to nestle against his chest. The moment was charged with an intimacy I didn't anticipate. I belatedly realized my guards were slightly down.

That was the second time that day. Damn, so much for my perfect control. Logan shifted under my slight weight at his shoulder. "Sorry," I muttered, building my walls back up.

"Is that how you control people?" he asked guardedly.

Rolling my eyes, I answered, "I can't make anyone do what they don't want to do. I can only provide my own emotions that click with their own, amplifying the process. For example, if you're angry, I can't make you happy."

"But you eased my anger," he pointed out, genuinely interested.

I shrugged, meeting his intense caramel gaze. "I can take emotions from people—suck them, if you will."

"That gives you power, energy?" he questioned, raising an eyebrow.

"Quite the opposite," I answered, flicking a glance at Kass, "it's intensely draining. Over the years, I have built a fairly large tolerance for other people's crappy emotions." I sighed, staring levelly so he understood it was his crap I was now sealing in a metal ball in my head.

"I thought you all gained your power from sex," Logan asked, definitely suggestively.

Lowering my darkened lashes, I peered up at him, letting just the tip of my pink tongue slip out to lick the side of my mouth. He followed the action, his own mouth slightly parting.

Leaning closer, I whispered to his entranced gaze, "I am a master of all emotions and sensations." Pulling back, I smirked.

We twirled effortlessly around the dance floor. I was actually letting him lead. A man who could dance, that was attractive.

I was about to continue my explanation when a sharp tap on my shoulder had me turning. "Thanks for keeping him company, I'm feeling much better," Lorraine said with a fake smile, as the irritation I had sucked from Logan bubbled to the surface.

Smiling, I inclined my head before sending a nod to Kass's disapproving gaze, followed by a shrug as I grabbed my clutch and headed out into the fresh night air.

Blowing out a deep breath, I slipped into a cab and relayed Blake's address, my mind roving over Logan and Lorraine.

I could understand why he had made it to the top of the shifter pack. What I didn't understand was why he had chosen a mate so poorly. Lorraine lacked political knowledge and physical abilities. Hell, she wasn't even a support system, which he would need. She could never be an asset in the challenging path he would undoubtedly navigate on a daily basis.

More importantly, it was none of my damn business.

Chapter 12

The cabby exhaled, twisting cigarette smoke tendrils oozing from his ancient mouth as he announced my total. I cringed, handing over the crisp bills to his greasy palms. Gross.

It was early still, according to Blake's schedule, as I pushed open the front door. He did say he wanted me to come back tonight, but an unlocked door? That had every instinct I had screaming, and I listened well to those.

I discarded my shoes, creeping silently, now that the creaking door had announced my arrival. I almost slid in a pool of blood. Regaining my balance with a loud smack against the plaster wall, I followed the trail to a human with his throat ripped out.

The asshole was heavily loaded with military-grade clothing and guns. I cringed, unclipping the .40-caliber pistol at his waist, waiting a breath to listen as I straightened back up. While my hidden knives were grand, I never turned down additional firepower.

I was really hoping Blake already had the cleaners on their way and my slow creep with a gun was overkill.

The kitchen was empty, along with the living room and parlor. I crept slowly up the stairs, my worry growing steadily as the blood stains and body count increased.

At the landing, I stepped over the human who had prepared my grilled cheese sandwich. I had a sinking feeling in my stomach. Steeling my emotions, I raised the gun, following the noises coming from Blake's bedroom.

I could hear him grunting, hear him fighting, growling, and threatening even though it sounded like he was gagged. Slowly, carefully, I slipped down the hall to the illuminated doorway as my core cooled and my breathing evened out.

This was what I was designed for.

Pointing the gun down the hallway, I stepped over and around bodies and pieces of bodies gingerly. There could not be many left, given the carnage. I had counted at least nine dead. Blake alone could handle that.

Hope is a tricky emotion. No matter what I tell myself or how I force myself to act, I always have hope, even in the darkest, sickest nightmares I call my memories, I always clung to the fabric of hope, although I didn't always know what it was called. I don't give up. I keep hoping.

I haven't decided if that is a good or bad thing.

So, when I heard Blake scream with the tearing of tissue, I hoped I was wrong about what had happened. Blowing out a breath, I picked up an unoccupied arm, flinging it down the hallway with a resounding thud past the open door. It gave the desired outcome, as several additional men, clad in the same military-grade equipment, fanned out from the room.

Too bad I was a faster shot, no hesitation to kill my greatest strength, if anyone ever asks.

Four went down like jelly, their brains spattering over each other and the walls. The fifth went back into the room, firing out. One human, I thought to Blake, this you should be able to fucking handle.

Sliding right next to the doorframe I waited a breath until I heard Blake grunt, followed by the rapid repetition of gunfire and a blistering pain in my left upper arm. Not waiting for an invitation, I flung myself into the room. My gaze settled onto the last man standing. I lunged, landing on him hard, only to be thrown against the wall. The fucker should not be that strong.

Where the hell was my gun?

"Pretty dress, vampire fucker," he said, admiring my now ruined borrowed dress. Oops. He shook his head. "What they got a normal man don't?" he rasped.

Fucker thought I was human. "Stamina, for one. Eons of experience, for second." I tapped my bottom lip while I pretended to think. "Third, they don't kill innocent bystanders," I hissed, bunching my quads and smashing into him, his knife digging deep into my stomach as we hit the floor.

Wrapping my hands on his throat, I slammed down with every ounce of energy I had, over and over again, until I felt his skull split and the pathetic excuse for a brain slide slickly out.

Grunting, I turned to look at Blake. Stupid, foolish hope.

"Here," I said, gripping the sides of my navy dress and ripping it over my stomach wound. I shoved the dead man away, pulling myself closer to Blake as he sat up.

He pulled himself towards me, closing the distance between us. His white shirt was stained red from blood. As he opened his mouth, I saw the missing fangs before he dropped his head to my gushing stomach wound.

"Drink; you need to heal," I encouraged, running my bloody fingers through his dark locks.

He drank deeply, my mind already working on a to-do list to tackle once he was finished. Poor Blake, this was a serious blow to his image, not to mention his body. He would regenerate the fangs, but the process was painful and long.

It was an extremely effective form of torture. If the humans were that knowledgeable in vampire anatomy, one shouldn't have taken out so many.

Blake leaned against my stomach, looking mildly better. "They were juiced," he said, his words garbled.

"On steroids?" I asked, shifting once he sat back up.

He shook his head. "Vamp blood."

"Oh fuck," I said, slipping back down. "Someone is really pissed at you."

...

Mallory was stitching up my stomach wound as we watched the bodies being assembled on Blake's driveway. Lights flashed from the police cars I'd warned Tate against calling. The officers stood on the fringes of the assortment of pieces of flesh that the techs were pulling out of the house.

Aside from the reporters yelling and the constant flashing of bulbs at the gate, it was silent.

Mercer stood up from one of the piles he was examining, coming my way.

"Ouch," I hissed at Mal. "I said I was sorry about the dress."

She glared at me. "It was on sale," she said again, slamming her first aid kit together and shaking her head as she stood up to head over to Blake.

"Olivia," Mercer stated tentatively.

"Mercer," I responded, looking up from my seat on the cold, concrete steps.

"Sure got yourself a mess here," he said, pocketing his hands.

"Nope," I responded, looking at him. "You have a mess here. What I have is a housekeeper and cook who was brutally murdered by humans."

He didn't have a single thing to say to that. He turned as Blake and Tate brought her body ceremoniously out of the house. I sighed, looking back at the press, hoisting myself up with a groan.

"Where do you think you're headed?" Tate asked hotly.

"We need to deal with the press. I have a plan." I wasn't waiting for his approval.

"Your idea to get the protestors to back off has worked well. I will allow this."

I raised an eyebrow at the use of the word allow, but I didn't have the energy to correct it.

Hobbling my way over, I reached the guard, who looked like an ex-Marine, and nodded to him. Surveying the crowd of reporters, I realized I knew nothing of the faces in front of me. Turning to the tall human, I asked, "You follow the news at all?"

He looked down at me, his stony features not changing. "I need someone who will tell the facts and not write something fear-based," I continued.

He turned back to the crowd. I thought he was ignoring me, but he called out, "Chin, front and center."

From the back of the crowd, a short, slightly overweight Asian woman in a gray dress suit came forward. "Yes?"

Tall and stony looked down at me. "I want you and one camera to come in," I said to her. She hesitated for only a moment before her cameraman slipped a camera over her neck, taking away the audio equipment. Once stony was satisfied she had nothing else on her, including her cell phone, we moved back to the bodies.

Chin was silent, so I began, "The humans were loaded up on vampire blood, as it is becoming common knowledge that vampire blood increases strength and healing abilities."

"What are the long-term effects of that?" she asked nervously.

I shrugged, regretting it as my stitches moved. "Vampirism," I stated.

She stumbled, staring at me. I gave her a moment to adjust before continuing, "So, the humans were juiced up and broke into a local vampire's home, killed his human helper, and began torturing the vampire."

She nodded and I gestured to the bodies, hesitating again as she snapped pictures.

"You were here the entire night?" she asked above the camera.

"No, I arrived from a party mid-torture," I stated tiredly.

"How do you know it was the humans and not the vampire who killed the helper?" she asked, gaining confidence.

"The vampire kills look like this," I said, pointing out the row of bodies. "The human had bullets shot through her," I said sadly.

"You sound upset about one housekeeper dying, not the dozen here," she stated more than asked.

"I am upset she was killed for doing nothing wrong, only her job. The rest made their choices and this," I motioned to the bodies, "was the consequence."

"Many would argue that was the just fate of someone who worked for the vampires," she said, done taking pictures but still staring at the bodies lined up, along with the few in bloody piles.

I shook my head. "That doesn't seem fair or just. It's just sad such fear exists."

Chin nodded, and I walked her back to the gate.

Looking back at the flashing red and blue lights, I heaved a sigh as Blake and Tate were in a heated conversation with uniformed officers, Mercer offering no advice or assistance. For a brief moment, I gave thought to helping, before remembering that the vampires caused this mess.

With a groan, I went to sit with Mal on the steps to wait it out.

"You could go help," Mal said, not bothering to look over at me.

"What would the fun in that be?" I asked, cringing as my newly formed stitches pulled.

Slapping me on the back, she stood. "Then come help clean the mess."

I huffed, staring up at her grumpily. "Alright," I conceded.

Between Mal, me, and the several vampires who had drawn the unfortunate cleanup duty, we had the house back in fighting shape a few hours after sunrise. Blake had not been back inside yet and I was mildly worried. Following Mal outside, I ignored her pointed glare at her bloodied, torn, and now bleach-stained dress.

I wasn't going to change and ruin my own perfectly good clothing.

Only Mercer remained outside with Blake and Tate, the bodies having been hauled away by the coroners. Blake's blue eyes were streaked through with blood from the stress and pain of being defanged. He needed sleep. Sliding up next to him, I slipped under his shoulder, wrapping my arm around his waist and bracing my legs wide for the extra weight he pushed onto me.

"We are done, Mercer," I said, turning Blake toward the house.

"Not until I say so," Mercer demanded, hauling me back around.

I smiled wickedly at Mercer, stepping right into his personal space as I slipped out and Mal took my place under Blake.

"Step gingerly, Mercer. You're pushing the buttons of a vampire who could use a fresh kill, and I might be willing to give it to him." His eyes widened as he stepped quickly back.

Easing myself on Blake's other side, I turned to Tate. "Get him inside," he growled.

Mal and I made quick work of that task, setting Blake down in the living room on the overstuffed, dark blue couch. Pulling back, I sat on the coffee table in front of him, holding his hand as his eyes rolled into his head.

Tate sat next to me, cutting deeply into his wrist before pressing it into Blake's mouth. Aged vampire blood would speed the healing process, but it would do nothing for the pain.

Blake drank deeply, his eyes, once open, never leaving my own and his bloodstained hand cradled gently in mine as I gave him a small smile. Then his eyes dropped heavily, his body taking over the healing process from the control freak.

Tate stood, flexing his healed wrist.

"You will watch him," Tate said.

"I don't take orders," I growled.

He turned, his eyes full amber, fangs descended. "You will watch him," he repeated as I snarled, bunching my muscles, ready to leap.

Mal stood between us. "Tate, Olie, back down. We've all had a very stressful night. Olie will stay here. Tate, let's go figure out who the hell leaked Blake's home address and supplied those fuckers with the heavy artillery."

Easing down from my crouch, I shifted to adjust the sharp tilt of Blake's neck and then remove his blood-covered shoes before resting his feet on the couch.

Mal sent an exhausted look at me before leaving. "Lock up, Olie."

I nodded when I wanted to snarl. Moving the coffee table away, I lay next to the couch for a few hours of shut-eye.

Chapter 13

My hip hurt, my stomach was on fire, and my left arm was throbbing dully, in rhythm with the gigantic ache in my head. Groaning, I turned on my back, staring up at the pristine ceiling. A cell phone was ringing annoyingly and repetitively as I dug around on the sofa.

Squinting up, I was glad to see Blake was sleeping through this.

"What?" I growled when I finally found Blake's annoying phone.

"Olivia," Tate hissed at me.

"Yes, Tate," I said wearily as Blake roused. Dropping the phone to my shoulder, I settled on my knees, smiling down at him. "Hey," I said softly, as his bright blue eyes focused on me and he touched my cheek gently.

He groaned, reaching out for his phone. "What?" he growled, possibly as annoyed as I was.

I pushed myself up and sat down on the coffee table, rubbing my shoulder to ease the tension.

"When?" Blake asked. "Who?" He looked up at me, rubbing his jaw. "I will ask." Ending the call, he pushed to his feet.

"Can I interest you in a shower?" he asked, extending a hand. "And a visit to the compound?"

Smiling, I forced the wince back down as I took his hand and we hobbled our way to his bedroom. We moved slowly, with a few grunts and groans, sharing hesitant smiles.

"How are you feeling?" I asked, impressed with the cleaning crew's work in his room.

He shrugged, heading straight for the bathroom. "About as well as can be expected, given I've been de-fanged." Rubbing his jaw slowly, he added, "Can't say I ever would have thought about that before last night."

I smiled, leaning against the large expanse of counter as he turned on the warm water. "The best forms of torture are ones you can experience for yourself," I informed him.

He nodded, looking back at me, his eyes searching my own. A close call with death was never easy. No matter how many I had, there was still that exhilaration of escaping to live another day. Torture, now that bred a whole new list of problems.

Blake smiled closed-lipped before chucking his shirt into the trash, followed by his shoes and pants. He didn't spare me a backwards glance as he stepped into the steaming shower, naked. Following suit, I pulled off Mal's ruined dress and undergarments, the cool air chilling my skin.

Blake still hadn't turned around as I placed my hand on the shower door, pulling the glass back almost timidly. Sex wasn't a new thing for me, but this felt different.

As I closed the door slowly, he turned to look at me with the forlorn face of a haunted, damaged vampire. I laid my hand against his chest and shivered when the warm water trickled over my fingers.

He wrapped his hands around my shoulders, pulling me into the spray of the water with him. Tilting my head up, I searched those blue depths, trying to understand why sex with Blake felt different, why I felt almost vulnerable.

The answer wasn't in his eyes or in the dark locks plastered to his forehead. Pressing up on my tiptoes, I gently touched my lips to his, unsure how painful that would be for him. His hand snaked up to tangle in my wet locks, pressing me firmly against him.

My instincts took the lead, my defenses dropping as I ran the pads of my fingers over his hardened body. His lips were firm yet gentle and neither of us dared a tongue, given his raw mouth. Cradling my face, he pulled away to look down at me as I looked up at my beautiful, damaged vampire.

"I want more than sex," he stated, now searching my eyes.

I blinked blearily, not understanding, as he continued. "I don't want sex to know I'm alive. I want to sleep with you because we have a relationship."

Tilting my head slightly, I found my voice. "I don't know how to have those."

Stroking my cheek, he leaned down to kiss me tenderly again, moving from my lips to my jawbone and, finally, my ear.

"No other," he said, pulling back to watch my expression.

"Exclusive?" The vampire playboy wanted exclusive?

He nodded. I wasn't sure I was capable of such trust. "Break your word, and I'll break your neck." I'm such the romantic.

He smiled, pushing my finger easily off his chest. "Same goes for you," he whispered, running his warm lips over my ear. My body involuntarily shuddered as my hands flexed on his biceps. Enjoying my reaction, he held me tightly while he worked on my other ear.

Panting, I stretched my neck up, closing my eyes and allowing Blake to caress my skin with his very talented tongue. My guards slipped further, which should have worried me, but what he then did to my breasts had my brain shutting down completely.

Pinning me with his rapidly warming body against the cool shower tiles, he pushed my legs apart with one of his own, groaning as he pressed his fingers gently into me.

"You smell divine, Olivia," he whispered against my ear, pushing more aggressively into me as a yelp escaped my lips.

Nuzzling my neck, he pulled out of me as a demanding growl left my lips. Speech was beyond me, but he was riding my emotions. I knew I was pushing out urgency and need. His eyes widened. He grabbed my ass and pulled me up as I wrapped my arms securely around his neck and locked my legs on the small of his back. With a swift, well-practiced movement, he had himself deep within me. I growled with pleasure, letting my eyes close.

Slowly Blake pulled out, moving only to push me back down again. Arching my back, I tilted my hips until he pressed me painfully against the tiles. Growling again, I tightened my grip on his backside until he moved again.

"Fuck, Olivia," he whispered, pushing forcefully into me. "You should have warned me," he panted, his eyes full amber.

I smiled, a gasp escaping me as his pace increased. "Less talking," I gasped, crying out as he increased his pace.

My arms locked around his neck and I leaned my head against his shoulder as my body shook with the raw desire he was building inside of me.

"Come on, baby," he whispered into my ear, the speed and heat pushing me over the edge as I screamed. Blake followed me into bliss, biting deeply into my neck and pulling much needed blood out. It hurt with no fangs to inject the blissful toxins into me. I held on until my vision blackened and I went limp in his arms.

It felt like hours later when I groggily awoke curled next to Blake, who was gently stroking my dry locks. Groaning, I snuggled down into him. "Hey, beautiful," he whispered, kissing the top of my head.

I again ignored speech as my contentment coated us both. "I should have warned you," I eventually whispered sleepily.

Being a succubus means my powers lie in influencing emotions. Sex is a recharge of my abilities, giving me greater control and depth. So why don't I shag everyone I've ever been attracted to? You'll see.

"Yeah, I think you just ruined me for other women," he chuckled, nuzzling my neck.

Tipping my head back, I tasted my blood on his lips, licking gently. "There is that." I pushed into a seated position so I could see him better.

"My shielding will no longer block out my emotions from you." I watched his eyes warily. This is why I don't take random lovers. Willing unions resulted in my shields not working. For many, it was too much to handle. For others, well, they viewed it as an annoyance.

"You are worried." He curled an arm under his head, lying on his side, watching me.

"Yes, but the bond will fade over time." I schooled my features not to reveal my worry.

"And if we keep doing this?" he asked, stroking my hair.

"I don't know," I answered softly, shrugging and breaking eye contact.

"Why are you sad?" he asked, tipping my chin back up. Searching my eyes, he smiled. "I don't mind it, Olie. In fact," he pulled me down next to him, "it made sex amazing, and feeling your contentment is even better."

I was silent. I didn't know what to say; the emotions in my chest were foreign. Anger, hate, frustration and guilt were emotions I knew well. What was happening inside me now, I couldn't name.

Chapter 14

Morgan gave Tate an annoyed look as Blake pulled more of the healing blood from his wrist. Idly, I spun in Tate's office chair, watching the serious vampires in sporadic views. What I really wanted was a few more hours of sleep. Feeding Blake twice in a short amount of time had taken a lot out of me, even with the recharge of mind-blowing sex.

Mal stopped my spinning with a hip, setting down orange juice and a sugary sweet breakfast spread.

"Thanks," I said, wolfing down the French toast.

She didn't answer me or stay to berate me again for ruining her dress, instead going to sit with the other vampires camped out around the room. I narrowed my eyes at her behavior.

I filled my stomach with the feast I was in desperate need of. Leaning back in the overstuffed red leather chair, I surveyed the vampires and their uncanny attention to Blake. I also noted the sly glances I was receiving.

What was up with that?

I snuggled in the chair more comfortably, not bothering to hide the yawn that forced its way past my lips. My eyelids became leaden; lethargy began to deaden my legs.

I snarled, meeting Mal's guilty gaze. "This was a very bad idea," I hissed, before the darkness fully claimed me.

A sedated dream state might truly be my worst torture: my guards are down, my emotions run rampant, and I cannot wake up from the nightmares, the hellish nightmares that define and degrade me.

The silver cell was cold. It was always cold against the metal, I thought idly, my brain still numb from the *terrors I had seen earlier. My body wanted to shut down, but I knew the man coming through the door wouldn't let me. It was his job to make me strong, make me better than my pathetic heritage.*

The door opened, outlining his jean-clad body, etched with muscle forged from the hard labor we endured here.

"Hi, beautiful," he said softly, crouching down in front of my body, which was curled into the fetal position I had forced it into after the beating I had suffered earlier.

I eyed him warily. He liked it when I was glad to see him, liked it especially when I was sad and cried. He didn't like it when I refused him. I wanted to refuse him, but letting him do what he wanted meant more freedom, and more freedom meant escape. I wasn't strong enough yet, but I would be.

"Hurt," I said sadly, the bloody lip and bruised face sending more shards of agony.

"I know, beautiful," he whispered, trying to tilt my head.

"Not beautiful," I said, hiding my head down.

"Hey, none of that," he murmured, sitting next to me against the freezing metal. He was warm and I couldn't help leaning into him.

"Good girl," he murmured, stroking my back softly.

Lifting my head, I let the tears trickle just slightly. He shifted me to his lap, cradling me, as it seemed natural for him to do. He liked it when I sighed contentedly, so I did.

"What do you want?" he asked gently.

I knew the right answer as my gaze betrayed me, glancing to the hard metal bed. I managed to contain the disgusted shake that wanted to break free. The last thing I wanted was his body next to me, inside of me. I hated it, and I wanted to rip his throat out. I could. I was strong enough to do it, but I had to wait, had to bide my time.

"Shower?" I asked hopefully, lifting my small head to his dark brown eyes.

"There isn't a shower here," he reminded me, the wrinkles on his face crinkling together as he smiled gently.

I had been to his place only once and it had been for a kill of a trespasser. I'll never forget her face as she screamed that she could help me. Fool, she had been caught; she couldn't even help herself.

Dropping my gaze, I nodded, then added timidly, lifting my eyes back to his, "Your shower?" I searched his gaze slowly.

He leaned back against the metal, studying me, and fear gripped my insides colder than the metal I had just been sitting on as I my heart rate accelerated. Had I played this wrong? Did he know I was playing him, that the only emotion I could ever feel for him was pure, undiluted hatred?

I started to talk, stammering, but he silenced my words with a forceful kiss. Yelping, I tried to return it, but he had me up in his arms too quickly.

I held on as the guards outside opened the door, hiding my head in his neck. "Did I do something wrong?" I whispered, terrified.

"No, baby girl. You're doing perfectly," he murmured against me, holding me tightly. I counted his steps and each turn, committing them to memory. I was grateful when his door finally opened. Gently, he set me down, and I took a look around, gingerly testing the strength of my legs.

The bed loomed huge and threatening, but I swallowed my bile, turning to smile at him instead. He liked the smiles when my shoulders weren't tense and hunched. He reached a hand out, asking, "Are you ready?" His readiness was already evident from the bulge in his pants.

Slowly, I nodded, taking his hand, being sure to keep my facial expression pleasant as my insides screamed to make this horror stop.

The screaming grew louder, and I placed the voice as Mal, followed by Tate and Morgan, bellowing in anguish. The prick of a needle in my arm had me jerking involuntarily as the steaming heat seared through my veins, pulling me into instant alertness and counteracting the first drug they had slipped me.

Mal was in front of me as my shields slammed back into place, panting, tears streaming down her own face. I stood and, with a snap of my arm, elbowed her skull, leaving a softball-sized impression.

I turned my gaze, dropping it on Morgan next. Flinging the ornate desk to the side, I stalked toward him, pulling out twin blades. He was leaning against the wall, a hand against his chest. I sliced open his stomach, feeling the warm blood spill over my hand, followed by his insides falling out.

Snarling, I felt the monster Selena had created trying to make its presence known. I forced it back. I couldn't lose that much control right now. I wanted to kill everything in this room, but I knew better.

But a lesson? A lesson was certainly in order.

I turned to find Tate righting himself, holding a hand out, attempting to use words to stop me, yelling for me to calm down, be reasonable, and listen. I stabbed him terribly close to his hearts, watching with pleasure as he looked down at the wounds, no doubt seeing his own fragile mortality dangled in front of him.

Letting his body weight pull the knife out, I stood above him, disgusted. I wanted to say something poetic and threatening, leave him with words that would resonate for decades after I stopped showing up on his doorstep. But I had nothing, only the raw, open wound the drugs had forced on me and the pain of reliving memories of a person I hated.

I walked out, noting almost happily that Blake was unconscious.

At least he hadn't betrayed me as well, yet.

Chapter 15

Leaving all of my responsibilities on the shoulders of others, I took the battery out of my phone, refusing to deal with anything other than my horrid memories.

In the dilapidated motel room, I pulled the cap off my second bottle of vodka. My bags littered the filthy floor. Thanks to Jerry's donation, I was up to two. Bracing my forearms on my knees, I stared thoughtfully at the dingy floor before I sat up, taking another swig, willing the burn to dull the ache inside of me.

The memories just wouldn't stop, wouldn't relent. I drank more.

I could still see his face when I let my mind wander. I could still feel his hands.

The empty bottle dropped from my fingers with a dull thud. My body shut down, refusing to take in any more toxins. This blackness was different. It was a welcome reprieve from the hellish nightmares I had endured.

...

Slowly, the dryness in my throat itched at my awareness, a reminder of the terrible treatment I had put my body through. I looked at my watch—two days had passed. Groaning, I sat up in the chair, my back popping as feeling returned painfully to my legs.

Sitting there, staring down at the brown, stained carpet, I mulled over the events that led to me a disabled cell phone and two bags that made up my entire, pathetic life.

Swallowing down my bile, I stumbled into the shower, cranking the water as hot as this rundown shit hole would let it go. I stripped down, stepping into the warm spray, enjoying the stillness, even if it was fueled by isolation.

The hot water didn't last long enough for my taste before I had to step out, wrapping myself in a towel. I wiped off the cracked mirror, half expecting to see that same thirteen-year-old girl who ruled my nightmares, not the twenty-two-year-old survivor.

Pressing my forehead against the glass, I fortified my walls, pulling the braided cords of pain down deep, leaving them with all the rest.

After dressing and packing up, I picked up the hotel phone and called a familiar number. "George," a gruff voiced answered angrily.

"It's time for a two by two with a ride for four," I told him, giving him the address as the line went dead.

Gathering my bags by the door, I kept an eye out the window, with its thin, peach-colored curtains.

Thirty minutes later, a blue sedan pulled up in front without the scantily clad, drug-using prostitutes it usually carried. Tossing my bags in the back, I slipped into the passenger seat next to George. "I fucking hate when you call," he growled, a cigarette dangling from his crusty lips as he hunched over the steering wheel, staring into the night.

Leaning against the seat, inhaling cheap perfume and expensive cigarette smoke, I reminded him, "You could have sent someone else."

He huffed, pulling a dangerous move as he merged with traffic while giving me a disbelieving glance. "And have ya cause more problems in my establishment?"

"Be grateful you are human as are your employees, George," I reminded him. If he wasn't, I'd have had his balls already. As it was, the most I did was demand free, anonymous transportation in exchange for taking care of the occasional Supernatural problem he might encounter.

George cast a nervous glance my way, and I didn't care if it was because of the silver knives strapped to my legs or the deadpan stare I was giving him, I wanted him on edge.

We pulled into the deserted back alley of the house where I had met Darren and Hannah. I stepped out, leaning down to make eye contact. "Take my bags to the manor, speak to no one," I demanded, slamming the car door. Probably shouldn't have slammed it, I chided myself.

I silently scaled the wrought iron fence and dropped, my combat boots hitting the ground softly. Crouching, I listened for sounds of approaching guards I assumed Logan would have posted. Nothing.

Keeping low to the ground, I slipped between the perfectly trimmed foliage, arriving at a tall, wide tree. The limbs were not low enough to climb, nor was it close enough to the house. Slipping into the open yard again, I wove farther, stopping behind a large rose bush to listen again. Shifters would smell me instantly. Still nothing.

I sighed. Perhaps I truly was paranoid with my electric fence and constant guards at the manor. Maybe, but as my nightmares reminded me, better safe than sorry.

Close enough to the house to be worried about the light shining out, I finally found a tree worth climbing. Clawing my way up so that I could see the second story, I was rewarded with a perfect view of Logan's back, on the phone at a sleek black desk, kicking his feet up. I watched through the Victorian square window that had clearly missed the memo that this house was modern.

Lying my stomach down on the branch, I settled in to wait here till I saw the target I wanted. In the waiting, I was more than willing to watch Logan in secret as he stretched, standing up from his chair. He was a beautiful specimen of shifter: wide shoulders, tapered waist, and a perfect air of menace. I sighed, thinking about Blake. Had I made a mistake with him?

At the time, it hadn't felt like one. I'd have to face him and get his take on what happened at the Centennial House, but I wasn't ready. A small voice in the back of my head whispered I had been used. I had long ago gotten used to the idea that I could be used and tricked in sex. My body and soul craved the physical connection as a means to stock my energy reserves.

A relationship, that was what Blake wanted, and, foolishly, I entertained the thought. Perhaps I should just swear off vampires as a whole. They certainly hadn't brought me anything worth my time or energy lately.

Adjusting on my branch, I sighed when Logan shut the lights off and called it a night.

Chapter 16

It took three days of living in Logan's backyard till I finally saw my prey. Three days of pushing my muscles through hours of misery to maintain a still position, all the while surviving off military-grade rations. Finally, Steven, in all his cocky, irritating, hate-inducing glory, walked in.

The dead place inside me thumped triumphantly.

Logan kept him across the desk with arms crossed, and while I couldn't read his lips, his body language screamed pissed the fuck off. I wondered idly what else Steven had done since attempting to kill me.

It didn't matter.

I needed the kill.

I didn't have the time or patience to hunt anyone or anything else. My stiff muscles protested at being used as I slipped off the branch and dashed to the front of the house, staying low in the bushes and waiting for a response from any nosey neighbors. The drapes all stayed in place and no one was about as I crept to the front of what could only be Steven's car. The color gave it away: the brightest, loudest orange I had ever seen, shockingly worse than Tate's car.

Settling my backpack in front of me, I pulled out the small tracker, slipping it into a secure location behind the license plate before darting back behind the bushes. Sighing, I stared down at my still disassembled phone, knowing I would have to put it back together in order to track Steven. I was dreading it, since I was certain my violent and bloody exit from the vampires' House had not gone over well. Shifting to sit on the cold, wet ground, I put the battery back in before I could decide to just kill Steven here and have the shifter nation also pissed off at me.

I often wondered how I had remained the primary Executioner for this long; I don't do politics.

Exhaling, I snapped the cover on the back of the phone, powering it up, angry with myself for wondering if Blake had tried to call or text me. Foolish hope.

Then a truly terrifying thought seeped into me. What if no one called, no one texted, no one gave a fuck that I went off the grid for almost a week?

That thought had my stomach dropping to the ground, and I almost missed activating the tracker on my end as Steven took off.

Did it matter if people missed me, if I were a large enough part of their lives to be missed? When had they become such a large part of mine?

I was going to have to put my current identity crisis on hold; I needed a ride. According to my phone, the manor was 3.7 miles away. I could jog it as fast as they could reach me.

...

At the manor, I punched in the code to the garage and stretched my side, waiting for enough space to slip in. I wasn't expecting Kass to be standing there, looking dumbfounded at me.

"Hey," I said, pulling keys for the SUV. I had learned my lesson with small cars.

"Olivia," Kass said as I unlocked my own beast, "where have you been?"

"Away," I answered with a half shrug, tossing my backpack in the passenger seat.

"Olivia," Kass repeated.

"What, Kass?" I asked, facing her, anger shortening my temper.

Her own temper hit me with force and I narrowed my eyes at her. "Control," I hissed, letting my own temper slip slightly.

Tilting her chin up, she swallowed, uncrossing her arms. "You are needed," she said, with emphasis on each word.

"I'm hunting," I said, slipping into the car.

"Olivia, we have a sit-in that needs your attention," she said, casting a look behind the open garage door.

"A what?" I asked, rolling down the passenger-side window.

"A sit-in," she repeated tensely.

"What the fuck is that?" I repeated as Grams came to the driver's side door, opening it.

"It is where four vampires will not leave our living room until they speak to you," Grams hissed, leveling me with an equally intense look.

I leaned my head against the headrest, closing my eyes. "I really would prefer to kill them," I muttered. "Well, at least three of them," I amended.

"That almost feels like progress," Kass said wryly.

Glaring at her, I clarified, "It's not." Reluctantly, I got out of the car. "Where are the fuckers? They have fucking awful timing."

The vamps were in the living room, as advertised. Blake was playing video games with Tommy. The others were sitting like stylish mannequins on the sofa.

"What?" I growled as I entered the room and all eyes turned to look at me. I braced my hands on my hips, the silver on my thighs catching their attention before it snapped back up to my glare. I wasn't over the incident and seeing them now, on their timetable and not mine, was doing nothing to ease it.

"Tommy, you should probably leave," Kass said, turning the TV off.

"Oh, come on, Kass, I never get to see Olivia kick vampire asses!" Tommy whined, following her out.

I waited for them to speak, although I only cared what Blake had to say.

He smiled at me, and I remembered he could still feel me. "Hey, beautiful," he said, smiling.

I faked a glare at his widening smile.

Turning my attention to the two Master vampires, I intently glared holes into their undead skulls. They shifted uncomfortably, probably with the memory of how close I came to killing them. At least, I hoped that was why.

Mal spoke first. "We didn't know, and were trying to figure out, what the bond would be between you and Blake."

I nodded and said, "Get out," before turning to Blake, raising an eyebrow.

"Olivia, we came to work this out," Tate said.

"Really, Tate? I don't see any chocolates or flowers, nor do I hear a fucking apology out of any of your mouths," I seethed fire, it uncurled from my gut into my veins.

Tate shifted uncomfortably. "You did almost kill me."

"Don't make me regret the almost," I answered hotly, crossing my arms over my chest.

"We didn't come here to fight," Mal said, trying to get through my thick skull.

"Then why are you here?" I yelled, fighting the urge to stomp my feet.

They all shared a shameful glance. "Fucking hell, you need me."

"Gunner, he made a shocking discovery with the DNA samples," Blake said, turning a wary eye to his Master.

"Lovely, let's go," I demanded.

Morgan growled, "He will only talk to you."

"Huh, sounds like he's smartening up nicely," I said, smirking. "I'll expect you all to be either gone or doing dishes when I return."

Tate unnecessarily cleared his throat. "We have Gunner at my compound."

"You kidnapped him?" I said in disbelief. "I'm gone for less than a week, recovering from your fucked up plan to gain information, and you idiots kidnap one of the best resources you have found? Brilliant, just fucking brilliant. Not to mention you are under tight scrutiny already. Well, let's go, kidnapping vampires, lead on to the hostage," I proclaimed, ushering them out.

Blake grabbed my hand, holding me from following them out. "We'll be right behind you," he told them, not looking away from me.

I waited until the door closed before asking, "You okay?" After which I silently yelled at myself for even giving a fuck.

He nodded, smoothing back a wild strand of my hair, worry clouding his features. "I could feel you, your pain, frustration, but I couldn't find you," he whispered. "Do not do that to me again."

I looked away. "I can try."

He cradled my face, his blue eyes intently searching my own dark green ones. "Don't do it again. I don't care if you shut the entire fucking world out, just not me."

I nodded, but it wasn't a promise I could make. Some scars, some memories I could never share. He engulfed me in a hug and I couldn't help the small sigh that left my lips at being back in his arms.

...

In the far back seat of the SUV, I contemplated all that had happened. I'd had my mind hijacked by dead shifters, someone was using dark magic to animate said shifters, and I had been hired and fired as liaison between the police and the Council. And who could forget about Steven? Not me.

Then there was Blake, a force I didn't understand, and that worried me. I had built and maintained elaborate guards around my heart and emotions.

Having another potentially so close to both was unnerving. The realistic part of me knew it wouldn't last long; I was bound to screw it up one way or the other, but that blasted hope gave us a chance at happiness.

I was stopped from entering the Centennial Compound due to my excessive weapons collection.

"Sir," the guard said uneasily to Tate, "she did just try to kill you."

"It was warranted," I said loudly, to everyone listening. "And furthermore, if I decide one of you or all of you need killing, I am perfectly capable of ripping off heads instead of slicing them."

"That was a bit over the top," Mal whispered as I was ushered through.

"Factual Mal, I deal in facts," I answered, taking in the numerous vampire eyes watching our descent into the basement.

More guards greeted us before we were allowed to see Gunner—that is, before I was allowed to see Gunner. I was assuming the rest were watching the plush underground living room from security cameras.

"Hi, Gunner," I greeted the overweight genius, sitting down across from him on the paisley couch.

He smiled meekly, his arms wrapped around a small, terrified female. "They took us at dinner."

I nodded. "They're assholes, interrupting a date"

"She needs medication to control her social anxiety disorder," he said worriedly, eyeballing my knives.

I nodded, leaning forward. "I can help," I said, reaching a hand out to her frail form. She flinched back.

I smiled. "What's your name?" I asked, keeping my hand out non-threateningly.

"Cricket," she chirped, peeking at me around Gunner's massive arms.

"Nothing is going to happen to you while I am here, Cricket. I guarantee it," I reassured her, pushing all my confidence into those words.

She nodded, leaning slightly away from Gunner. "Why do you want to touch me?" she asked warily.

"I can put people at ease sometimes," I answered, not sure how much of the supernatural Gunner had enlightened her on.

After giving a long glance at Gunner, who nodded his head soundly, she reached out her fingertips, just brushing my own. It was enough. I reached for her nervousness and fear, braiding it down and compressing it.

She sighed audibly. "Wow, thanks! That's better than my meds."

"No problem," I answered, with a gentle smile

"So, I hear you have made progress," I said, addressing Gunner, clasping my hands in my lap.

He nodded. "Babe, wait in the room, please."

She left, casting a long look at what I hoped was a genuine smile on my tense face. Once the door closed, he leaned forward, his round glasses slipping down his equally round face. "They were supercharged."

"I don't understand," I said, shaking my head.

"They were genetically predisposed to become Supernaturals, and my guess, judging from the tests I was able to perform, is that once they had changed into either shifter or vampire, they would have been ahead of the pack in abilities."

I sat there staring at him for long moments before asking, "Who were?"

"The children. It was present in the young ones, but once puberty hit, their openness for change grew exponentially," he answered, pushing his glasses up as I sat back in the couch, nodding.

"I really need to see that teacher," I muttered to myself.

Chapter 17

I accompanied Blake and Tate to drop off Gunner and Cricket, personally seeing to it that they were compensated for their time under lockdown. Blake, Tate and I next headed out to Mr. Davis's residence, in hopes of finding out how our Puppet Master was able to locate the children.

Gazing out the window in the back seat, my eyes saw none of the beautiful countryside we traveled through, my brain working on theory after theory.

"Did you hear me, Olivia?" Tate asked, peering behind at me.

"No," I answered, still looking out the window.

"I asked if you had heard from Mercer," he said.

Turning toward him, I shook my head. "No, not since Blake and I saw him last. Why?"

Tate smiled, turning to look at me. "Apparently, the Governor made an example of him, reprimanding him quite harshly in front of all of his peers."

"Why?" I asked, not following.

Blake looked at me from the rearview mirror. "For breaking the arrangement with you," he answered.

"I don't see why it matters; I'm still working the case," I said, looking between both of them.

"Yes, but when that information went public, the headlines put a great deal of bad publicity on the Governor and his staff for not using all available means to track the killer." Tate smiled. "It gave us a bit of good press for once."

"Needless to say, you probably have a few messages from Mercer," Blake informed me as I looked at my now reassembled phone.

"Fuck," I whispered as the tracker I had placed on Steven's phone lit up, close to us.

"What?" Tate and Blake said in unison.

"The tracker I put on Steven's car. He's close, less than a mile."

"Do you want to follow him?" Blake asked as I watched the red dot flashing furiously in front of me.

"No," I said, sighing. "My personal vendettas can't get in the way of figuring out who the Puppet Master is, now that we have this lead."

"Dammit," I hissed, watching the dot disappear off the screen. It only had a three-mile radius, and now the bastard was gone yet again.

"We will get him, Olie," Blake said, as I scowled at the guard gate we were passing through.

...

There are kills to send messages and there are kills of necessity. What we were looking at in Mr. Davis's home was a kill of necessity. It was good news for us that we were making the Puppet Master nervous, but bad news for Mr. Davis.

His front door was ajar when we entered, but there was no sign of forced entry; he knew his killer. The vampires smelled death instantly, though it took me a while longer. The kill was fresh. Tate and Blake pulled in long breaths as they navigated through the front rooms and into an office.

Mr. Davis sat back against his leather chair, a single gunshot wound between his eyes. Thick, sticky blood dripped out the back of his head.

I dialed Mercer's number, not surprised when he picked up on the first ring. "Olivia," he said awkwardly.

"We have another Puppet Master murder." I relayed the address, adding, "Hurry up, I can only keep the vamps from investigating for so long," before ending the call.

Sitting down on the steps outside, I was grateful the sun was starting to set so I wouldn't end up burned. Tate and Blake sat on either side of me.

"Thoughts?" I asked.

"We are getting closer," Tate said.

"I agree," Blake added. "Do you think it's strange that Steven was so close to here? The kill is fresh."

He had voiced my own thoughts. "I would love for him to be involved, but I am also prejudiced in thinking he had a hand in it." Thinking about it more, I suggested aloud, "We could always call Logan to confirm his whereabouts."

Tate scoffed, "Sure, you two get along wonderfully."

"No, but poking at the hornets' nest has yielded results so far," I answered with a shrug.

"Lion's den," Tate corrected. To my raised eyebrow, he added, "Poking at the lion's den has yielded results, but be careful. They bite."

I smiled, showing my flat teeth. "So do I."

The silence stretched on as I worried my bottom lip, thinking of impossible scenarios that would involve Steven, but all were heavily steeped in my deep prejudice against him. Even I recognized they held no merit.

Tate shifted as Blake stood, stretching and announcing, "I'm going to walk around."

"Want me to come with?" I asked, leaning forward, ready to stand.

"No," he said with a smile. "I'll yell if I can't kill it."

"Ha, ha," I chuckled, rolling my eyes as he brushed my shoulder walking by.

Tate picked at the manicured lawn next to us on the stairs, casting me long looks before I finally asked, "What, Tate?"

"I am sorry for causing you unnecessary pain, Olivia," he said, watching me closely. Important facts to note: he didn't apologize for drugging me, nor for attempting to extract information against my will. He didn't regret those items. But it was more than I had gotten from the others, and, to be honest, I liked Tate. He allowed those in his House more freedom than most. I could appreciate that in a vampire.

"Apology accepted," I said, looking back toward the driveway before adding softly, "You could have just asked."

He cleared his throat. "I was hoping you would say that."

I should have seen that one coming.

"Ask away," I said, leaning back against the stairs, forcing myself to relax.

"What are the consequences of sleeping with you?" he said warily.

"A person who sleeps with a succubus or incubus is bound to our emotions. The stronger the succ or inc, the stronger the emotions are felt," I answered, feeling Blake had surely told him the same.

"And what if he no longer wants to feel everything you do?" he questioned.

I sighed, "Then no more sex." Leaning forward to watch Tate, I added, "Blake knows all of this. I told him everything I know."

He nodded, looking towards the blooming night sky. "What will prolonged contact with you do to him? Will it hurt him?" he asked, his eyes yellowing as he looked back at me.

I wanted to be angry, wanted to tell him it was none of his fucking business, unless he was fucking me, but I didn't. He was Blake's Master and I certainly didn't want to cause problems for Blake or make additional messes he would have to clean up. So I put my big girl panties on, and fuck, are they uncomfortable!

"I don't know what it will do to him. I don't believe he will suffer any ill effects. If I did, I wouldn't have slept with him," I answered, remarkably surprised at my maturity.

"He is family," he said tensely, and I understood, nodding.

"I won't hurt him, Tate," I said softly.

He shook his head, smiling. "You really haven't dated before, have you?"

"No, why?" I asked, suddenly very insecure.

"Have you ever been in love, Olivia?" Tate asked me, still smiling to my scowl.

"No," I responded quickly.

He nodded, now watching the full dark littered with stars. "It's a wonderful feeling, even if it is too fleeting."

I nodded, happy to see the lights of a vehicle approaching. I wasn't expecting the speed or the sudden stop that had gravel flying.

"Olivia, you are so fucking lucky I don't know your middle name," said a very cranky black man, throwing himself out of the Beast, "or I would use it to scold you for your disappearing act."

"Hi, Jerry," I said timidly. "Point of fact, I don't actually have a middle name."

"Don't you even think of giving me that line," he said, charging in front of the Beast to pull me standing before administering a proper shaking. "Do you have any idea how worried we all were?"

I opened my mouth to answer, but he charged right along. "And leaving poor Blake, the man was damn near crazed looking for you. And let's not forget me!" he yelled.

I tilted my head at him. "Why are you yelling?"

Mercer came from the other side of the Beast. "The more upset they are, the more they care," he said before walking to the house.

I squeezed Jerry's forearm before he could shake me again. "Sorry," I said simply, as his lanky arms engulfed me.

"Bad enough I had to hear from Mercer you were back," he muttered into my red hair.

"How did you two end up talking?" I asked, pulling back as we followed the rest into the house.

"With you being out of the picture, Mercer reached out to the only other person he had worked with in the Supernatural community."

I shrugged, "Good for you."

Jerry scoffed. "Like he had any other choice. I am the best in the business."

"Does that mean you are finished carting around pain in the ass clientele?" I asked, bumping his shoulder good-naturedly as we entered the last resting place of Mr. Davis.

"Nah, this gig ain't busy enough for me to quit my day job," he answered, throwing an arm around my shoulders.

"So, where is the dead guy?" Mercer asked, inhaling. "Doesn't smell like death."

"I'll stay here and guard against return visitors," Tate announced. I didn't believe him for a second as he pulled out his phone to make calls.

"It doesn't smell like death *yet*," Blake corrected. "The kill is fresh," he added, looking at me intently waiting for me to disclose the tacker.

Blowing out a breath, I peered at Jerry, who had one raised black eyebrow, watching me. "I might have put a tracker on Steven."

"The one who tried to kill you?" Mercer asked, snapping blue gloves over his worn hands.

"Yeah, that one. Anyway, as we were coming into the community, he was less than a mile away from here," I said, wondering if they would come to the same conclusion I had.

Jerry was silent for a few moments as Mercer handed the rest of us gloves. Finally, Jerry asked, "You think he is trying to fuck your investigation?"

"No, I think he is playing some part for the Puppet Master," I answered honestly.

He nodded. "Possibly."

Mercer spoke up, "We will request an alibi for tonight."

I nodded as we headed into the home office of the late Mr. Davis. One shot to the head finished him, no torture, no undead shifter, possibly a living shifter had done the dirty work. His dirty blond hair needed a cut and stuck out at odd angles, eerily setting off his eyes, glazed over in death.

Unlike his students, he had died instantly in his plush office, his body still in the leather chair behind the matching deep red monster of a desk.

The men surrounded the corpse as I wandered into the library, taking in the fancy book titles. Most of them had to do with education, but judging from the leather-bound spines, they must have been expensive.

Stopping short, I scuffed my boot against the hardwood floor. This book I knew. Pulling it down, I gently ran my hand over the cover before reaching to the space where it had rested, my fingers probing for a secret lever. A click and a hiss greeted my search as Blake came up to my shoulder. "What you got there?" he asked, taking the book from my hands.

"Think of it as *How to Be a Witch for Dummies*, the ancient version," I answered, watching the book case slide backwards, revealing a black abyss my eyes couldn't see into.

"Who told you about that book?" Jerry asked, tucking it into his jacket pocket protectively.

"A witch," I answered simply. The truth was far more complicated than that.

"That witch still alive?" Mercer asked, joining us.

"Nope—and I didn't kill her, either," I said before the question could be asked. Turning to Blake, I asked, "Can you see in there?"

He nodded. "Can you?"

I shook my head, interlacing our arms. "Shall we?" I asked with a smile.

He nodded. Jerry braced his hands on my back, and I assumed Mercer would work something out.

Darkness pressed around us as we left the well-lit office behind. Blake moved slowly and easily down the darkened corridor.

"Dammit," Mercer cursed, and I smiled, leaning closer into the vampire I was developing a fondness for.

Blake pulled me closer, pausing for a moment. I could hear him flip a switch before the hidden room was showered in pale ambient light.

"Whoa," I muttered, taking a step away from Blake.

"Son of a bitch," Jerry added behind me.

"Devil worship? You can't be serious," Mercer said, pulling up the rear.

We all turned to level him an annoyed gaze. "After all you have learned over the last few weeks, you still believe this to be the work of a devil?" Jerry asked, irritated.

"A devil, not *the* devil," Mercer repeated, growing confused as he looked around the dimly lit room at the hanging herbs.

Jerry shook his head, bending down to the pentagram in red. "Paint, no blood," he reported. I nodded, blowing out a breath, taking in the ancient texts, the jars filled with hard-to-find ingredients such as bats, and the modern laptop sitting next to a new journal.

I made my way to the journal as Blake sat down at the laptop.

"So what exactly does this tell us, except for the fact that the professor liked to dabble in the dark arts?" Mercer said, holding his hands wide, not daring to move farther into the space. Peeking at Jerry, I hid a smile behind Blake as Jerry stood up, pointing a gloved finger at the clueless police officer.

"Dark arts? What is this, a damn video game?" Jerry demanded.

"Fine, what is the politically correct term for all this nonsense, witch?" Mercer asked, clearly not giving a damn about upsetting Jerry.

"Being called a witch in the Supernatural community is fairly close to an insult. While at some point in our history they did yield impressive power, currently they only exist to annoy me. A mage is probably a more accurate term, but not applicable to a human. Secondly, just because there is a pentagram on the ground doesn't make this devil worship. More importantly, most of the Supernatural community doesn't believe in the existence of a Devil, or God, for that matter."

"Wait, you're telling me all you Supes don't believe in God?" Mercer asked, shocked, as he cautiously moved a clump of thyme hanging from the ceiling.

"You have to understand," Blake said, his fingers flying over the computer, "even apart from those of our kind who witnessed the birth of human religions, many of us have been alive long enough to watch humans change, modify, or exploit those religions for personal gain."

I scoffed. "It doesn't take hundreds of years to see that," I added, not looking up.

Blake continued, ignoring my remark. "Granted, there are those few who genuinely do good in this world, but it doesn't require a belief in a higher power."

"What do you believe in?" Mercer asked Blake, tapping a glass of newt eyes.

"Don't ask," I said, watching him. "Each race believes in something different, and it's all hogwash."

Blake stopped typing to look at me. "Excuse me?" he said, shocked.

I rolled my eyes at him, ready to answer when Jerry yelled, "You gotta see this!"

Turning, we crossed the small room quickly to see the hidden trap door Jerry had discovered beneath the floorboards.

"What could have him so paranoid that he needed a hidden compartment in a hidden room?" I asked, looking over Jerry's shoulder at the dark wooden box he had just opened.

We listened to Jerry read off the complex experiments and tests that had been done.

"The professor isolated a gene that indicates if a human would make a superior shifter or vampire?" Mercer asked, shocked. I'd forgotten that I hadn't filled him in on Gunner's earlier discovery. It didn't matter, anyway. This was a Supernatural issue, not a human one.

Mr. Davis's involvement and death were simply proof humans did not belong in our affairs.

"Yes," Jerry answered solemnly, "and guess who his test subjects were?"

"The same families that are now in the morgue," I answered, leaning back in the black office chair and staring at the dark wood ceiling. "How did a human stumble upon something we didn't even know about?" I asked, turning to Jerry.

He shrugged. "Science," he answered in one word. "I assume the answer must be here in his journals."

Blowing out a breath, I asked, "Is there anyone not dead on the list?"

Jerry scanned the list. "Yes, twin siblings," he said excitedly, looking at me. "I have the address."

"Let's go," Blake said, leading the way back into the darkness.

Chapter 18

Two dark-haired, dark-skinned teenage girls stood huddled on their lawn in their matching pink bathrobes as Mercer explained the situation to their parents.

"Glad I'm not him right now," Blake muttered.

Looks of shock passed across their faces. The mother grabbed quickly for the girls, following her husband to a police SUV and to safety. The dad stood holding open the door, watching the surroundings. He was a big man, but even his abilities wouldn't keep his daughters safe.

I could, though, and I would.

Mercer's awkward demeanor spoke volumes, and the glances from his fellow police officers told the rest of the story well. He was an outcast for playing with the alleged demon.

"Everything appears normal," he said.

I nodded. "You shouldn't leave anyone here. If he shows up, I'll know."

Mercer rubbed the stubble on his wide chin. "Having backup wouldn't hurt."

"If you leave any humans here, they will be dead if the Puppet Master comes looking for the twins," I told him, watching him look over the others. "It's your decision."

Turning to Blake, I said, "I've about had enough fun for tonight."

He nodded, slinging a strong arm over my shoulders, drawing me close as we met Tate at the SUV.

I caught a catnap, sprawled across the backseat, waking up as we came to a stop. Groaning, I pulled myself into a seated position, not liking the fact we were at the Centennial Compound.

Blake opened my door, raising both hands in an attempt to calm me. I growled.

"We need to make a few phone calls, and we can use the command center to organize everything," he said, pulling me out by my arm.

Huffing and disheveled, I followed him into the house. Whereas before, I had been stopped for my weapons, this time, I just decked the vamp on guard duty who grabbed me, and kept walking.

Tate and Blake exchanged glances. Hey, not my fault their security didn't have a better communication network.

Down in the basement, I asked, "How did the Puppet Master know about the kids?"

"We have tech breaking apart the computer now to see who the list was sent to," Mal said, typing away.

Resting in the plush couch, I shook my head. "It must have been a face-to-face meeting. I doubt, with all the secrecy, he would have just emailed the list over."

"Whatever, if it's in there, my guys will find it," Mal answered with certainty.

"Do you think this has anything to do with the attack on Blake's place?" I asked, resting my exhausted head.

"No," Mal said shortly.

She didn't meet my eyes, but I could tell she knew something she wasn't sharing. Perfectly fine, I can tell when I'm not wanted.

"Lovely. If that is all squared away, I'm going to check with Logan on Steven's alibi," I said merrily, turning to Blake, engrossed in a computer. "I'll grab a ride with Jerry," I said as he looked up for a brief moment, smiling.

Calling Jerry, I found him wrapping up at the professor's house. "Just call when you're close," I said, going outside to wait. The protestors were fewer and those who still were there looked terrified as I walked by. Good thing my plan had worked; otherwise, I'd be killing them.

Twenty minutes later, Jerry pulled up, watching me warily as I climbed into the SUV, smiling. "What are you so happy about?"

"Nothing, I just enjoy a good pot stirring," I said with a smile. "But don't worry, I called Logan. He's expecting us."

Jerry put the car into drive. "But does he know what to expect?"

"I hope not, that would ruin all my fun," I answered with an evil grin.

Chapter 19

Logan growled at me from across his lush desk before answering, "Absolutely not." His caramel eyes glowed as his lion beat against his self-control.

I smiled, leaning forward. "I was really hoping you would say that."

The three of us lumbered down into the basement training room—no need to destroy Logan's office, yet.

"This is asinine," Jerry informed me, taking a seat on the metal bleachers of the shifter training room located under Logan's current residence.

I smiled wider. "It's the only way to get the information I need."

Jerry looked at me, not believing a word as I shrugged out of my impressive weapons arsenal. I could have pulled the whole "Council card" on him, but I needed a good fight, and Logan, without his shirt on, was going to give it to me. I couldn't help but wonder what he would taste like under my lips.

Quickly, I shook my head. Were those thoughts allowed when one was having a "relationship?" I didn't have a clue, I had never in my life worried about such silly concepts as "exclusive." But I was worried now, worried I may have made a mistake, worried I would unquestionably ruin things with Blake, and worried I'd fail the whole damn Council.

Besides, I didn't need this man scenting my attraction.

I put my game face on as Logan began circling me. He was all predatory grace in this moment, ruggedly built, solid muscle. He moved with the agility of the lion pressing against his skin.

His carefully groomed features were gone, replaced by the hunter he truly was, and I basked in it as I lunged for him. He danced away, smiling as we continued to circle.

I expected some taunt from him, some low blows, but nothing. We circled in silence, our true natures fully exposed. His legs bent in anticipation of his own lunge as I tried to dance away.

I wasn't fast enough, as he caught me around the middle, landing heavily on my torso.

The air flew out of my lungs as I punched him hard in the shoulder. We had agreed to no face blows. I pulled back to slam him again and he blocked me easily. He then pulled back and hesitated, giving me the opening to buck him off by thrusting my hips up and unseating him.

I wasted no time in lunging at him, using my momentum to take him down. We rolled as I tried to come up on top, only to have him take a cheap shot at a kidney. I threw an elbow, successful connecting with soft tissue.

I'm fairly certain we would have gone on for hours more, but Lorraine walked down the stairs, screeching, "What the hell is going on down here?" with her hands pressed against her thin hips. "It sounds like a herd of rhinos, and I have company," she hissed, stomping her foot impatiently.

I giggled, and Logan, still on top of me, tried very diligently not to share in my mirth.

Clearing his throat, he said, "Sorry, dear, we are done," and quickly moved away from my body.

She nodded before taking her upturned nose away.

Logan turned to me, and I could see the regret at our match being cut short as he nodded and said, "I'll find out where he was."

I nodded, still laughing as I gathered my weapons.

...

I climbed the stairs to Blake's bedroom, turning over the key he had left for me in my hands, still feeling very strange about having a boyfriend. I had never used that term for any male in my life, ever. So what had changed? When had a one-night stand become not enough? Maybe it still was, maybe I was just being weak, bending my will to his. That idea didn't sit well with me as I opened his bedroom door.

He lay there, still, the dark sheet draped dangerously low as heat instantly flooded between my legs. Chewing my lip, I was weighing if I was too tired to jump him, when he cracked an eye, smiling. "You smell divine."

My grin widened as I went to him in bed, decision made.

Chapter 20

I awoke to Jerry in my face, shaking me. Batting him back, I glared up at him. I'm not a morning person.

"We have problems," he said, shaking me again. I shoved him away from me and growled.

As Jerry took a step back, Blake laughed, coming out of the shower. "I told you she isn't a morning person," he said, coming around the bed to kiss my temple. Snuggling in his embrace, I inhaled the scent of soap.

"You failed to mention violent," Jerry said. I glared at him again, forcing him to fidget in his black, pressed suit.

"Give me a minute," Blake said to Jerry, stroking my face.

"Fine, but we need her, shit is going down," Jerry said, slamming the door behind him.

With a sigh, I lay my head back down on the fluffy pillows, stretching my limbs and groaning.

"You are needed, Olie," he said softly into my ear.

"Why?" I asked, my voice muffled by the pillow.

He stroked my arm lightly. "You have been called to Logan's grandfather's plot."

I groaned, rolling to my back. "Jerry can handle it."

"He didn't get an invitation and neither did I," he said, pressing a gentle kiss on my lips. Heat instantly flooded my body and I leaned up to dive deeper into those sweet lips.

Pulling back, he smiled, saying, "I'm afraid I must deny you this morning."

I pouted as he picked me up out of the bed.

...

It was too fucking early for this shit or maybe too fucking late. My days, nights, and mornings were a complete disaster with the schedule I had been keeping, and, after the amazing sex with Blake, a day off seemed to be in order. But no, not according to the head of the shifter nation, who we were still waiting on.

Tate toured the property as I sat on a headstone. "Really, Olivia?" he whispered.

I didn't bother with an answer as Mercer came from the trees. "This place is freezing."

"It's the magic," I explained, idly feeling it prick along my skin under my leather jacket and jean clad legs, braced wide.

Darren exited his flashy sports car, looking haggard as he made his way to join us. "Where is he?" he asked, coming to stand before me.

"Damn if I know," I answered with a shrug, just as exhausted. The directions from Logan had been exact: wait in the center of the shifter cemetery at noon with only Tate, Mercer, and Darren. It truly made the man look paranoid. I would have liked having Blake and Jerry there, although perhaps that made me paranoid.

The actual piece of property, located ninety minutes outside St. Ann, was breathtaking, with sweeping trees and rolling hills dotted with plots carefully hidden from the road. We were all seated under a weeping willow. Well, I was seated; the other three just looked uncomfortable.

"What's the matter, boys, don't spend much time around the truly dead?" I asked, my foul mood pressing against my barriers.

None of them dignified that with an answer. Shrugging, I looked out towards the rest of the cemetery and the crypt high on the hill. This didn't feel like the same place as in the vision I'd had, but looking up there now, I had the distinct impression that was where I had been.

I had just stood up, about to head up there, when I felt the ground beneath my feet rumble. "What the hell?" I asked, looking down as the ground cracked. An ugly wail sent chills to my gut, a dreadful suspicion seeping into my thoughts.

"What's going on?" Darren asked me, his dark eyes starting to shift.

"We walked into a trap," I answered, holding perfectly still, as though that would stop what was crawling its undead way out of the ground.

"Trap?" Darren asked, looking around as the ground beneath his feet began to split. "Logan wouldn't have—" He stopped mid-sentence, looking up at me with a mix of annoyance and disgust as a bony hand clenched around his foot. "This is disgusting."

I nodded as an entire arm pushed out of the ground, the fingers coming even with my hip. This was a hefty one, chunks of ligaments attached to rotting muscle. I rolled away from the tombstone as the other arm exploded from the dirt and watched Mercer and Tate tackle their own undead problems from a crouch.

Big and nasty came up belting unintelligible words from a jaw hanging partially down, eyes glowing deep red. He rounded on me, pulling his long legs from the broken coffin with a final snap.

"Hey there, pretty boy," I said, smiling. "Come and get me."

He didn't need a second invitation, launching at me with claws extended, swiping wildly. I leapt back as the claws sliced through my dark turquoise t-shirt.

"You're lucky that wasn't my leather jacket," I scolded. The force of the swing made the ugly unstable as it lumbered back to find me again.

"How do we kill these things?" Darren yelled, landing a solid right hook into a skeleton's jaw.

"I don't suppose you have a blow torch hidden in your brassiere?" Tate asked me, ducking under a wild punch.

"I don't even know what that is," I answered, dipping back out of range of the next swipe.

"Your bra," Mercer answered, shooting at the skeleton head. Chunks of brain and skull plastered Tate.

"Really!?" Tate said, annoyed, brushing chunks off his expensive suit.

Mercer shrugged. "Worked, didn't it?" he said, indicating the now truly lifeless body of the shifter.

"It did," I said, shocked, standing out of my crouch. Vital mistake. Big and ugly's next swing found home, launching me across the cemetery and smashing my back and wrist against an angel statue. Well, it used to be a statue. As I rolled to the softer ground, white plaster wings sprinkled my body. I groaned.

"Ouch," I muttered, pushing onto my knees, leaning heavily on my elbows. The ground beneath my body shook as the giant took awkward steps toward me. Fuck.

Scrambling upright, I used the now broken angel for support.

"Aim for the head!" Tate yelled at me, taking down another shifter. "These ones are different than the other."

Well, no shit they were. I was still conscious, for one thing. Although, to give Tate credit, I hadn't thought of that.

Pulling a long blade from the holder at my back, I dodged left, using the shifter's own unstable thighbone as a step to give me the height I needed to slice his undead head off. Landing on my feet, I held still, waiting, holding my breath, to see if it really did work.

The snarled skeleton head rolled down the hill to the broken angel statue, the red eyes reduced to empty eye sockets. Pushing out a relieved breath, I turned to face a massive pair of jaws. This was going to be one of those days.

Honestly, I can't say I was too upset. I like killing things. Hell, it's probably one of the few things in life I really love. Even though they were already undead, I'd still like to think it all counted toward my average.

The four of us sliced, diced, shot, and, in Darren's case, half shifted, his clothing straining at the seams from his massive thighs and wider torso, to eliminate each and every threat. Towards the end of the battle, when only a few undead were still able to fight, I turned toward the crypt, my nagging subconscious making me uneasy. I thought it was my hopeful imagination that saw the white-blond head of Steven in the distance. My mind went black and I was looking at the vile Steven close up before the connection was cut off.

I stumbled from the brief moment of connection before growling and taking off at a sprint. I wasn't going to make it; a full football field separated me from the murderer who had drawn us out and attempted to eliminate us.

But I hadn't survived this long by ever giving up. I pumped my legs as I continued uphill, forcing the muscles to respond after the brutal assault moments earlier. Darren caught wind of my attempt, running on all fours, loping faster than I could toward the crypt.

I was going to be more than a little ticked at him if he took my kill from me. Anger helped push me to go faster, but there was no comparison to the swiftness of the half-lion in front of me. Snarling reached my ears from the crypt, violent blows sending shock waves through the ground as I tore around the side of the structure to find Darren holding a quickly healing gash along his side.

He looked at me, all the anger and hatred barely contained under the surface of those dark, chocolate brown depths.

With a growl, he hefted himself off the ground, standing feet taller than me. "Your suspicions are correct, Olivia." Brushing off the dirt from his scuffle, he looked down at the wound closing upon itself, trailing thin rivets of crimson down his side.

"Steven," I said, following Darren's gaze to the forest where he had retreated. I debated a moment, my body shifting forward as I thought about going after him.

Darren hefted an oversized paw on my shoulder, stopping me. Looking up at his face, he shook his head, lines of worry present on his forehead. "We are in no shape to go after him. As powerful as he is, we will need a mage of our own."

I growled, knowing he was correct and not enjoying it. "Besides," he said, turning back to the mess of body parts, "we have to take care of this mess. With Steven's powers, we could spend days out there and not find him."

I groaned, which ended in a whine, hating the fact that he was right on both accounts. At least I didn't stomp my feet.

Chapter 21

"Unbelievable," Logan said, surveying the damage we had inflicted upon the shifter graveyard. "What do you have to say for yourself?" he asked, rounding on me, anger rolling off him in powerful waves. "And what could possibly possess you four to think that I would call a clandestine meeting out at a graveyard? How did that little nugget of information not have any of you realizing it was a trap?"

"You are such an ungrateful asshole!" I answered, limping over to him, "You are far too selfish to understand what is happening here! One, we know Steven is the Puppet Master; two, we kept the undead from wreaking havoc outside this graveyard; and three, you are a terrible leader!" I screamed at him.

Logan growled, his caramel eyes glowing as his fangs descended in his mouth. "You will show me respect." His beast pushed to the surface.

I licked my bloodied lip, watching his eyes follow my movements. "Make. Me. Asshole."

He flexed his hands. I was waiting for claws to sprout when Jerry stepped up. "You guys alright?"

"No," Logan growled through clenched teeth.

I snarled at him, my anger seeping out my skin.

"Olivia!" Blake yelled, running to my side. "Down," he commanded. I snarled at him as well.

"Control your woman," Logan hissed demeaningly at Blake.

"You better shut up, shifter. She is borderline berserker. I will not step in her way if you push her much more," he said, holding his hands up to me, reaching out.

"Berserker? She isn't hurt that badly," Logan said disgustedly.

"Let him feel it, baby," Blake said, smiling knowingly.

Always a practical problem solver, that Blake. I dropped my guard, letting the pain in my leg seep into Logan along with the throbbing in my temple, not to mention the gash along my back. He staggered, and I grinned, my true evil nature loving to share my pain.

"Enough, my love," Blake said, touching my face gently, reminding me there were rules in this world I unfortunately had to obey.

I nodded, folding myself into him, pushing up my barriers, and heading to the car.

"Let me handle this, Olivia. I don't need any more dead shifters at your hands," Logan bellowed to my back. Right, because clearly I am the only one who dismembered the already dead shifters.

Tate, Mercer, Blake, and I got into the SUV. Blake had driven out upon hearing about the very cleverly laid trap and the fact the asshole had damaged all of our vehicles. Darren was livid.

"What now?" Mercer asked, checking the rounds in his gun from the backseat.

Shifting in the seat next to him, I organized my thoughts. The killer had been identified. Darren, who was now arguing with his brother, had given me the positive ID of Steven. Killing him was not only sanctioned but a necessity in order to keep the peace between humans and Supernaturals.

"Are you really going to let Logan handle this as he is demanding?" Tate asked, leaning between the seats to look at me.

"No," I answered, rolling my sore shoulders. "I'll petition the Council for immediate action, pulling all the resources we have to find Steven and eliminate him. Leaving this in Logan's hands will undoubtedly lead to more deaths from his incompetence," I concluded, calling Grams on my phone.

"You do realize his brother is marrying into your clan," Tate prodded, feeling good after going a few rounds with things it was legal and encouraged to tear into little pieces.

"Yeah, I have no problem with Darren. Logan and his fiancée are social-climbing idiots," I responded, reaching back to see how much blood I was losing from the wound on my back. It was a steady drip that would eventually seep through my jacket. "Do you have any bandages in here?" I asked.

"Yeah," Blake said, instructing Mercer on where to find them as I stripped out of my jacket and shirt.

Chapter 22

"What do you mean I can't kill Steven yet?" I yelled, slamming my open palms against Grams's desk. Killing was what I did, what I excelled at. My entire existence was defined by killing the bad guy.

Slightly cringing, she answered from her plush chair. "We have to give Logan twenty-four hours before we start our own attack."

"That's bullshit," I said, pacing the room. My wounds were healing nicely after a few rounds of mind-blowing sex with Blake.

"Those are the rules," she answered, turning back to her computer.

Groaning, I slammed myself into her bright blue modern couch. "I should change that rule," I muttered.

"Relax, Olivia, you only have twenty more hours to wait, and you are needed at Kitten if you're up to it," she said carefully, not making eye contact with me.

I huffed, storming out to play video games with Tommy until my Kitten call.

...

I was on for every song at Kitten. As we neared the ending scene, the beat slowed, no longer inducing quick hip thrusts from me as the stage emptied, leaving me and a lone incubus. His power washed over me, calling to my own, and I surrendered, stroking the naked flesh of my stomach. I trailed a hand playfully up to linger at the side of my breast, adorned with a dark, glittery bra, before continuing my self-exploration up to my pronounced collar bone and soft neck.

Noise from the dinner crowd died off as the dance continued, my power of seduction washing over everyone. Servers stopped to gawk, plates of food forgotten in their arms. My gentle swaying changed as Luke, the European incubus, lightly laid his hands on my flesh above my low-slung skirt, making an enjoyable show of pushing his gloriously bare and oiled chest against my back, our hips snug together.

As I lifted both hands above my head, our emotions swirled and mingled, both of us testing and enjoying the heightened feelings we were building.

His calloused hands stroked slowly up my sides as our hips kept perfect rhythm together. Trailing the same pattern that I had explored with my own hand, Luke kneaded my sides, his fingers leaving depression marks as he traveled my slick body. With his mouth blissfully close to the sensitive spot below my ear, I arched my back into him, stretching, pressing my breasts into his waiting hands.

We felt more than heard the collective gasp from the crowd.

His hands rested there for a brief moment before he spun me to face him.

I settled my hands on his muscular shoulders and he reached for my thigh, pulling it tight against his hip. Smiling, I leaned into him as the song ended, darkness sweeping our bodies and desires.

"Careful," he whispered in accented English.

"You afraid?" I whispered back, sliding my body towards his, his fingers pressing into my back.

"You are a taken woman," he reminded me.

That was the shock of cold water I needed. I pulled him off the stage and into the dressing rooms. He was careful not to meet my eyes as my barriers slammed back into place.

I could still feel Luke's desire and his self-control, restraining him from pulling me into the closest with a locking door and finishing what we started on stage.

His words remained with me, "taken woman," and I wasn't entirely sure how I felt about them.

Did I enjoy the respect of the exclusivity arrangement with Blake? Or was I annoyed at others deciding who or what I was allowed or expected to do based upon a label I had agreed to? Thinking about it made my head hurt.

Slipping out of the rigid, glittering costume and into soft jeans and a black shirt, I gathered my belongings, heading out back where Jerry was waiting for me.

Phone pressed to his ear, his usually carefree expression was replaced by anger and concern. Not bothering to acknowledge my arrival into the Beast more than to shift the car into drive, he headed out of the alley.

I waited, sensing the change in him, watching closely as he tightened his grip on the steering wheel.

He was driving too quickly, throwing me against the car door.

"Jerry?" I said, asking what was wrong with a single word.

"Mark's been hurt," he answered, running a red light. "They took him to a hospital."

"Why the hospital? That's a terrible place for an injured shifter," I said, grabbing onto the oh shit handle as we made a left that rocked the SUV.

I watched his jaw clench before he answered softly, "They didn't think he would make it to Gunner's."

Any response I had died on my lips.

...

I dislike hospitals for a variety of reasons, but let's start with my childhood experiences of being strapped down to a pristine white bed while having surgeries done on me. Shaking from the inward tension, I slammed an extra set of barriers on my emotions, holding my body rigid as I followed Jerry through the mass of hallways.

"I'm sorry, sir but you cannot go in there. He is too unstable," said the nurse, placing a restraining hand on Jerry's chest, shaking her head sadly. "We can't afford any human casualties."

Jerry pushed her hand off, storming into the room. I followed. "No worries, we aren't human," I told her, smiling at her bewildered expression.

Yelling drew our attention first. I heard Logan's voice, followed by Kass's shout of "Leave him alone!"

The grunting and the popping of a taser being fired was not a good sign, and Jerry took off at a sprint, crashing into the room, shielded from the outside hospital by only a thin blue privacy screen. Following behind him, I pulled the screen back, taking in the scene before me.

Mark lay badly broken, half on the bed with his legs sprawled limply over onto the floor, as Jerry throttled the security officer who had sent painful electricity into his dying lover. I stepped over the fight as the other guard attempted to pull Jerry off. I rested my hands on Mark's raw back, not flinching when his bloodshot eyes focused on me.

Pulling a deep breath, I closed my eyes, focusing on pulling the pain from Mark's body. The sheer weight of it had me staggering as he made a mournful cry.

The noise had Jerry jumping to his feet, ready to take me on as well. Thankfully, Kass pushed her way between us, hands outstretched with a pleading look on her face.

"Get the doctor," she ordered Logan.

I had assumed he would argue, but only the sound of his rushed footsteps reached my ears. Tilting my head back, I sucked more into my already aching body. Thankfully, Mark's beast stayed silent. Drawing on that energy would have made me useless and just as violent as Mark.

"Help me get his feet up," Kass gently instructed Jerry.

I felt Mark's body moving under me, and I shifted with him so I could lean against the hospital bed, shifting my hands to his battered chest.

Running footsteps announced Logan's return with the doctor.

"I'm sorry, I can't help your friend. Aside from the fact he is a danger to everyone here, I know nothing about shifter medicine," the doctor stated as Logan growled.

"He isn't a danger anymore," I grunted, squinting my eyes open. "As long as I am touching him, he won't hurt you."

"As for the medicine," I continued, my knees going weak, "he is the same as humans, just with a higher pain tolerance."

The doctor scoffed. A painful moment of silence stretched out into the already tense room.

"Alright," he agreed reluctantly, "we need to move him into surgery."

I lost track of time, of the yelling and the beeping of machines, in my fight to stay conscious and keep Mark calm. At some point, Jerry had to pry my fingers off of him, whispering he was going to be okay.

That was the last thing I remembered.

...

The next thing I knew, I was waking up stiff and sore. I peeked at my surroundings, annoyed and starving. "She's waking up," Kass said, blowing out a breath of air as she sat with me on Logan's couch.

"Why are we at Logan's?" I asked, shifting my hips, attempting to sit up. It was clearly too soon, as I toppled back into the couch.

"Easy," Kass said. "We needed a safe place to reconvene."

"What happened to the manor?" I asked, attempting to sit up again.

"You won't want them there after what happened with Steven," Logan said from behind me. Groggily, I turned to face him, my head feeling too heavy for my neck to support.

"What the fuck did you screw up now?" I yelled before passing out again on the sofa.

When I woke up, my eyes focused on Mark, sitting on the couch across from me, his bloodied face healed with only scratches and a broken nose to show, his leg in a cast. "You look like shit," he said, grinning at me.

Rolling to my back, I pressed the heel of my hands into my temples, which didn't help to stop the pounding there.

"Come here, I want to give some of your pain back," I croaked, crooking an index finger at him.

Jerry came into my line of sight, sitting on the arm of the couch Mark was on, beaming. "Now, Olivia, that ain't no way to accept a compliment."

Lifting my head a few inches off the pillow, I gave him my best annoyed look.

He continued, unbothered, "I am sure Mark was just about to confess his never-dying gratitude for saving his life." Rounding on his partner, he gave him a warning look, crossing his arms over a very neon pink polo.

Mark shifted uncomfortably, casting a furtive look my way. "Yeah," he said, rubbing the back of his neck, "thank you, Olie." His sincerity reached his eyes as he finished.

"Enough talking. I'm starved," I said, not wanting to have a heart-to-heart about saving Mark.

Logan picked that moment to walk in tensely with Lorraine, who said, "Finally, you people can get off my designer couches."

"Someone please hit her," I said, throwing an arm over my face.

Mark chuckled as she continued, "I see no reason why they couldn't have stayed at the hospital." She stormed out.

Mark snickered and I looked back to Logan, who watched his fiancée walk away with a slight twitch in his jaw. "Just the picture of shifter hospitality," I goaded. My injured condition earned me a few one-liners.

Logan looked back at me and growled low, and I couldn't help but join Mark in laughing. Shifters are pack animals, and they enjoy and thrive on having others around. Thus, as the soon-to-be pack mate of the leader of the

U.S. shifters, Lorraine would be hosting her fair share of injured shifters, and hating every minute of it, apparently.

Was it wrong that I enjoyed that fact?

Blake picked that moment to walk in a side door, sauntering up with the most amazing smelling food ever.

"Who's your daddy, baby?" he asked, holding the bags up.

I gave him a pained smile before croaking, "You are."

Annoyance flashed across his face. "You again underestimated how drained she is from keeping Mark's pain under control," he said, glaring at Logan.

"I'm not her babysitter," Logan informed Blake. I scowled at him before returning my attention to Blake with a smile.

Sitting up slowly, I patted the couch next to me. With an annoyed growl, he set the bags on the coffee table. "We need to talk," he snarled at Logan, motioning with his head to Logan's office.

Rolling my eyes, I slid to the floor and leaned my back against the couch. I was happy when Jerry started unpacking everything.

"Can you hear them?" I asked Mark.

Tilting his head, he focused on where they had walked out, and shook his head after a moment. "The office is soundproof," he said with a shrug before looking back at the mouthwatering food. "I hope he brought enough for both of us."

Mark and I devoured the food and leaned back heavily. I smelled the hospital still on me and cringed. "Jerry, can you help me to a shower?" I asked.

He nodded, making sure Mark was good for a moment before guiding me to a guest room. The hot water sliced through the ache between my shoulders, pounding my lower back as I shifted and arched, sighing. Beyond the bathroom door, I could hear the door to the guest room open and close loudly.

Turning off the shower, I pulled a plush cream towel over my body before running a second towel over my wet, short locks.

Opening the door, I peeked out at Blake sitting on the bed, legs wide and muscular arms braced behind him. Heat instantly flooded my body, sending my pounding headache away for a few blissful moments.

Amber lit his gaze as I dropped both my towels, coming to stand before him. His eyes roved my body, taking their time before meeting my own sea green ones. Resting my hands on his shoulders, I straddled him, bringing our lips together. His hands spread wide on my back, pressing me closer to him. Smiling against his lips, I obliged him, settling my hips down on his pressing erection.

With a growl, he flipped us, pinning my hands above my head, arching my aching body against him. His soft mouth trailed down my jaw line to nibble at the soft flesh of my breast before his cool tongue swept over my pebbled nipple. My hands found his hair as I tried to pull him back to my lips. A warning growl accompanied him pushing my hands away. "I will tie you up," he warned, which only made me rub my naked flesh over and against him more.

Smiling at me, he kissed me slowly, with a cautious swipe of his tongue, heating when mine reached to meet it in his still injured mouth. Locking my ankles around his waist, I pushed the soft folds between my legs against him. "You're overdressed," I whispered as his mouth found my other nipple.

Shifting down, he smiled at me between my legs, my breath catching. "It's all that is keeping this slow," he said, breathing onto my heated core.

"Blake," I whispered.

Flicking his tongue, he hit my nerve center, causing me to writhe with pleasure. "I do love how you shave for me, Olivia," he whispered, before using just the tip of his tongue to tease my core. I arched as he pressed his hands against my hips, keeping me in place as he explored farther. The soft sensations he was building had me forgetting there were other Supernaturals here who, if they wanted, could hear every whisper and moan.

I couldn't have cared less.

Bucking against him, I begged with just his name, "Blake." I reached down to run my fingers through his dark hair. He looked up, pleasure at his skills showing in his amber eyes. He soon discarded his clothing, landing heavily on top of me.

I smiled, locking my legs around his hips, kissing his lips and tasting myself, which only had me applying pressure to my ankles in order to bring him fully into me. Pulling back and leaving off foreplay, he looked down at me seriously as he slipped into my waiting warmth, sending my eyes closing and my head arching back. "Look at me," he commanded.

I did, thinking he was lucky I took his commands in the bedroom. His mouth hung open in bliss as he moved within me. Shifting my hips slightly, I clenched my muscles, enjoying his groan as he nipped my neck. Slowly, furious strokes had me pushing against him for more as I suckled his bottom lip. As he pulled me up into a seated position, we moved in harmony, driving me to the edge faster as I whimpered his name.

My breathing was ragged and Blake pulled a few breaths as well as I squeezed my ankles tighter, feeling my entire body clench in pure release. Slamming back onto the bed, he kept up his pace as my vision cleared and his body arched in his own release.

Blowing out a shaky breath, I wrapped my arms around his wide shoulders, my contentment seeping into him.

Chapter 23

Reluctantly, I followed Blake back into the den, plopping back on the couch that I had passed out on earlier, feeling in perfect health. Mark watched us with a raised eyebrow. "It just isn't fair that you can heal with sex," he said, looking down at his broken leg.

I shrugged, snuggling next to Blake. "But I can't shift into an animal and run under the full moon."

"True," Mark said, nodding. "It sure pissed off Logan," he said with a chuckle.

I shrugged, not giving a shit if Mr. High and Mighty got his panties into a twist.

"Yes, now that you are done," Logan said from behind us, "let's get down to business."

I didn't bother to look at him. "You still haven't found him?" I asked, checking my industrial watch.

"Oh, no, we found him all right," Mark said. "Who do you think did this to me?"

Tilting my head, I guessed, "The undead?"

"No. Steven has a few new skills, including magic, that blasted the shit out of me," Mark said, shaking his head.

I turned to Jerry. "How?" I asked.

Jerry shrugged. "There are various brutal ways he could be augmenting his power so quickly, but most leave behind a body trail, so I'm not sure."

Shrugging, I nestled closer to Blake, knowing it was only a matter of time before I was on the hunt for Steven myself. "It doesn't matter. The twenty-four hours has expired, so it's now my turn to find the fucker and eliminate him," I said.

"Everything always ends in death with you," Lorraine said, standing next to Logan, "which is why Logan wanted to find him first."

"He did. Look how well that went," I replied, feeling steel settling over me. "Let's get Mercer involved, and are there any other executioners in town?" I questioned Jerry.

He nodded. "Blue is."

I smiled. "Perfect."

...

Now that Logan was willing to cooperate, we had Steven's home address. I did my best to leave the place in shambles.

"How did you get a tracker on him?" Blake asked, raising a well-shaped eyebrow at me as we ransacked Steven's temporary home.

"When Steven was at Logan's, reporting in," I replied, rummaging through a well-organized drawer.

"Why?" asked Jerry.

"Why what?" I asked, flipping over the mattress. Nothing, dammit. Better check inside of it, I thought, smiling as I pulled a knife from my boot.

"Why were you stalking him?" Jerry rephrased, rummaging through papers.

I looked at him. "To kill him."

He nodded, having no response for that.

"I nary seen another reason Olivia uses the buggers," Blue offered with his heavy Scottish accent.

I shrugged; he was right.

Stopping in my manic searching, I took a look around the sparsely furnished house. According to Logan, Steven had been here for almost six months. Yet there wasn't enough stuff: not enough clothing, nothing in the kitchen, nothing in the trash. As I exited the bedroom, something was bothering me, nagging at my subconscious.

Mercer was running Steven's cell phone, credit card, and bank statements back at the station, and from the lack of an excited phone call, I assumed he was coming up as empty-handed as we were.

Turning, I took in the pristine kitchen, then the undented sofa in the living room. Not a nick on any of the doorjambs, not an ounce of mold in the bathroom. Opening up my emotional senses, I picked up nothing, a void. Slamming my fist against the table, I caused Blake to peek out from the bedroom.

"This isn't his place," I hissed.

"I don't follow," Blake said, watching me closely.

"Logan lied." I kicked the coffee table into two pieces.

"I doubt he ever lived here. The emotional levels should register with me, but there's nothing, not a whiff," I said, sitting down angrily. "My tracker only works within three miles and it will take too damn long to track him down with it, if he hasn't already ditched the vehicle."

"What the fuck am I going to do?" I asked, tilting my head back and hitting the thinly covered wood frame too quickly.

"We'll figure it out," Blake said, running his fingers through my hair.

"You do know of a way," Blue said, leaned against the hallway wall, his short stature and cobalt gaze reminding me of things I'd rather forget.

I growled at him.

His posture didn't alter. "You know I'm right."

"Yeah, and it also hurts like a mother," I answered, slamming my arms across my chest. With a sinking certainty, I knew Blue was right. It was my only trustworthy option and I wasn't going to allow Steven any additional time to kill innocent people.

It's Logan responsibility, anyway. If he had handled his shit, I wouldn't be in this situation.

"That's it," I said, sitting up suddenly.

"What?" Blake and Blue asked in unison.

I smiled. "We are going on a field trip, boys."

Sliding into the passenger seat, I asked, "Logan at home tonight for that shifter meeting crap?"

Jerry nodded, slowly removing the toothpick he had been chewing on. "Why?" he asked cautiously.

I smiled, shrugging. "Just want to pay a friendly visit," I said as Blake closed the door to the backseat.

Jerry took a slow look at Blake, who shrugged. Starting the Beast, he murmured, "I hate it when you're happy." Casting a sidelong look at me, he added, louder, "It means you're going to do something stupid and enjoy the hell out of it."

Blue came up to the rolled down window. "I gotta see 'bout a few matters, now that I'm home. I'll be seeing ya, Olie."

"Bet your ass, Blue," I responded. He smiled, the exhaustion and unshaven stubble evidence of a hard run. I hated to bring him into this, but I needed the backup.

Jerry was right, I was ecstatic. I finally had a real lead, a viable option, and a plan. So my plan might involve beating the shit out of Logan. I saw no downside to that one. I giggled, and Jerry sunk lower, mumbling to himself.

"Mark there?" I asked, smiling widely, using muscles I hadn't used in a long time.

He nodded, not looking at me.

"Fantastic."

We pulled into the shifter compound, which now had a few guards out and about, but not enough by my count, especially if what I was guessing was true.

When there is unrest in the packs, an Executioner is called upon.

Skipping up the steps, I rang the bell with equal measures of annoyance for taking so long to figure out the clue and excitement at the thought of harassing Logan.

Kass opened the door with Hannah on her hip, who squealed when she saw me. "What are you doing here?" Kass asked warily, shifting Hannah.

"Taking care of business. Stay with Jerry," I said, kissing Hannah's cheek, brushing by her and Kass.

I followed the voices, seeing Darren first, sitting bored and looking down into his glass. His brother sat behind an ornate desk, a new addition to the house, as were the gargoyles out front.

"You knew," I said softly, as all eyes turned to my leather clad form.

"Knew what?" Logan asked, standing while buttoning his camel jacket uncomfortably.

"You knew," I said again, louder. "You fucking knew that the killings were shifter related and did NOTHING!" I screamed, slamming my fists on his desk. "I wasn't the first one to have these visions. I was just the one who did something about it," I hissed, watching his face pale.

Standing back up, I snarled, "I'm right, and you know it," my disgust for him dripping from every word.

Darren came from behind, standing next to me. "Please tell me she's wrong," he said, horror shading his features.

Logan closed his light brown eyes, shaking his head.

"Oh, no, just wait a minute, you bitch," said Lorraine, pushing toward the front of the crowd. "Those were just nightmares, nothing more. The fact that you have your wires crossed doesn't mean Logan does as well," she stated, hands on her hips, her snooty face inches from my own.

I smiled and she wilted, but not far enough as I slammed my crown into her nose. "Oops, my bad," I said, still smiling as the blood began to gush. No one made a move to help the conniving, materialistic, selfish bitch.

Crouching down, I tilted my head at her. "Listen well, human, these matters do not involve you. Do not mistake your species again," I added softly, as Logan hauled me up by my shirt. Finally, a good fight, I thought, smiling as he threw me onto the designer antique couch back, smashing the delicate wood trim as it fell to the ground under my weight.

"You fucking know I'm right," I yelled as he barreled at me, his face a mask of rage.

Smiling, I twisted left, giving him a swift kick as he went by. "Gotta fight smarter than that, sweet cheeks," I taunted merrily, jumping to the other side of the couch as I eagerly watched him strip out of the camel jacket, breathing heavily.

"You're going to pay," he growled.

"Bring it on," I taunted. He flew over the couch, tackling me. Ouch, didn't see that launch coming. Our momentum carried us into the ornate desk, smashing the back of my head.

Grunting under his weight, I taunted, "That's what I'm talking about."

Logan pulled back a punch, a moment of indecision crossing his face, before Lorraine's scream of outrage echoed through the halls. He landed the punch home. Blackness crossed my vision as I pulled my right leg, pinned so perfectly between his legs, up into the family jewels. I didn't get to see his priceless expression of pain as I rolled away, shaking the blood from my nose as my vision returned.

I smiled on all fours, watching him rolling around before I leaned back, popping my nose back into place. Giving Lorraine a bloody smile, I informed her, "That's how it's done."

"Logan, kick her ass!" she screamed, sandwiched between two beefy shifters, who didn't appear thrilled about guarding her.

Slowly, with ample amounts of groaning and more than a few of my favorite curse words, Logan made it to his knees, looking back at me. Seeing what I could only imagine was a foolish grin and a bruised face, he laughed.

"You are psychotic," he said slowly, pushing to his feet.

I shrugged, standing, hands on my hips. "Be honest, tight ass, you needed it. No one else gives you a fair fight."

He laughed harder. "You are not a fair fight. The odds are heavily stacked in my favor."

"Wanna keep going? I am more than game," I answered, rolling my aching shoulders.

"LOGAN!" Lorraine screamed, and we both cringed.

Blake left his post at the door, coming behind me and whispering in my ear, "Baby, life with you is never going to be dull." I shrugged as he kissed my cheek lightly.

"Dull is highly overrated," I said, smiling up into those bright blue eyes. The blood drained from my face and my eyesight blacked out. I heard myself choke, falling into Blake's arms.

"Baby, Olivia, no," he said, slapping my face. "Olie, baby, stay with me," he demanded as we slipped to the ground.

Pale pink of a nursery assaulted my senses, the smell of baby powder and an ivory crib.

Sucking in a breath, I found myself on the ground with Blake in my face. "BREATHE!" he screamed, cupping my face as I pulled oxygen into my lungs, arching my shoulders off the ground.

A yellow, fur-covered hand with black talons gripped the ivory crib, and it creaked in the silence of the darkened home.

Logan had his lips pressed against mine, blowing in air as I came back, my eyes rapidly blinking as Blake thumped on my chest. I squeaked as Logan pulled back, bellowing deeply, "BREATHE!"

A whimper escaped as the cracked, decrepit clawed hand touched the peach blanket, gently pulling it off the sleeping form of the newborn girl, her hands swaddled in pale yellow mittens.

I screamed, thrashing against Blake and Logan.

Pink lids were closed, content in the sleep of innocence. The clawed hand rested gently on her head. I could feel the baby's contentment, love. It seeped from her body into the room, her emotions coating the undead. She was a succubus and she would be powerful. Steven could have found her anywhere; no one suspected they would be killed just for being a Supernatural.

I was crying. Logan's arms circled under my bra, binding me to his chest as Blake straddled my chest, holding my shoulders into Logan. Darren and Jerry each had one of my legs.

I drew a ragged breath, as the dead shifter slowly clenched his hand and the newborn's skull cracked, making the only sound to permeate the silence. It left the parents alive. I could feel Steven's smugness, knowing the pain he was causing.

A desperate, pathetic, hopeless sound reached my ears, and I realized it was me, my lungs, my voice producing the wail.

Logan arms loosened as both Jerry and Darren let go of my legs. I heard the clink of glass, and I assumed Logan poured himself a drink. Blake cradled my face gently, asking, "Baby?"

A sob made it past my lips. "It killed again," I whispered, closing my eyes. "A newborn, days."

Blake pulled me into his body, holding me close as my emotions shut down.

I heard someone ask muffled, "Is it always this bad?"

Kass answered, "At first, no; she could break it and trace the undead to wherever it was killing." She sighed, resting her hand on my head. "She, Blake, and Tate destroyed that one, but then Steven called another."

"Our grandfather," Darren said softly, pressing a glass of water into my hands. I pushed tightly into Blake, struggling to control my emotions and angry that he could feel them. I should be better than this. I should be able to protect him.

"It's okay, Olivia," he whispered into my ear. "Don't worry about me."

"Doesn't he try to fight it?" a voice asked.

Peeking around Blake's shoulder, I saw the speaker, a man with an auburn head of hair cropped close, dressed in relaxed back dress pants and a skin-tight shirt.

"He did," I said softly as all eyes turned to me. "His strength was why I couldn't breathe, why I couldn't regain consciousness. He tried to show Steven to me, but all I saw was darkness."

I sighed, closing my eyes, handing the glass back to Darren. "It's time," I said softly, pulling out my phone as I struggled to stand with Blake's help.

"Yes?" Blue answered.

"It's going down now," I said, not elaborating. His silence was broken only by a sigh.

"What exactly is going down?" Jerry questioned me with a raised eyebrow.

I made a grimace, answering, "Blake is going to drain me to the point where my heart almost stops."

"No," Blake answered immediately.

"I don't have a choice. Between waiting for Logan and his idiotic plan to find Steven and wasting time ransacking the false address he gave us, I don't have any more time," I answered. The newborn's death was my fault.

"I can hear you," Logan said, draining his glass and pouring himself another.

"And?" I asked, raising an eyebrow. "This is your entire fault."

"No," Blake said, pulling back to look into my eyes. "No, I will not risk your life."

"I don't have a choice. I will not go through that again."

The auburn-haired man spoke up. "How did you avoid the visions, Logan?" The question was heavily underlain with insult.

"Sleeping pills," he said softly, perched on the broken couch, taking a long swig of his drink.

"They were not real, and how does anyone know what she is seeing is real? She could just be delusional in addition to psychotic!" Lorraine screamed.

Someone growled at her, to my shock. "Remember what she said—" the auburn-haired man said softly.

"Alec," Logan warned.

He turned away, but I caught the glowing in his eyes. I turned to Blake. "I have to do this."

His eyes were misty and I hated myself for it. "Stop it," he whispered, nodding. "Olivia, I could kill you," he reminded me. I didn't need the reminder.

"I trust you," I said simply and for the first time in my life.

My brain understood I should be terrified, whispering those words to a man I was sleeping with, a man I was already needing and depending on, but my heart rejoiced at the admission. Common sense told me to pull back, demanded I stay aloof, but the walls I had constructed were crumbling. I knew there was no going back, and if I were very, very honest, I didn't want to. That simple fact terrified me more than anything else.

I had denied myself many things in this world and the idea of a lifelong companion was one of them.

He sighed and Jerry added, "It will help regenerate your fangs."

Blake nodded, still not looking away from me, caressing my face. Pressing a firm kiss against my forehead, he pulled the knife from my boot and I couldn't help but smile at how well he knew me.

He moved behind me and I eased into the strength of his chest as I tilted my head, now staring at the ornate desk. Inlaid into the thick wood surface was an intricate floral pattern I hadn't noticed earlier. I forced my mind to focus on beauty and strength as Blake cut into my jugular. Blowing out a breath, I cooled my core. I could do this. I trusted Blake. I just had to find that place again where Steven called the lion. I could do this. I had to; there was no one else.

My lids grew heavy and my foot thumped once as my survival instinct tried to stop the vampire pulling out my life force.

"Forgive me, Olie," Blake whispered when he was finished.

"Don't leave me," said the thirteen-year-old inside me.

"Never," he promised. As blackness swarmed my vision, his cobalt eyes were my last sight.

I had been to this place once before when I had almost died. Cultures call it different things, but it had always felt like twilight to me, when you can't tell if the sun is rising or setting and the things that go bump in the night start making an appearance.

I thought this was the place the lion had taken me. Here's to hoping I was right, as my eyes flew open and I sat up abruptly.

Looking down, I saw my body as wispy smoke intertwined with my physical body. It had worked; I was here. Fantastic, I was dying. Standing, I stumbled slightly, unused to the lightness of my body, knocking over the glass of water on the table.

"Oops," I muttered.

Blake sighed audibly. "It worked," he said, more to himself. "Forty-five minutes, baby, and not a second longer."

I squeezed his shoulder, looking down. I expected to see my same leather pants, ass-kicking boots, and blue shirt. Instead, a black dress drifted on me, moved by a breeze I couldn't feel. Odd, yet the oddest thing was the thick red cord that disappeared into my chest. Touching it lightly, I felt shock waves, screams of the victims I had watched, the bellow of the lion trying, fighting, and always reaching me.

Removing my hand quickly, I walked out through the front door, past the worried looks from my friends and the stony denial of Logan. It was asinine that I had to clean up this mess. It was his and his alone, yet here I was, straddling the line between the living and the dead in an attempt to solve all his problems.

I should just take over the whole damn shifter nation if the head of the damn U.S.A. branch can't keep his ducks in a row.

Chapter 24

My rope ended at the docks, and I honestly don't know why I was surprised. It was dark, dingy and dirty, with plenty of places to hide and lots and lots of boxes to shove over and trap an unknowing victim.

Twisting my way toward the center of the building, I noticed Steven had carved himself out a nice little place to play, with jars of paste and herbs circled around a shallow brass bowl, dimly lit by the fading sun, sending orange hues across his annoying face. I wished I could kill in this form; it would solve all my problems quickly and painlessly, not to mention there would be no trail back to me.

The sound of crying had my smoky head shifting to the side. My mental ranting was silenced as my eyes rounded in horror. Trapped in a large dog crate were the twins, their thin forms huddled together, careful not to touch the sides of the metal enclosure. Squinting, I could see orange power twisting over the black metal. Son of a bitch.

Steven's magic had a color; this was far worse than I imagined.

Like a rocket, I shot back to my body, being pulled rapidly, the sleeping city flashing by in hues of bright whites and pale blues.

Slowly, I drew a deep breath, feeling fatigue in my limbs. Clenching my fists, I whispered, "He has them."

"Who?" asked Blake from far away.

Rolling to my side, I forced my eyes open, meeting Logan's gaze. "The twins."

...

"I realize it may be 'ard to understand through me accent, but me answer is no," Blue said again, tilting his head at a sharp angle to argue with the impossibly tall Logan.

"He is one of my mine," Logan growled, leaning menacingly towards Blue.

"How decent of you to admit responsibility now," Blue said, his cobalt blue eyes dancing merrily.

I smiled from the couch I had earlier recovered on. Unfortunately, sex wouldn't pull me back from this one. I needed time to replenish the blood I had lost. An IV drip taped to my wrist greatly sped up the process.

"Let us not forget yer previous attempt to gain control of this situation led to Olivia having to save yer arse once again," Blue said, his lips turned up in a smile; he was enjoying the goading.

Blake paced behind me, on the phone with Tate in low whispers.

"The vampires are going?" Logan asked, losing ground.

It took all my strength, which wasn't much, not to laugh aloud. Blue grinned, answering, "Aye, they are."

Logan's jaw muscles twitched as Blue continued, "Aside, someone be needed to tend to Olivia," he said, blasting me with a full Highlander grin.

My mouth hung slack as I met Logan's wary gaze.

In the silence, I heard the click of Blake hanging up. Turning on my back to look up at him, I pleaded with my eyes not to let them leave me alone with the pain-in-the-ass shifter.

He leaned down, resting his lovely chin on the couch back. "Sorry love, someone does need to stay here with you, and if Logan goes with us, no one will listen to Darren." He met Logan's gaze for the next statement. "And they need to listen to Darren on this one. After all that has happened, it is important he secure his position."

Huffing, I crossed my arms, pulling the IV and scraping my underarm with my watch, hissing.

Jerry walked in the front door, followed by the no longer limping Mark. "Leave Mark with me," I suggested hopefully.

"Sorry, sister, I am not leaving Jerry's side. He is going to need all the support he can to fight off the bad mojo magic of Steven."

"Shit, I forgot to tell you, Jerry, his magic is orange," I said, worry creasing my features as I rolled to my side.

"Orange?" Jerry repeated.

I nodded, searching his face, the hard lines in his forehead creasing as he said, "I am going to need more supplies."

Mark watched him retreat into the kitchen before turning to me. "What does orange mean?"

"That he has moved above the average abilities. Mage's ranks work much the same as a rainbow: red, orange, yellow and so on. To move up in the ranks takes a great deal of time and effort; Steven has been planning this for some time."

Mark nodded as Jerry came back out. "What level are you?" Mark asked Jerry with concern.

"High enough to take his ass out," Jerry responded.

Mark just nodded, throwing me a last glance before following Jerry out.

Blue crouched by my head, stroking my temple before placing a kiss there, turning, and leaving silently. I watched Logan's house empty of shifters, vampires, and a few trusted human police, leaving the place feeling empty and watchful, or perhaps that was just me.

"So, you and Blue," Blake said lightheartedly, sitting on the coffee table in front of me.

I smiled at his attempt at a joke. "No, there never was me and Blue. I taught him how to fight, how to kill, and gave him a job."

Blake nodded, knowing full well what Blue meant to me—but did he know what he himself meant to me? Being bound to my emotions guaranteed he knew how I felt, but not why.

Clearing my throat, I was shocked at the hot tears I felt. "Come back to me," I whispered, unable to articulate all the reasons why I needed him. All the change had forced its way into my soul, and I hoped desperately that I would be given the opportunity to explore all these new sensations with him at my side.

My words were inadequate. Blake bowed his head to me, kissing my pale knuckles. "Always," he promised, his eyes somber with the battle ahead.

I nodded, feeling a tear slip down my cheek as the door closed behind him. Closing my eyes, I was aware of Logan's stare. "Go ahead and say it, Logan," I said.

He remained silent and I didn't care to hear his disapproval of me. I ignored him and tried to ignore the nagging voice in my heart that demanded I go by Blake's side.

When I had my emotions under control, I opened my eyes to find Logan watching me with understanding. After all, his brother was facing down a powerful mage as well.

"TV?" he suggested, holding up the remote.

"Sure," I agreed, needing something to keep my mind off of everything.

Lorraine slammed doors from the second story, letting us know just how upset she was. Neither of us gave a shit.

The question slipped out before I even realized it had. "Why do you put up with her?" I immediately regretted asking. "Never mind; it's none of my business," I said, turning back to the TV, careful of the needle in my wrist.

Logan sighed, surprising us both with an answer. "I don't know. Why do you stay with Blake?" he asked.

Rolling to my back, I pushed up against the armrest to look at his haggard appearance before answering, "Because I am so tired of being alone."

Lorraine slammed another door as something delicate crashed to the ground. More of her yelling followed.

"Is it worth it?" I asked, suddenly genuinely interested.

"Is what worth it?" Logan mumbled, still staring upstairs after Lorraine's cursing.

"Having a mate?" I asked, turning on my side, sliding back down.

Logan narrowed his caramel eyes, watching me. "You should know that answer."

"I don't. I've never had a relationship before, never had restraints and commitments." I shrugged, turning on my back, staring up at the ceiling.

"It can be," Logan answered hesitantly.

I nodded, restlessly turning on my side to watch the sunset through the plantation shutters. Deep reds turned into purple, bleeding away to pink before the giant ball was swallowed up entirely. My nerves grated as I chewed on my lip, my stomach a mess.

Casting a glance at Logan, I saw that he mirrored my own anxious state, staring blankly at the TV blasting some news channel, waiting for news that mattered.

Chapter 25

I slept, arms crossed over my middle, breath coming and going in easy exhales, too spent to be worried about the front door being cracked open.

"What are you doing here?" Logan asked. My lids flew open from the hostility in his voice. I was careful to keep my body still.

"We need to talk," Steven's pathetic voice announced.

My easy breathing became labored as the giant remnant of Logan's grandfather walked in behind Steven, closing the door and lumbering in a dark trance, his eyes a burnt red.

Taking a deep breath, Steven let it out as a loud sigh. "You have taken our clans on the wrong path," he said, beginning to pace, as I pushed myself into a sitting position, watching him intently.

Throwing a hand to indicate me, he continued, "You've aligned us with the succubi, allowed your own brother not only to impregnate one but marry one as well." Steven shook his head, pacing in front of the TV. "Let's not even get started on her corruption of the innocent Hannah." Steven stopped, pulling off his glasses to clean them on his dress shirt.

He cast a desperate look toward Logan. "I should be able to kill you, to take over and lead us down the noble path we were born for, but I want you to be a part of that picture," he said hopefully, placing his glasses back on his ugly face as Logan sat ridged in his chair.

"You have killed innocent children," Logan stated.

"Bah, freaks, all of them! We are the true shifters, the true bloods, and we shall make our clans great once again," he said, the future glimmering madly in his eyes. "We are the rightful rulers of all the Supernatural races, we are the superior life form," he claimed, gaining strength, puffing his chest out. "We shall force the humans into slavery, as is fitting for them, and rule all," he finished. I was impressed with his commitment to insanity.

"We cannot enslave humans," Logan said, adjusting in his chair to give the appearance of relaxed nonchalance, while his energy vibrated with alert rage, ready to pounce on the rogue shifter.

Steven sneered with an ugly look on an already ugly face, and I cringed.

He rounded, catching my disgust. "Demon," he insulted.

I rolled my eyes. "Why am I not passed out right now?" I asked. I was genuinely curious, and, as any good movie watcher knows, the villain always loves to boast about his brilliant plans. Too bad we were going to ruin those.

He scoffed, throwing a disdainful look at Logan's grandfather. "Yes, I have heard of your ability to link with my pet. Not sure how you managed it, but it only seems to happen when I force him to do something he finds distasteful. Surprising, considering he was known as the Terrible, Destroyer of Many, that now he flinches at disposing of a few impurities."

"How did you fool me?" I asked, worry growing for Blake and the others.

He growled at that question. "I didn't. Your minions successfully ruined my ritual killing of the twins, but not before I trapped them in the warehouse." He adjusted his stance, insecurities showing as his shoulders hunched forward. "You will reveal how you did that before I bleed you," he hissed, his beady eyes narrowing.

Swinging my legs down, I slipped the needle out that was delivering sweet blood to my arm.

"Doubtful," I taunted, resting my forearms on my thighs, gathering my strength, reaching for my dark pools.

Steven foolishly walked closer, the front of his gray slacks brushing against the steel coffee table.

I knew my eyes were dead, knew the beautiful sea green I was used to see in the mirror had changed into the dark green of a forest possessed by night, where the truly disturbed beings lurk. He didn't notice the change or didn't care; it made no difference. Darkness began to coat my cells, unleashing the killing beast I kept just below the surface.

From the corner of my eye, I saw Logan leaning forward in his chair, muscles bunching under his shirt, deadly eyes trained on Steven. I felt his shift, the unbridled power being released, stroking against my own. I couldn't help but smile.

Steven sneered. "What the fuck are you smiling at, bitch?"

My grin widened. "You had the dead perform your demented deeds, used others' hands to end life, took the coward's way out," I said, leaning forward, watching his jaw clench as I reduced him to the pompous ass he was. "You forgot we are true killers," I informed him, my voice softening. "We are the reason darkness is feared, the ruthlessness that keeps order in a chaotic word. We are contained by the rules we choose, and you, Steven, have walked straight into our judgment."

I might be half-dead, but his death was guaranteed this hallowed night.

He looked nervously to Logan, whose fangs had lengthened, his massive bulk forcing apart the seams of his clothing. Logan chuckled softly, his eyes twirling as he licked his lips.

"You forgot," Steven said, straightening his hunched shoulders out, "I have the undead on my side."

I smiled before pointing to Logan's grandfather. "Sit," I commanded, drawing power into my words. He did so without hesitation.

Steven's eyes widened behind his wire-rimmed glasses as his most valuable pawn obeyed my command. He was left with only his own abilities to finish us. Judging by the fear that now stiffened his limbs, he didn't think it would be enough.

"Never bring a knife to a gun fight," Logan said, standing slowly from his chair.

I couldn't help but join in with a dark chuckle.

Steven turned to his dead shifter sitting on his heels, his elongated thighs feeling no stress as he watched us, his empty eye sockets glowing a dim red. My heart felt the pain Logan's grandfather did, caught and forced between worlds. His destroyed body caught in mid shift, unable to become his true lion form, he managed in a half shift, his human body lengthened to unnatural proportions.

He was grand in life and equally impressive in death.

I watched Steven muttering words I couldn't understand and didn't care to, his last, futile attempt to once again force his minion into doing his evil bidding. What he didn't understand, and, I admit, I didn't either, was that Logan's grandfather's energy was bound to mine, intertwined and pulsing inside of me.

He would obey me exclusively.

Slowly I stood, navigating the new sensations of power throbbing inside of me. My vision took on another layer as I saw the orange cord connecting Logan's grandfather to Steven. Reaching out with my own muted red power, I tugged gently against the cord, feeling the pop of release as Steven's gaze found me, shocked.

Blowing out a breath, I maneuvered the cord back to Logan's grandfather, feeling it pulled into his decaying chest.

That's when shit got weird.

The power cord disappeared into his chest, and instantly, he was bathed in golden light too painful for my eyes. I turned away, feeling the heat of magic on my back.

A deep growl had me turning around to an older, yet regal version of Logan: strong, naked shoulders, caramel eyes, and strands of gray hair wound through dark blond. His eyes narrowed, crow's-feet sprouting up, as he took a powerful step toward Steven.

Steven regarded him in awe, mouth hanging open before turning his wide eyes to me. "How?" he asked, before being thrown across the professionally designed living room.

I smiled, leaning against the arm of the couch, watching the destruction as Logan came to stand next to me, hardly containing his violent nature. "Can we move this outside?"

"Sure, as long as you have a great explanation for the neighbors and news crews," I reminded him.

He growled low as Steven was thrown through the banister of the second story, his body flopping back down. His cries reached us, pathetic attempts to beg for his life, to explain how he only had the best of intentions in mind.

I scoffed, enjoying the sound of bones breaking. I had been forced to do things against my moral code, and I understood how Logan's grandfather needed to punish Steven. It helped ease the pain, the guilt, and the self-hatred.

Lorraine picked that moment to come down the stairs, screaming.

"Fuck," I whispered, turning to look up at her ashen face.

"Go back to your room," I ordered her without thinking. She screamed again, unable to move as the lumbering giant tossed Steven's body precariously close to her own.

"Shit," I whispered, turning to Logan for assistance only to find myself staring directly into his beast. I averted my eyes as quickly as possible, but it didn't matter.

"Get away from me, Olivia," he whispered hoarsely.

Smart enough to listen, I dashed up the stairs, pulling Lorraine behind me. As we turned the corner, Steven's body threw plaster down on us as he hit the ceiling and groaned weakly.

Pushing us into the first open room, I slammed the door and locked it, pressing my back against the wooden barrier, feeling good about our near escape as I sucked in oxygen, slightly light-headed.

Logan's grandfather was pulling energy from me, not a lot, but in my currently depleted state, I felt the difference.

I had just opened my mouth in an attempt to calm the still-screaming Lorraine for my poor ears' sake, when a solid force connected with the door at my back. Holding my breath, I waited a heartbeat, hoping it was only Logan's grandfather still throwing around Steven before the force connected again, splintering the door.

Without thought, I pushed the now hyperventilating Lorraine into the bathroom, slamming the door closed behind her as I turned to face Logan's wild eyes.

"Easy," I said gently, holding a hand out.

He cleared the distance between us easily in one leap, pulled my body into his, and nuzzled his five o'clock shadow into my neck.

I sagged against him, relieved. In my current shape, I couldn't stop Logan from killing me or Lorraine. I could slow him down, but even at full capacity, a fight to the death between us would be close.

His warmth seeped into my body as my arms wrapped around him, my eyes closing as I felt his energy pushing into my own to help support me. I sucked in a shocked breath. What the hell was going on?

Outside the door, the noise had stopped. I opened my heavy lids, heaving a deep sigh as naked Grandpa stood outside the destroyed door with Steven's head in his hand, dripping fresh blood onto the carpet.

"You may want to consider tile," I muttered, feeling Logan release me, turning to survey the scene.

He sighed, annoyed and back in control.

We both turned as the bathroom door opened and a tear-stained Lorraine emerged. I cringed seeing her; she was not a pretty crier.

"Logan," she wailed, throwing herself into his side.

Untangling myself from him, I felt my core cool reluctantly at the reminder of who and what we were. Logan didn't take his eyes off of me. Energy did weird things to people. Certainly, after all of this was over, we would get a killer laugh at the absurdity of this situation.

Shaking my head, I turned to Gramps. "Release me," he commanded.

"Do you know how?" I asked, looking down at the head of the now dead mage who could have answered that question.

He growled as I scratched my head.

"I have an idea," I said, feeling exhaustion seeping into my bones. "Logan, you good to drive?" He nodded, still awkwardly holding Lorraine.

"Let's take this party on the road."

Chapter 26

Pulling up to the dilapidated warehouse, I could hear my trusty band of fighters arguing as they battled against the energy field keeping them locked inside.

Gramps awkwardly got out of the backseat, still carting around Steven's dead head. I wasn't sure if he even realized it, but I certainly wasn't going to bring it up, considering his unstable mental faculties.

"Logan!" Darren yelled, attempting to warn us as we walked to the metal rollup door, "it isn't safe!"

"I believe we are in the clear," Logan answered, motioning to the head hanging down from his grandfather's hand.

"Shit," Darren muttered as I took in the orange field holding them in.

"Everyone alright?" I asked.

"Yeah," Darren responded, "pissed as hell, though."

I smiled. "I can only imagine. So any ideas on how to get you out of here?"

"None. Jerry took Blake and Blue to try and gather supplies for some super magic, and when they came back—" He shrugged. "That was a bit ago. None of our cell phones work. This barrier is no joke."

"How can it exist if Steven is dead?" Logan asked.

We all shrugged. Magic wasn't something I dabbled in.

"Twins alright?" I asked with a sigh, resting my hand against the field.

"Yeah, just shaken up," Darren answered, casting a look over his shoulder.

I nodded, my eyes no longer seeing into the warehouse, but only the energy running through the shield. Cords of burnt orange tangled with brilliant yellows weaved together with blood reds in my mind, and I pulled against them, gently at first, curious, before I tugged again, feeling a give.

"Get DOWN!" Jerry screamed, right before I pulled with all my strength.

The cords snapped like an elastic band pulled past its capacity, flinging outwards with a force that smashed me against the car window, shattering the glass as the cords sucked into my body.

"No one TOUCH her!" Jerry screamed again as the pounding footsteps slid to a stop uncertainly.

Drawing a ragged breath, I had to blink a handful of times before I could actually see the sky above me, before rolling to my side on the black car.

"Fuck," I whispered, feeling my entire body pounding.

Jerry looked down at me, pissed—actually, livid. "What the fuck were you doing?" he demanded, his teeth clenched.

"Oh, you know, attempting to blow myself up," I replied, sitting up, regretting it as my head swam and I sagged back down.

"How the fuck did you do that?" he asked, glaring at me.

Pushing all the way up, I saw Blake's worried face come into view. "It had bands; I broke them," I said with a shrug.

"No, how did you absorb Steven's power?" he asked again, dark eyes intent on my own.

"Uh, I … oh, shit," I muttered, casting a glance at Logan's grandfather. "Probably when I freed Gramps, which would also explain why he's still functioning."

Jerry nodded, watching me closely as I stared back at him, unblinking. I suppose getting himself trapped in a warehouse was bound to make him cranky, but I wasn't in the mood.

"Do you have any idea what you have done?" Jerry hissed at me as I stood on unstable feet.

"No, Jerry, I do not, but you speaking in cryptic questions sure as fuck isn't going to help me figure out how to fix it!" I yelled back, cradling my head.

Jerry stepped back as I leaned heavily against the damaged car. "We need to go," I reminded him as the sirens wailed in the distance. I would explain everything to Mercer, just not right now. Being detained with a naked dead shifter didn't seem like a good idea, not to mention the head he was still clinging to.

...

Walking into the crypt where Gramps was laying, the destroyed plaque dust beneath our feet, I focused on what Jerry had tersely told me.

"Draw all of the magic into yourself from him, every last drop. It is the only way he will have peace," Jerry had said intently.

"Right, because clearly I, the succubus Executioner, can see magic," I mumbled to myself.

"What?" Jerry asked from the doorway.

"Nothing," I answered, my irritation and anger wanting out of the tight confines as I bound them deeper inside of me.

My anger left a red trail as I pushed it deeper and locked it down tight. Sighing, I tilted my head to see the orange surrounding Gramps.

"Oh shit," I whispered, raising a hand and seeing the faint outline of Steven's magic surrounding it.

Finally, now we were in business. Drawing the magic as I manipulated my own emotions, I pulled, twisting and sucking every drop of orange that wanted to stick to Gramp's body.

From the gasps and muttering, I assumed it was working.

Magic, unlike my emotions, burned hot, pricking my skin, boiling under the surface, and, also unlike my emotions, it was damn hard to control. Strands kept reaching out, trying to get back into the now lifeless body.

Once I felt fairly confident I could remove my focus from the magic and walk toward the open door, I did so very ungracefully and without help.

Panting from the effort to contain the magic, I looked into Jerry's cold eyes.

"Done," I told him as I pushed myself up.

"This is going to hurt," he warned, his voice emotionless.

"Bring it on," I demanded as he reached out and gripped my hand.

Fire sliced through the veins he pulled the magic from, tearing apart the delicate framework of my body into a thousand pieces. I was certain, even with my advanced healing, I would never recover from it. The orange magic screamed as it was pulled, echoing out of my mouth in a pitch so high I could never produce it on my own. Throwing my head back, I could see Jerry's own dark energy pulsing as he absorbed the new influx of power.

His dark power silenced the voice and left me dry. Shoulders hunched, I looked at him with new understanding. He wasn't just a driver and magic dabbler; Jerry was a powerful mage who could level city blocks if he decided to.

So why was he hanging around my little old town pretending differently?

As he saw the knowledge in my eyes, his shoulders straightened, preparing for words every smart person would have said.

I've never been accused of being intelligent, but I have been called a whore and a violent, mindless demon. All those I could relate to. Whatever secrets he was hiding, I wouldn't be the one to force them to light.

Instead, I just nodded. "Done being cranky?" I asked, rubbing the hand he had touched.

Shock registered across his features for only a moment before he put on his good ol' boy smile. "Nope, not hardly. We still got a hell of a mess to clean up."

I groaned, trudging past him back to the cars.

He was right, though. We did.

Chapter 27

"I cannot believe I let you drag me here," I hissed at Grams.

"Relax, Olivia, they don't know if we're Supernaturals, only that we are part of the Council, here to support the vampires and update the public on the death of the horrible person responsible for killing all those innocent families," Grams said, smoothing out her black pant suit. She looked good, unlike me in my jeans with a turquoise tank top under my leather jacket. I wasn't sure what confidence I was supposed to be bringing to the table.

Tate nodded at me across the long white table with some random sport sponsor logo behind us, printed on cheap plastic. Really?

Logan and his band of shifters were nowhere to be seen. While it was his total and complete fault that Steven was allowed to become so out of control, it was politically better if only one group of Supernaturals were present at this press conference wrapping up the Puppet Master case.

"Ladies and gentlemen, if you will all please take your seats, we can begin the update from the Supernatural Council," Governor Hash began with a fake smile on his slimy face. That man sent disgusting shivers down my spine every time I saw him.

"But before we do, I would like to say a few things." I scowled, should have seen that one coming. Grams kept her calm and composed smile. "We have done everything in our power to identify and stop the supernatural monster behind these senseless and brutal killings. The Supernatural Council has been assisting our lead Detective Mercer on the case and he has the update on the gritty details of how this went down. For now, please know that everything has been taken care of, and the threat eliminated," Hash finished, his eyes attempting to intently relay that everything was under control.

He was a fool; tomorrow there would be another monster to vanquish, another Supernatural or human psychopath walking free, created in the darkest places of their own psyche.

I glanced at Mercer's face turning red. Apparently, he didn't enjoy public speaking. Stepping stiffly to the podium, he fidgeted with his jacket before stuttering into the microphone. My chair, scraping against the stage, was brutally loud in the silence. I smiled at Mercer as his shoulders relaxed. "Actually, I'd like to hand this off to Olivia, who has been working with me."

I smiled, clapping Mercer on the back. "We can finally say we have successfully ended the rampage of the killer named the Puppet Master."

"Where is he?" asked a reporter.

"Dead," Mercer said, his shoulders stiffening back up.

"Why did it take so long and so many deaths before you found him? Was it due to the Supernaturals who kill everything in their path?"

"Only the ones who deserve it," I said, leaning toward the microphone as Mercer went back to his seat.

"Who made you judge, jury, and executioner?" the reporter asked, with pure hatred lacing his words.

"No one, those are constructs of your justice system," I answered him honestly, wrapping down the need to kill him. I certainly didn't want to prove his whole mindless killing theory was accurate.

"It seems like a poor way of dealing with your problems, killing so many," he said with a flick of his pen in his notebook.

"We protect our own from any and all threats," I answered.

"What about your own threat to us?" he asked with plain hostility.

"You create enough threats for yourselves," I answered right back, quickly.

"No, we protect everyone and give the accused rights, something you and your kind could never understand," he finished, his lip curling in malice.

"You are telling me you are happy with your current system of dealing with sex offenders?" I asked, astonished at the thin reporter who began this dialogue. My eyes roved over the crowd. "You are perfectly happy that they are arrested, if the children they abuse are ever brave enough to come forward and if someone believes those children, then go to trial, where they may or may not be found guilty, serve their time, and are released back into the community?"

No one spoke up.

"That is a pathetic attempt to protect your innocent children. The Supernatural Council, when given evidence of a Supernatural sex crime, eliminates said Supernatural. They kill them, they destroy the body so it cannot be reanimated, and protect the children. Because we understand something you clearly have yet to comprehend: hurting others by choice is a choice that will always be made again."

"But you sickos have sex clubs," a blond, middle-aged woman in the back yelled out.

"Correct, and no one there is forced to be there," I answered, growing bored.

"How can you be so certain?" the annoying, skinny reported asked, clearly having been thrown a lifeline.

"Because we have a reputation," I began, "of being ruthless to those who force others into the sex clubs, who use drugs to coerce. But more importantly, we have a reputation of protecting our own," I finished with heat.

"You are inhumane," the blond woman said again. "You vamps feed off our blood."

"But we don't kill," Tate said over the chorus of outcry.

"Show them, Tate," I said, slipping off my leather jacket and pulling my hair out of the way. He stood up abruptly, his eyes ambering.

"Are you mad, showing them what they fear the most?" he hissed at me.

"No one does well with lies and attempts to please. Show them the truth, that you can stop when you want and don't hurt me," I said, ignoring the yelling happening behind him.

He was silent for a moment before he agreed, stepping behind me. "If Blake asks, this was your idea."

"Fine," I said, as the crowd grew silent.

Tipping my head to the side, I gave him full access, watching the crowd as they waited with all the anticipation of an audience at a magic show.

Slowly, he lowered his head so I could feel his breath before his fangs descended. At least, I assumed they did, based on the crowd's united gasp. "I hope you're right about this," he warned before breaking my skin. Instantly, the contentment and safety of his bite overwhelmed my senses, and I pushed that emotion out to all those present, visibly relaxing my body against him.

"It doesn't hurt," someone gasped.

"It almost looks pleasant," said another, shocked.

Finishing, Tate sealed my wounds, seductively licking his bite for the audience. "Any other takers?" he asked. Hands flashed up from the audience as Tate smiled. "I should really make you head of PR," he murmured, pleased.

"Not on your undead life, buddy," I said, slipping my jacket back on.

Passing by Grams, who was shaking her head, I shrugged, "I got it done."

"Yes, and by what means?" she asked disapprovingly.

"By whatever means necessary to overcome their fear," I answered, leaving the press conference.

...

I threw my bag down in Grams's study, disgusted, annoyed, and frustrated with a world I didn't much enjoy or like right now, and let's not forget had just busted my ass to save.

"Blasted humans," Kass said, plopping into the red modern chair I hated before digging into her purse for chocolate.

Settling down on the slanted arm next to her, I reached for her candy. "Hey, back off the pregnant lady's stash," she warned.

I laughed, popping the dark chocolate in my mouth as Grams walked in, stretching her shoulders.

Chapter 28

My mouth wouldn't stay shut as Kass and I accidently spied on Grams and Mercer involved in a low conversation at Luigi's. I was shocked when Grams laughed, her eyes dancing with mirth as Mercer leaned forward, covering her hand with his own larger one.

"When the fuck did this happen?" I asked, still staring in shock.

Kass sipped on her lemonade before shrugging and smiling broadly. "Sometime around when you went missing. He stopped by the manor to look for you and found Grams instead."

"I'm not sure how I feel about this," I said, meaning every word.

"Oh stop," Kass chided me. "She's a woman who has her own wants and needs," she finished heavily, emphasizing needs.

I made a face. "She has never had those…" I floundered for the right word before borrowing Kass's, "needs until now."

Kass crossed her arms, regarding me with brown depths. "How would you know? This is the longest you've been back that I can remember."

"Really, you are going to start with that?" I asked, instantly annoyed, as I drained my wine glass.

She shrugged before adding, "You are not the only Executioner, Olivia."

"True, but I am the best," I answered hotly, annoyed as my work ethic was dragged into question yet again.

She said nothing to that, smiling as Blake and Darren approached. I never would have imagined myself double dating before. Kass's comment stung as I realized Blake might also have a problem with how often I worked away from home, and a longing for being single again instantly flooded me. Life was so much simpler.

Kissing me on the cheek, he whispered, "What's wrong?"

"Just found Mercer and Grams out together," I said, shifting my worry.

"Is that a bad thing?" Blake asked, accepting a menu he wouldn't need from the waiter.

"I don't know," I answered with a sigh.

Dinner went well, and, afterwards, Blake and I headed back to his place. His fangs had fully regenerated, thanks to a life-altering dose of my blood and a little help from our mage.

Lying in bed with him as he stroked my hip after a passionate lovemaking session, I told him. "I have to leave tomorrow. Something is sucking humans and shifters alike off the radar in Kentucky."

I lacked the nerve to look him in the eyes.

"When will you be back?" he asked, nuzzling my neck.

"I don't know," I whispered.

"Promise you will come back to me," he asked, his hand sliding lower.

"I promise," I whispered.

Connect with Me!

Thank you for reading *Dead Shifter Walking*!! I greatly appreciate your support and I whole heartedly hope you enjoyed it. If you did, please consider leaving me some love on the platform you purchased on.

Want to connect on Facebook? Look me up at KimBairAuthor

Prefer twitter? @thekimbair

Join my mailing list to be first in the know: www.thekimbair.com

I am always looking for beta readers to help me iron out the kinks, if you would like to join please email me at kimbair@proton.me

Thank you and happy reading!!

More books by Kim Bair:

Dead Shifter Walking, The Succubus Executioner Book 1

Demigod Down, The Succubus Executioner Book 2

A Witch's Fury, The Succubus Executioner Book 3

A Council of Betrayal, The Succubus Executioner Book 4

Death of a Succubus, The Succubus Executioner Book 5

Legacy of the Succubus, The Succubus Executioner Book 6

Creation of the Dual Shifter, The Dual Shifter Executioner

The Mel Files

Andy's Origin, The Andromalius Chronicles